THE SIGN OF THE GALLOWS

THE SIGN OF THE GALLOWS

Susanna Calkins

Severn House Large Print
London & New York

This first large print edition published in Great Britain and the USA in 2022 by Severn House, an imprint of Canongate Books Ltd, 14 High Street, Edinburgh EH1 1TE.

First world regular print edition published in 2020 by Severn House, an imprint of Canongate Books Ltd.

severnhouse.com

British Library Cataloguing-in-Publication Data
A CIP catalogue record for this title is available from the British Library.

ISBN-13: 9781448308699

Typeset by Palimpsest Book Production Ltd.,
Falkirk, Stirlingshire, Scotland.
Printed and bound in Great Britain by
TJ Books, Padstow, Cornwall.

Acknowledgements

Creating a novel is never a solitary endeavor. I'd like to thank my agent and friend David Hale Smith for believing in my Lucy Campion mysteries, and for Severn House for allowing Lucy's journey to continue with *The Sign of the Gallows*. In particular, I'd like to thank Kate Lyall Grant for her kind support of the story, Rachel Slatter for her insightful editorial feedback, and Natasha Bell and Katherine Laidler for their work on the manuscript.

A number of good friends encouraged me as I wrote the draft, most notably Lori Rader-Day, Jess Lourey, Terri Bischoff, and Erica Ruth Neubauer. I am always appreciative of the support of my wonderful children, Alex and Quentin Kelley, who allow me the space and time to write. I am hugely grateful to my husband Matt Kelley who, as my first reader, knows my characters and this world almost as deeply as I do, and will let me know when I've gone astray. It is to him I dedicate this book.

One

London
November 1667

The north-western road to St Giles-in-the-Fields was darker and more desolate than Lucy Campion remembered. She shifted her peddler's pack, full of *True Accounts* and *Strange News*, her shoulders aching under the familiar strain. She'd taken the longer path to avoid the outskirts of Covent Garden since it still teemed with people displaced by the previous year's Great Fire. Now she was beginning to regret that decision.

'Why sell at this market?' she muttered out loud, despite being warned about her habit of talking to herself. She continued trudging along the old cow path carved out through thick forest, patches of fog obscuring the hundred yards ahead of her and behind. The fire had not spread this far west, and the trees that surrounded her were dense and old. Although the trees helped block the wind, the occasional icy gale still sliced through her thin woollen cloak and dress. At least the earlier snowflakes had melted already, leaving the path muddy but not so wet as to soak through her pointed leather shoes.

This morning, at Master Aubrey's request, she was heading to ply their trade at a new market along the northern edge of Westminster, an

1

unlicensed gathering of merchants that had sprung up a few months ago. She'd brought some pieces they'd recently printed in the workshop, mainly tracts detailing the Earl of Clarendon's latest treachery against King and Parliament, though she'd tucked in a few murder ballads and recipes since they always sold well in crowds. So far, she'd encountered only a few merchants here and there, on their way back and forth to London, hawking their wares.

She stopped for a moment, trying to get her bearings. Probably a few hundred yards from the crossroads with the old hanging tree. A long time ago, local villagers would hang murderers, witches and other miscreants from the old oak tree there, before such executions moved to the Tyburn Tree. Suicides still found their way, though, committing their most desperate act, knowing they could not be buried in a church's sacred ground. Poor families and relatives of criminals might bury their dead here too, if they could not pay for a proper church burial.

Lucy sighed. She'd forgotten about the hanging tree when she chose this path. As a child, she'd learned to pass the crossroads quickly, her mother warning her about ghosts that lingered there. *They're waiting to latch on to a weak-willed mind. A ghost will catch hold of your skirts and follow you home! There they will stay, tormenting you all your days, causing mischief and filling you with melancholia until you die and suffer the same fate as them.*

Her steps slowed even as her heart beat faster. *Shall I turn back?* she wondered, coming to a full stop. Every click in the woods, every animal rustling, every shadow in the trees was bringing her to a state of high alert. For a moment she stood there, listening to the sounds around her, the thumping in her chest and the shallowness of her breath resounding in her ears.

Then she slapped her forehead. 'Such nonsense you spew, Lucy Campion,' she said. 'What would Master Hargrave say of your foolishness?' Thinking about the magistrate, whom she'd served for several years as a servant before becoming a printer's assistant, began to steady and calm her. She continued to admonish herself silently. *He'd say that your imagination is tricking you! He'd tell you that more often than not there is a scientific and rational cause for magicked happenings and strange tales. He would certainly say that there is nothing to fear at the crossroads.*

Thus restored, Lucy stoutly moved forward. It was then that she heard a cart moving rapidly ahead of her, though the fog was still too thick to make it out. She stood aside to let the cart pass her by on the narrow muddy lane. At the sound of men shouting, she knew something was amiss.

Out of the mist, two men came racing towards her, pushing a wildly careening wooden handcart in front of them.

'Good heavens!' Lucy cried. 'What is amiss?'

One of the men was looking over his shoulder, as if they were being pursued by something dangerous. A highwayman? A ghost?

Seeing her, one of the men stopped short,

releasing his hold on the handle, confusing the man who'd been looking behind. The abruptness of his action caused the man to stumble and send the handcart veering towards her.

Without thinking, Lucy tried to lunge out of the way of the cart. At the same time, the other man, in an effort to stabilize the cart, ended up pushing it directly into her path. The cart caught her in her lower limbs, and her pack flew from her shoulder as she flung up her arms. Unable to catch herself, Lucy fell straight backwards, smashing her back and head on to the ground. The breath was knocked right out of her, and for a moment everything went dark.

'What the—' she heard one of the men exclaim. 'Why'd she do that?'

Blinking, Lucy looked up only to find the two men staring down at her, a similar chilling expression in their dark brown eyes. They looked alike – most likely brothers or cousins. Probably in their later twenties or early thirties. One of the men was clean-shaven, but on his neck she could see a swirling tattoo of some sort of fierce animal, marking him as a sailor or convict. The other man had a neat light-haired moustache and dark russet hair.

The more the men stared at her, the more uneasy Lucy grew. *Why hadn't they left yet?* Both men looked burly and strong – labourers, possibly tradesmen. Her pocket was well hidden under her skirts and contained only a few coins to provide a bit of change as needed. But none of that mattered if they had ill intentions towards her person.

'What do we have here?' the clean-shaven man asked, looking her over.

What should I do? Where should I go? Lucy cast about wildly. The trees on both sides were dense and fearful, and she knew her skirts would catch and trip her if she ran. Her limbs suddenly felt heavy, and her feet became anchored to the ground. *Why can't I move?* Her sense of panic grew. *Run!* she told herself. *Run!* Still she couldn't move.

Then she saw that the man was looking down at one of her tracts. Some of the penny press from her pack scattered and began to blow about in the rising wind. Picking it up, he read the first part of the title with ease. '*A True Account of a most barbarous monster . . .*' He stared down at her. 'What kind of peddler are you?'

Still trying to catch her breath, Lucy just waved futilely towards her pack.

'Bookseller,' the moustached man said, guessing correctly.

Lucy slumped back, her heart to her chest, wheezing. Try as she might, she could not draw breath back into her lungs. Still fearful of the men's intent, she began to scramble backwards, her skirts catching in her shoes.

'Now where are you going?' the moustached man asked. 'We're not done talking.'

'Leave her alone,' said the man with the tattoo, crumpling up the tract and tossing it over his shoulder. 'Pike, we must go.'

Moving past her, the man who'd been called Pike gave her a mocking glance. 'Stay out of our way next time, would you?'

Thankfully, the men sauntered off, continuing southward along the dirt lane. Whatever had unnerved them earlier appeared to have subsided, and they appeared deep in conversation. Still hunched on the ground, Lucy watched them go, her hand on her chest, trying to breathe.

Fortunately, the cold air flooded back into her lungs and she gulped it in as if she'd been drowning. She struggled to sort herself out, and to her annoyance she found that she was trembling. Then indignation and anger filled her as well. *Why did they rush at me that way?* 'Didn't even check to see if I was hurt,' she grumbled as she began to brush herself off. 'A pox upon them both.'

Only when a white paper blew by her did she snap back to attention. 'Oh no!' she cried. Pulling herself up on shaky legs, she began to retrieve the pamphlets and broadsides that had blown out of her pack, hoping none were destroyed. The wet ones she might be able to dry off and still sell, but those that had got bogged down in the slick mud would be hopeless. Master Aubrey wouldn't be pleased when he saw the ruined pieces. 'I'll get a scolding for sure.'

Experience had taught her that there was no use explaining to Master Aubrey that the poor state of the printed pieces was not her fault. He expected her to take care of their stock at all costs, protecting their tracts and pamphlets as if they were made of precious metal, instead of their true flimsy and ephemeral nature. Fortunately, he did not box her ears as he would his apprentice Lach.

Unlike Lach, she'd never been Master Aubrey's true apprentice. The Stationers' Company still had strict standards on who could be apprenticed, but since the calamitous years of plague and Great Fire, everything had been disrupted. She'd been able to seize opportunities that she'd never expected, and she hoped to learn as much as she could before the world returned to its senses and strict guild rules were once again enforced.

Besides, she certainly didn't want to get on the wrong side of Master Aubrey. Having been with him for over a year, she'd hoped to write more pieces for him and to be given more responsibilities at the shop. She looked sadly down at the tracts that were a bit soggy from their time on the damp winter ground. Carefully, she slid them back into her pack. *Maybe I can still find a way to sell some of these. Murder, at least, always sells.*

Continuing on, Lucy limped towards the crossroads, keenly feeling the bruising impact of the collision. Her head and back hurt from the fall, as did her legs where the cart had struck her. Perhaps there'd be some healing medicines to be had when she reached the market. Why had those men been running? What had they been running from?

Then the mist cleared, and Lucy stopped, the answer to her question taking form. 'Oh,' she exclaimed, putting her hand to her heart. Her pack slid from her shoulder, landing on the ground with a small thud.

There, dangling from the hanging tree, was a man's body.

She just stared at the corpse, suspended about two feet in the air. She found herself focusing on the man's torso, unable to look up at his face. He was clad in a tradesman's hearty grey wool coat and breeches, and his boots were of a durable and expensive leather. This was no doubt what had frightened those men so. 'Say a prayer, say a prayer,' she admonished herself, before quickly muttering a few words that were half charm and half an offering to the Lord.

Although she wanted to hurry past the terrible sight and continue on to the market beyond, Lucy could not help but study the body a bit more. There was something odd about the corpse. It seemed to lack the rigidity of death and not a single fly, rat or crow had discovered it yet. Indeed, it reminded her of the freshly dead criminals who'd been hanged at the Tyburn Tree, which she'd witnessed first-hand several times, having been sent by Master Aubrey to sell murder ballads and last dying speeches to the crowds gathered at the public spectacle.

Mustering all her courage, she reached up and pushed the man's foot, feeling her stomach heave as the body swayed at her touch. A quick glance at the man's face showed that he also lacked the waxy pallor and decay of most corpses: it was mottled and spittle still dripped from his mouth. Indeed, except for the grotesque angle of the way his head lolled against his chest, he looked almost as if he might have been asleep.

She sniffed. The stench of death was not yet upon him either, although she caught the faint smell of wine. 'He couldn't have been dead very

8

long,' she said, stepping back, continuing to regard the body. 'He must have been drinking before he died, poor sot.'

Unlike those pitiful souls executed at Tyburn, this man's hands and legs hung free, not tied or bound in any way. Certainly, there were no weights on his feet, which prisoners could pay for to hasten their deaths. From her knowledge of the public hangings, it might take a man twenty minutes or more to succumb to the rope, unless he had paid someone to pull on his legs to help death along and end his earthly suffering. Not a peaceful death. Lucy sighed. A suicide to be sure, and a recent one at that.

A small step stool under the body confirmed that point. It had been kicked over. Closing her eyes, Lucy imagined the bitter scene. The man must have stood on the stool to first loop the rope around the tree branch and then, after placing the noose around his neck, kicked over the stool to ensure that his desperate act was realized.

'Who were you?' she said to the corpse. She touched the man's hand, which still had the slightest bit of warmth to it. Grimacing, she drew her hand away. 'What drove you to such a state? What dreadful melancholia overcame you, to take such an action?'

She looked around. Such a forlorn spot. Perhaps he'd hoped to be buried here as well. Maybe he'd been concerned about his soul tormenting his family. Maybe he'd hoped to keep his act hidden. *Except, shouldn't his family know? Wouldn't they wonder what had happened to him? Should I tell someone?* Being friendly with the magistrate as

9

well as the local constable made her keenly aware that such an unnatural death needed to be reported to the London authorities.

Her attention was distracted by something hanging from the man's broken neck. Peering up at it, she could see it was an ornately carved and expensive-looking gold ring hanging on a silver chain. Standing on her tiptoes, she tried in vain to look more closely at the ring, which was still about a foot above her head. *I'd wager that ring could help identify him.* A tear unexpectedly appeared in her eye. *Not if someone steals it from him, though.*

'The truth must be out,' she declared, righting the stool. 'Your loved ones must be told where you are. Otherwise the authorities will just cut you down and throw you in the potter's field, if they don't just bury you here.'

Stepping on to the stool, she was now at eye level with the man's chest. She couldn't bring herself to look up at his face, so she looked at his heart instead. 'Maybe you had no one to care for you – maybe that is why you brought this dreadful plight upon yourself. But I imagine that someone will be looking for you and wondering what might have happened. This news, though tragic, may be helpful.' She looked at the man. 'What do you think?'

The corpse swayed slightly in the breeze, almost as if the man were agreeing with her. She took that as a sign to continue. Looking around, she quickly unclasped the chain with the ring, removing it from around his neck. As she jumped down from the stool, sudden misgivings came over her. *What if someone takes me to be a common thief?* There were hefty penalties for being caught stealing from corpses, from a spell in the stocks to time spent in jail. She sucked in her breath. *In for a penny, in for a pound.*

Just then, she heard voices coming from the direction she had travelled. Picking her pack from the ground, she ran into the copse of trees on the other side of the lane, her heart beating furiously as she peered out through the leafless branches.

To her surprise, the two men who'd knocked her down earlier had appeared, now dragging their handcart behind them. *Why did they come back this way?* she wondered, starting to tremble. As she watched, the men went to stand before the corpse. The one named Pike tapped on the man's boots. 'Like I told you, Dev,' he said. 'Seems foolish to leave all this to thieves.'

'I could have told you that,' Dev grumbled. 'You're the one who took fright. Go ahead and take his boots. Should bring a bit of silver.'

Pike complied, yanking at the man's boots without bothering to unbuckle them. 'Leather's hardly worn at all. Don't even need new soles.' He threw them in the handcart. 'Why don't you check his pockets, Dev. This here was a man of means.'

For some reason, both men laughed. Dev poked the man's jacket, withdrawing a timepiece and a pocket with a grin. 'I thought he might have something like this on him.' He looked inside the pocket. 'A few coins as well.' Tucking both items into his coat, he patted the man's

11

stomach. 'Thank you kindly, good sir. Anything else you'd like to offer us?'

As Pike laughed, Dev straightened up abruptly and stepped back, an odd expression stretching across his face. 'Say, Pike, I thought you knocked that stool over before we left.'

Lucy sucked in her breath. *What did he mean by that? Why would Pike have knocked the stool over?* Her mind began to reel. *Had Pike and Dev helped the man commit suicide? Helped him die?* Such a thing went against the Lord's will and was viewed as akin to committing murder.

Pike looked down at the stool. 'That's true. I did.' Then he looked up at the dead man's face, studying him. 'Something else is peculiar, too. Something is missing.' Then he snapped his fingers. 'Hey, what about the ring that was around his neck? Could it have fallen off?'

Hidden behind the trees, Lucy froze. The ring Pike was referring to was in the pocket she kept fastened beneath her skirts. *What if they come looking for it?* Dev's next sentence confirmed her mounting sense of panic.

'Nah, I think someone took it.' Dev began to tap his fingers on the handcart's handle. 'Someone who needed to stand on that stool.'

They looked at each other. 'The book peddler!' they exclaimed in unison.

Dev nodded. 'She was heading this way when we left her. We haven't seen anyone else on the road since then.'

'That's right!' Pike replied. 'Shall we go after her?'

Lucy didn't catch what Dev said next, but the

lewdness behind Pike's guffaws caused her cheeks to burn and her legs to tremble in earnest. She pressed against the tree, praying that she would not collapse. They would certainly hear her if they did.

'She was scared witless already,' Pike said. 'She's probably halfway to the next town by now, she was so afeared. We couldn't catch her even if we wanted to. Let's go.'

The men left then, continuing back down the path in the direction she'd encountered them earlier. 'What should I do?' Lucy asked herself, once she had regained her composure. 'I think I need to inform Constable Duncan about this body and give him the ring. Master Aubrey will be upset, I know, but my conscience tells me I need to do this.' Her chuckle was feeble. 'Besides, maybe I can write this as a true tale.'

Two

As Lucy limped down Fleet Street, where both Master Aubrey's print shop and Constable Duncan's jail were located, a tall and elegant figure unexpectedly blocked her path, causing her to stop mid-step and her heart to leap. It was Adam Hargrave, the magistrate's son, beholding her with a somewhat amused air. His dark hair was tousled, and his cheeks were a bit ruddy, as if he'd been in the wind for a while. He spoke just her name, as if he'd not been away from London for months. 'Lucy.'

'Oh!' she exclaimed. 'Adam!'

His name, said so familiarly, hung in the air, causing her to flush. For so long, when she had served in the Hargrave household, she'd called him 'Master Adam' or 'Sir'. Yet that had all changed more than a year ago when he'd asked her to stop addressing him in such a formal fashion. Still, circumstances between them had changed again before he'd left for the New World and that previous familiarity no longer felt appropriate.

'Lucy,' he said again. In his slight smile, she could read his hesitation now. For a second, she thought he was going to embrace her, which would have been shocking indeed, but he didn't. 'I did not expect to see you so soon.'

'Soon?' She hadn't seen him for several long

months, and the last message she'd received from him was that he was helping the colonists set up their legal systems. She'd had two letters from him since. Deep inside, she'd thought she might not see him again, although another part of her had never given up hope.

'I stopped by Master Aubrey's to see you and he said that you would be out for the day, having risen early to sell on the northern outskirts of Westminster,' he explained, still watching her intently. 'I had planned to stop by this evening again. So this is great fortune indeed. There was something I very much wished to discuss with you.'

'Oh,' she replied, not sure what to say. What could Adam wish to discuss with her? Then the memory of the corpse and the two men came back to her. 'I was just on my way to see Duncan.'

A disappointed look crossed his features, before it disappeared back into the courteous mask he used to wear when she was still serving in his father's household. 'Of course,' he said. 'I won't keep you.'

'No, no!' she replied, hurriedly trying to explain. 'I've just found a dead body hanging from a tree. It looks like suicide, and I thought it best to inform Constable Duncan, but there was something odd that I wanted to tell him, too.'

'A suicide?' His manner became more businesslike then. 'By all means, you must bring this to the proper attention. Lead the way. I shall accompany you.'

* * *

15

As they walked to the makeshift jail on Fleet Street, Lucy filled Adam in on what she had witnessed at the crossroads. She didn't mention the ring that she'd lifted from the body. *No need for him to think I've taken to grave robbing in his absence.* She spoke quickly, trying to keep her mind off the pain she was feeling from being knocked over by the thieves' handcart. She was also trying not to think about what Duncan would say when he saw Adam again at her side. For his part, Adam listened quietly, an intent expression on his face.

Given that it was nearly noon, Fleet Street was full of its usual hustle and bustle: women carrying baskets on their heads, men leading single-horse carts through the narrow passage, children pushing wheelbarrows to and from the market. Most of the shop doors and counter tops were shut tight, though, with fewer goods being displayed as storekeepers sought to ward off the winter chill and snowy rain.

Looking up at Adam, Lucy wanted to ask him about what he'd been doing in the colonies, and what had brought him back, but so much had passed between them that she didn't know what to say. The closeness they had enjoyed a year ago had dissipated after some misunderstandings and her own sense of confusion about her place in the world.

When they reached the Fleet Street jail, she knocked on the door. The jail had only been intended to be temporary, a holding place for tavern louts, petty thieves and prostitutes, created out of an old candlemaker's shop after the Great

Fire. However, even as Newgate and Fleet Street were once again accessible, this tiny jail had remained, overseen by Constable Duncan, a former soldier from York.

Constable Duncan opened the door, dressed neatly as always in his red uniform, his dark brown hair carefully trimmed, and standing with a soldier's upright bearing. 'Lucy,' he said, his York accent evident. When he saw Adam, his pleased smile disappeared. 'Master Hargrave,' he said, giving a curt nod. 'It's been a while.'

'Constable Duncan,' Adam replied, his manner equally stiff.

For a moment, the three were silent. Duncan had never thought Adam was serious about Lucy and had made his own interest clear. After Adam left England, Duncan and Lucy had grown closer, although she'd still held him off.

'What is it?' Duncan asked, turning back to Lucy. 'What brings you here?'

'On my way to St Giles-in-the-Fields, I came across a dead body, hanging at the old oak tree at the crossroads on Drury Lane, just before that road meets up with Holborn. I don't think the man had been dead for very long. I thought you should know.'

'I see,' Duncan said, his manner growing professional. He gestured to Hank, who'd been working with him for the last few years. 'Sounds like a suicide. I know the spot. Let's check on this. Grab the handcart, will you?' He pulled a long knife from the drawer and affixed it to the belt he wore buckled around his waist before pulling on his heavy grey woollen coat. 'Sounds

17

as if we'll need to cut him down from the tree. We can wheel him over to the potter's field from there. Perhaps there'll be a means to identify him.'

'Wait, Duncan! There's something you should know,' she said. 'Before I'd reached the crossroads, these two men came running out of nowhere. They knocked me down and—'

'What?' both men exclaimed at once.

'Why didn't you tell me?' Adam added, his eyes running over her apprehensively. 'Are you all right?'

Lucy held up her hand to ward off their anxious enquiries. 'I'm fine. When I first saw them,' she explained, 'the men looked afraid. I thought at the time that they were being chased. They had these terrible looks on their faces, as if they'd seen a ghost. I thought it was just because we were at the hanging tree. When I saw the corpse a few minutes later, I thought that was what had spooked them.'

Adam and Duncan both nodded. Such beliefs were common enough, even if they personally thought such superstition was fiddle-faddle.

'After they knocked me down, we went our separate ways. Or so I thought.' No need to tell them how frightened she'd been when the men stood over her. They were clearly worried enough.

'This was not so?' Duncan asked.

'No. They doubled back, returning to the hanging tree. Luckily, I heard them, so I had time to hide.' Her lip curled at the memory. 'They stole a few things from the corpse. His boots, pocket and timepiece.'

'Grave robbers,' Duncan said, making a disgusted grimace. 'A common enough practice. Unfortunately, it's almost impossible to capture them, let alone arrest and bring them to justice.'

'That is certainly so,' Adam agreed. 'For such mercenary louts, stealing a dead man's coins and boots easily outweigh their fear of ghostly spectres.'

'I don't think it's so odd that they stole from the corpse,' Lucy clarified. 'Something else struck me as odd. One of the men said, "I thought we knocked the stool over." Why would he have said that? It's true, the stool was knocked over, but I righted it.' When both raised their eyebrows, she hurried on, not wishing to explain why she'd been standing on the stool. 'Then the other man remembered that the body had been wearing a chain with a ring on it around his neck. If they were so scared when they encountered the corpse, would they have lingered long enough to note such a thing? I can't imagine this to be so.' Both men were still listening intently. 'Don't you see what this means? They must have been up close to the body for some reason. Perhaps . . .' she trailed off as she began to recall other details.

'Perhaps what?' Duncan asked.

Lucy paused. 'Perhaps they helped the man kill himself.' She continued to speculate out loud. 'When I saw them, they were pushing an empty handcart as they were running away from the gallows. Maybe it was not a suicide at all.'

'Indeed,' Adam said. 'That is most certainly odd. Perhaps a physician should come to see the body?'

Duncan nodded. 'Yes, that seems a good idea. I'll stop by to see if Doctor Larimer can spare the time to accompany us. Otherwise, we will bring the body directly to him, so that he may examine it at his residence, as is our usual practice.'

'Lucy,' Adam said, his earlier amused smile returning to his face. 'Where is the ring now? You said the grave robbers had pilfered the dead man's pocket, boots and timepiece, but you did not mention the ring.'

Her cheeks flushed. 'Oh! I forgot!' Reaching inside her skirts, she withdrew the embroidered pocket and fished out the ring, still connected to the silver chain. She held it out defiantly.

'Oh, Lucy,' Duncan sighed. 'Why did you take it?'

'I thought it would help to identify the man's body, in case his loved ones did not know he had died. I know I was not wrong either.' For the first time she noted the details of the ring, causing her to almost drop it in disgust. 'How peculiar! On one side there's a cherub's face, while the other side has a grinning skull. Such an odd and morbid piece.'

She passed it to Duncan, who held it up so Adam could view it as well. 'The band is gold,' the constable said, holding it close to the flickering light of a candle rising out of the brass holder attached to the wall. 'There appears to be an inscription, but it's quite worn down. Hand me that flea glass, would you?'

Lucy handed him the flea glass he kept on a small table in the corner, and he continued to look at the ring intently. A moment later, he sighed and handed both the ring and flea glass to Adam, who similarly positioned himself under the candle's tiny flame. 'Can you make it out? I believe the inscription is in Latin, but I can't quite discern the letters.'

Accepting the items, Adam studied them for a moment. 'The writing is faded, although it is definitely Latin.' He paused. '*Memento mori.* "Remember that you will die." Or "Remember that you have to die."'

'Why would someone inscribe this on a ring?' Lucy asked.

'I imagine it's something akin to *carpe diem* – seize the day,' Adam mused. He glanced at Lucy. 'An important sentiment, given the precarious nature of life.'

Lucy shuddered. 'Why would he wear it around his neck?'

'Perhaps it didn't fit him any longer? Maybe his fingers were swollen. We'll know more when Doctor Larimer examines the body.' He turned back to Lucy. 'I'm sorry that you witnessed such a sight. I'm certain that it was a shock. Why don't you head back to Aubrey's? Maybe you can rest a spell?'

'Shall I lead you to it first?' she asked, her heart sinking at the thought of making the long journey back to the hanging tree. The injury she had sustained earlier was starting to take its toll.

'Thank you, Lucy,' Duncan replied. 'There's no need for you to come along. We should be able to find the corpse without you. I know the crossroads of which you speak.'

21

'I'll see her back to Aubrey's,' Adam said, edging closer to Lucy.

Duncan frowned, looking at them back and forth. Lucy had never shared anything of her feelings about either man with the other, but the rivalry between them had long been there. She could feel an odd tightening in her chest. She didn't look at either of them as she left, Adam a step behind.

Lucy didn't live too far away from the constable's jail on Fleet Street. For more than a year now, she and her brother, Will, had been living above Master Aubrey's shop, along with the master printer and Lach. The lodgings were small but suited them all well enough, even though the harsh smell of smoke from the Great Fire had lingered for months. Divine providence had seen fit to spare Master Aubrey's shop and home from the conflagration, which was a true miracle given that half of Fleet Street had gone up in flames and nearly twenty thousand homes and businesses had been otherwise destroyed. Although Master Aubrey did not talk about it much, Lucy suspected that he was deeply grateful that his life and livelihood had remained intact, and as such had not minded another mouth to feed.

Without a word, Adam took the peddler's pack from her shoulder and hefted it on to his own. With his other hand, he gripped Lucy's elbow. 'Slowly,' he murmured.

'How does Sarah fare?' Lucy asked, trying to keep her mind off her pains, which were steadily worsening with every step. She had not seen

22

Adam's younger sister for quite some time. As a Quaker, Sarah Hargrave was still traipsing around the New World, following her Inner Light to deliberately defy political and religious authorities there as a sign from God. Believing themselves to be akin to the Old Testament prophets, she and the other Friends spent most of their time in the Massachusetts Bay Colony, where the laws were the harshest and where Nonconformists were treated most horribly. They spent their days berating the authorities there, often dressed in sackcloth and ashes, deliberately inserting themselves into troublesome positions so that they could martyr themselves for their faith. Tarring and feathering was a common enough punishment, although Lucy had once met a Quaker whose tongue had been cut out of her mouth for speaking against the governor there.

'Sarah's activities concern me greatly,' Adam said. 'I do understand she is following her conscience. I just wish her conscience might sometimes see fit to lead her towards a less dangerous path. When I saw Sarah last, she'd just been in the stocks.'

'In the stocks! Oh no!'

'She was fine. Just had some tomatoes and eggs in her hair, which she took pains not to wash away for some time. She did not appear to have been physically harmed.' He scowled. 'Friends view such torments as travails to be endured in their devotion to their Inner Light.'

'I saw your father recently,' Lucy said, changing the subject. 'He appears to be doing well.' *Except for missing you so greatly*, she added to herself. Master Hargrave did not confide in her of course, but she could tell from little things he'd say, or even in his silences, that he was lonely with his son away. He'd lost his wife during the plague, and his daughter was living a life that was hard for him to support, although he'd become reconciled to their differences over time. Still, the soreness of Adam's absence no doubt ran deep.

Now Adam's smile grew. 'I did stop in to see him this morning soon after I arrived. He told me you'd visited him on occasion. He also said that he'd been teaching you chess.' He looked at her. 'Truly, Lucy, I thank you for caring for my father.'

'I stop by to visit him, as well as Cook, Annie and John, whom I still view as my own dear family. As for chess, I will never be a match for him, but I have enjoyed learning the game. It is good that you have returned so that he may have a worthy partner.' She paused. 'Your father has always been dear to me. I never find it a burden to visit. Quite the opposite, in fact.' Then she returned to what he had just disclosed. 'You just disembarked this morning? Why did you not take to your bed? You must be so very weary.'

'I was, but I'm not any more.'

Lucy kept tugging at her cloak, wrapping it around her to protect against the wind. She was trying not to limp, but it was getting harder and harder to hide her pain. She slowed, putting her hand to her stomach.

'Lucy! Are you all right?'

She nodded, gritting her teeth as she did so.

The stiffness in her joints was getting harder to bear.

Adam smacked his head with his palm. 'I'm a doddering sot! You said you were injured, that a cart ran over you? I should have attended to this straight away. Let me take you to Doctor Larimer. He must see you at once.'

'Oh no!' Lucy protested. 'The cart didn't actually run over me. I just banged into it and got knocked backwards on to the ground. I will be all right. I'll just set type for a while. I can do that sitting down.'

He took her arm and gently helped her the last few steps to the shop. When they reached the door, they stopped. 'Lucy, I—' he started to say, when the door was flung open.

Master Aubrey's red-haired apprentice Lach was staring at them. 'Oh, *sir*, I wasn't expecting to see *you*.' He gave Lucy a wicked smile that made her face flush.

'I'm back,' Adam said easily, not discomfited by the apprentice's mischievous remarks. 'Is Master Aubrey about?'

The master printer appeared behind his apprentice. 'Greetings, Master Adam. I'm pleased to see you've returned.' He rubbed his hands. 'Are there some pieces I may interest you in for you or your father?'

Adam bowed his head slightly. 'I will return soon enough. However, I must tell you that I believe Lucy must be seen by Doctor Larimer. She was injured this morning and—'

'What? What's wrong with her?' Master Aubrey asked, while Lach looked her over impudently.

'Seems fine to me,' Lach commented, regarding her still-full sack.

'I *am* fine,' Lucy said quickly. 'Truly. Perhaps I may just sit for a spell.'

'Lucy, you can barely walk. You're in pain.' Adam turned back to Master Aubrey and handed him Lucy's pack. 'Let me call for a chair to take you to Doctor Larimer. I'll be right back.'

'A chair! Oh no!' Lucy cried, but Adam ignored her. He left to hail a sedan chair, one of those fine chairs hefted by a man or two, which were used mainly by the wealthy, the elderly and the infirm to get around the crowded city streets.

'Didn't sell much,' Lach commented, looking at her bag.

Master Aubrey looked at Lucy. 'You do seem pale. Have the good physician examine you and return as soon as you can. We must set the type for a new tract this afternoon. It's in three parts and may take us into the evening.'

Seeing that there was no room to argue, Lucy gave in. 'I may have a story for you as well,' she teased, still trying to hide the pain from her bruises. 'I'll tell you what I encountered when I get back. You'll never believe it! There's even a ghost or two! A true tale indeed!'

'What? What! What was it?' Master Aubrey shouted, as Lach exclaimed, 'Don't go. Tell us!'

Just then, Adam walked up, followed by two men carrying a sedan chair between them. Such luxury! Lucy again began to demur, concerned by the expense, but Master Aubrey wagged a finger at her. 'Lucy!' he said. 'Do as Master Hargrave says. It's for the best.'

'Very well,' Lucy said, reluctantly agreeing. She let herself be helped into the chair, with its luxurious cushioned seats and curtained windows, and leaned back, trying to ignore Lach's mocking comments as they set off down the street.

Three

The swaying walk to Dr Larimer's took about twenty minutes, which was quite long enough for Lucy to be seated in the covered sedan chair. Her head pounding, she thought several times she was going to be sick with the motion. Adam walked alongside the chair, his hand resting on the curtained window frame, so that his fingers were visible to her the whole while. Now it was Adam's turn to talk, chatting about different news of London that he'd taken in earlier that day.

He's just trying to keep my mind off my injuries, Lucy thought. As much as she hated to admit it, she didn't think she could have made the long walk to the physician's residence on her own without some difficulty.

When they arrived, Dr Larimer's young servant Tom shouted when he saw Lucy being helped out of the sedan chair by Adam and went running inside for help. A moment later, Mrs Hotchkiss, the physician's housekeeper, came out, brushing her hands on her skirts. She looked from Lucy to Adam in dismay. 'Lucy Campion!' she exclaimed. 'What have you been doing to yourself? Are you injured?'

'She needs to see the physician, if you would, madam,' Adam said.

Lucy felt embarrassed by the attention. 'Oh, I can wait—'

28

'At once,' Adam added firmly.

'Of course, sir,' Mrs Hotchkiss replied, acknowledging his position and status. 'He is with a patient, but I'll fetch him. Please wait in his study.'

Lucy and Adam were ushered into Dr Larimer's study, and Lucy looked around. Earlier that year, she'd spent some time in the doctor's home, looking after a patient, a woman she'd discovered, incoherent and alone in the vast expanse of the city that had been destroyed after the fire. She had got to know the members of the Larimer household quite well during that time.

Although he was with a patient, the physician came out to see her immediately. 'Lucy, my dear! What has happened to you? Got yourself in trouble again?'

'In a way, I suppose, sir. Although I think trouble ran into *me*.'

'What? How's that?'

After Lucy quickly explained what had happened, Dr Larimer nodded. 'Ah, yes, I know about this. Constable Duncan stopped by a few minutes before you arrived with news of a suspicious suicide. I sent Sheridan to accompany him and to return here with the body if necessary.' He led Lucy to the bed where he examined patients. 'So you were run over by a cart? How inconvenient!' Despite his jovial tone, Lucy detected an undercurrent of worry.

'I wasn't actually run over by a cart. I was just knocked over,' Lucy repeated, starting to feel resigned when both men looked at her sternly.

'Wait outside, if you would,' the physician said

29

to Adam, gesturing towards the door. 'I need to understand the extent of Lucy's injuries.'

A short while later, Dr Larimer helped Lucy to stand up and move over to the chair. 'I do not think there was any internal injury done,' he said. 'Although that bruising will be painful and the stiffness will most likely linger. Wormwood tea for you. I shall let Mrs Hotchkiss know.'

'Wormwood,' Lucy said. 'I had quite a bit of experience making that when I was here. I can make it myself when I return to Aubrey's.'

'Nonsense. You'll have it here under my supervision.' He gave her a stern glance. 'Be certain to drink it slowly. If you feel any pain in your stomach, stop immediately. With such an injury, we cannot yet rule out internal damage.'

That was certainly true. She remembered being at the deathbed of a man who'd been run over by a cart. His suffering had been great indeed, and she would not wish such an end on anyone. 'Thank you, Doctor,' Lucy said.

When the physician opened the door, they could hear a great clamour out in the hallway. 'I've brought the suicide,' she heard Dr Sheridan call out, sounding annoyed. 'Against my better judgement.'

'I insisted,' Duncan replied. 'I trust Lucy when she said that something seemed off about his death.'

'Just so,' Dr Larimer said. 'All right, wheel him into the surgery down the hall. We shall do the autopsy there.'

Lucy stepped out of the room then, just in time

to see Duncan and Hank push the man's body to the closed room at the end of the corridor. When he saw her in the doorway, Dr Sheridan glared at her. There was little love lost between her and the physician's assistant, even though there'd been a thawing of sorts this past year. 'Causing us trouble again!' he muttered.

'What was your opinion of the body, sir?' Lucy asked. She was genuinely curious, but she tacked on the honorific to appeal to his sense of pride.

Both physicians glanced at her in surprise, though Dr Larimer's look was far fonder. 'Ah, Lucy. You remember the right questions to ask.'

Dr Sheridan shrugged, directing his answer to Dr Larimer. 'The body was clearly hanged, although it is not completely certain that the man committed suicide. A few indicators suggest that someone may have assisted in this most desperate act.'

'Could he have been murdered?' Lucy asked, thinking about the activities of the two men she'd seen at the site.

'I hope we will learn that from the autopsy,' Dr Larimer said. 'Doctor Sheridan, please go and prepare the body. I shall be along shortly.'

'Lucy, what are you doing here?' Duncan asked, entering the room. 'Did Doctor Larimer check you for injuries? Are you all right?'

The room was suddenly starting to feel very cramped and hot, and Lucy sat down in a nearby chair, her arm to her forehead.

'Lucy, would you like some mead?' Duncan asked, filling a tin cup of mead from the pitcher on the side table. He looked at Dr Larimer. 'Is there some medicine you can give her?'

'I am all right,' she said, hoping she did not sound petulant. She just wanted to lie down and rest. Thankfully, Mrs Hotchkiss arrived then with a cup of steaming wormwood tea, which she accepted gratefully. 'This will help.'

Dr Larimer insisted on waiting while she drank half of the liquid, asking her questions about her health as she drank. Finally, he seemed satisfied with her responses. 'Your colour is improving, too,' he said. 'We shall just keep an eye on you.'

Feeling a little revived, Lucy began to think more about the body. She remembered the conversation about why the man was wearing the ring around his neck. 'Were the man's fingers too swollen to wear a ring?'

Dr Sheridan stepped back out then, scowling when he heard Dr Larimer address Lucy's question. 'His fingers will have swelled in death. Still, most people who've been wearing bands on their fingers for long amounts of time will have notable lines there from being pinched or rubbing the skin. Or, depending on the ring's metal, there might be some discolouration. Sometimes, too, for men who spend their days in the sun, there may be lighter skin where the sun could not tan. Any one of those things may help us know.' He nodded at Sheridan. 'If you would check, sir.'

'Why doesn't everyone just come along?' Sheridan asked, giving Lucy a mocking grin. 'The body is ready for autopsy.'

'I don't really need to see the body again—' Lucy began.

32

'Please, I insist.'

Lucy wasn't sure if Sheridan was trying to torment her or if he truly wanted her to come along, but, resigned, she and the others trailed into the autopsy room, where the man's corpse awaited.

Despite living in Dr Larimer's household earlier that year, Lucy had not spent much time in the space where the physicians conducted autopsies. The powerful smell of the room assaulted her nose, and she put her hand over her mouth. Even though there were sachets of rosemary and lavender all around the room, their cloying perfumes could not quite mask the more pungent stench of death.

The corpse was on a table in the centre of the room, a sheet covering his now-naked form. The clothes the man had been wearing were all dumped in a basket in the corner. They'd clearly been cut off the man's body with the pair of sharp scissors now resting in a tray with the other surgical instruments.

'So quick, Sheridan,' Dr Larimer murmured to his assistant, looking pointedly at the pile. From his tone, Lucy could not tell if he was complimenting his assistant or not. She suspected not. Dr Larimer tended to be far more meticulous and thorough in his actions.

Not replying to the senior physician, Dr Sheridan examined the man's hands one by one, then turned back to the others. 'A cursory inspection of all the man's fingers reveal that he did not habitually wear a band.'

'So perhaps the ring belonged to someone else,' Lucy mused, still standing a few steps away. 'I wonder what that might mean.'

Adam was staring at the man's face. 'Lucy,' he said, 'does this man look familiar to you?' His voice was strained, worried. 'I feel I've met him before.'

'I never observed his face in detail,' she replied, trying not to shudder. 'I couldn't bear to look long on his countenance.'

'Please look,' Adam said. 'I know it is not a very becoming sight, but I must know.'

'Certainly,' Lucy said. Ignoring the nausea that surged up when she looked at the dead body, she peered more closely. He was clearly now in the grip of rigor mortis, not the malleable form she'd looked upon that morning. His hair was thick and black, though trimmed neatly as befitting a rich tradesman's status. The earlier flush to the man's countenance had faded to the sickly bluish colour of death. His eyes were still closed but his features did not look recognizable. 'I don't think I know him. Why? Do *you*?'

Adam continued to stare at the corpse. 'I don't know. There's something about him.'

'Maybe this will help you remember.' Dr Sheridan pulled back the white sheet to expose the man's upper left arm, exposing a tattoo of a sea serpent. They all stared at it.

'No,' Lucy said. 'I've never seen this before.'

Adam studied the tattoo, eventually shaking his head. 'No, that doesn't look familiar to me either. Still, there's something about this man. I hope I can remember.'

Lucy and Adam walked slowly to Master Aubrey's. She was grateful that Adam had not insisted on another sedan chair for the journey back to the printer's shop, although he moved at a slower pace through the streets to accommodate her halting movements.

'Have you remembered where you've seen him?' Lucy asked. 'He appeared to be a tradesman. Perhaps you have been to his shop or he has made a delivery to your father's household.'

'That could be it, but I just can't recall. Certainly, it could not have been a recent encounter.' He sighed. 'With any luck, my slumbers will be restful and I might recall how I may have known him.'

They fell silent then, each to their own thoughts. Finally, Lucy broke the silence. 'Adam, what's it like in the New World?' she asked. She'd read the strange and fantastic tales of the colonists as well as the native peoples who preceded them.

He hesitated. 'Rough. I do believe in the opportunities there, but people age quickly. The environs are quite difficult. I have heard the winters there take on an ungodly chill. There has been much sickness that I am wary of, too.'

Will you be returning soon? Do you see a life there now? Why did you return? These questions hovered on her lips but she did not speak them. A sudden aching in her chest told her that she could not bear to hear his reply.

'Well, Lucy,' he said when they reached the shop. 'Do take your wormwood tea as Doctor Larimer has prescribed.'

35

Lucy waited to see if he might mention anything of seeing her again, or bring up wanting to speak to her, as he had earlier that day. When he didn't, she gave a tight nod and pushed into the printer's shop.

Four

After tossing and turning for a long while on her straw pallet, Lucy finally got up and opened the shutters of her tiny room. It was still dark, maybe several hours before dawn. Her stomach was not hurting any more except when she touched it, but her back was still paining her a bit. She must have hit a root or something when she was knocked to the ground, although, as the physician said, she'd certainly been lucky not to have sustained more serious injuries. Still, the purple bruising all over her body was a sight to behold.

Lighting one of the long tapers she kept in a small box, Lucy sat down at her table and pulled out a sheet of paper. Dipping her quill in the ink, she thought for a moment and then began to write: *A True and Fantastic Tale of a Corpse Discovered at a Crossroads.*

Chuckling to herself, she continued weaving the tale of why the man had killed himself, deciding that he had 'hoped to escape the Devil's madness'. Such language would appeal to her readers, and she could already imagine the woodcut of the Devil terrorizing a man that would accompany the piece. Master Aubrey had printed several of her pieces to date, all of them 'Anonymous' as befitting her status as a woman and former servant.

Setting down her quill, she massaged her fingers and palm. The physical act of writing was still painful and frustrating for her, as she had not learned to write until her later adolescence, although the joy of seeing her true accounts in print had outweighed her pain. Like most born into servant families, she'd only received a piece-meal education, learning bits and pieces from dame schools – run by old women tasked with teaching children their letters so they could read the Bible for themselves. Things had changed when she'd joined the magistrate's household at the age of sixteen. When Master Hargrave had brought in itinerant scholars from the great universities to tutor his daughter, she'd found ways to listen in on the lessons and develop her understanding of the world.

Reading over what she had written so far, she thought about bringing in Bedlam, having visited that godforsaken place for lunatics earlier in the year. However, there was something truly pitiful about the inmates there, and she did not wish to add to their pain by mocking them. Should she include ghosts instead? Why not?

Thinking about ghosts reminded her of the odd ring that she'd removed from around the man's neck. *Memento mori*, Adam had said. *Remember that you will die.* Or was it the other phrasing? *Remember that you have to die.* Did the ring mean something?

She wrote the words down on a different piece of paper, not sure if she'd spelled them correctly. Latin was not a language she knew well at all, although she could sometimes recognize it now from reviewing the tracts of other booksellers. She drew a little picture of the ring from memory.

'Shall I include the ring and those words in my true tale?' Lucy asked herself. 'No, someone might think I robbed the body.'

Abruptly, she pushed the paper away and replaced the plug in the jar of ink. The ring reminded her of Adam and Duncan, and the uncertainty of her feelings for each. Duncan, she knew, wanted to marry her. He'd been married once before, when he was very young, but his wife had died when they still lived in York. Recently, though, he'd mentioned how he'd like to wed again. She was less sure about Adam, and she was even less certain of her own heart. He'd once expressed an interest in becoming betrothed, but then he had left for the New World, which had wounded her.

What had he wanted to tell me today? she wondered. *Perhaps he wanted to tell me he was marrying someone else?* Even thinking that caused a deep pain in her heart. 'Although it would be easier if that were the case,' she said, slumping back in the chair. Duncan, she knew, would be a very good husband, and she was more suited to the station of a constable's wife. He'd make her a good home; she knew that, too.

Except that it was hard not to recall the passionate kiss she'd once exchanged with Adam, during the plague, when the world still seemed upside down. He had promised her a new life and he'd done so much for her brother. There had been a moment when she'd thought she could marry him. As the dust had settled, though, the differences between their positions in life had seemed too great. Still, he was so caring and attentive when he thought she was injured. Perhaps there was a way for the distance between them to be resolved.

Fretfully, she picked a small wooden box off her table. This box contained some of her most treasured possessions. She picked out the letter that Adam had written to her before he had left for the New World. She smoothed it out and read it again, a rush of emotion flooding over her as she read his elegantly penned words again.

> My heart will be sore without you, my dearest Lucy, but perchance you will one day travel to this strange New World where, as Sarah has told me, the birth right of men is less fixed. I have heard tell, too, of several petticoat authors among the colonists. Perhaps, one day soon, even a female printer may find a way to ply her trade.

At the time, she hadn't known if he'd return, and she had begun to ease her heart with Duncan's attentions. Later, Adam had sent her two other letters as well, one which she received in late June, and the other in late September. In neither letter had he mentioned his plans to return to London. They focused mostly on the challenges they had with enforcing laws in the colonies – that the laws of England were harder to apply in the colonies.

Things are rougher here, to be sure, Lucy, but there is much that is good and worthy as well. There are opportunities that I can foresee.

He did not mention setting up a printing press or bookseller again, as he had in the earlier message. Much of it was matter of fact, but there was a questioning sense there as well.

'Why did he come back?' Lucy asked, putting her hand to her forehead. She put the letters in the box, not sure what to do about the tugging at her heart.

'Dunderhead!' Master Aubrey said, lightly boxing Lach's ears the next morning. He pointed at the woodcut of a witch that the apprentice had been inserting into the Goodly Cruff's homely remedies. 'This is not a Devil's piece. Honestly, I don't know what to do with you.'

Lucy leaned over his shoulder. 'Oh, Lach,' she said, hiding a smile.

His apprentice grinned cheekily. 'Did you look at the ingredients? They are much the same as the witch's brew we printed last night.'

Master Aubrey cuffed him again. 'We want people to buy them, not feel they are being magicked.' He looked at Lucy. 'What say you, lass? You've been a bit quiet today. Indeed, I'm fearful of your mild temperament. Usually, by this time of the day you and Lach have thrice bickered.' His brow furrowed. 'Have you taken your tisane for healing? We need you back well, in spirit and in body.'

41

Stifling a yawn, Lucy pulled the short piece she had penned about the man's death and handed it to the master printer. 'I am greatly improved, thank you, sir. I did wake up last night, and I couldn't rest until I'd written this tale.'

'What's this?' he asked, glancing over her words. 'Honestly, Lucy, your hand is still so ill. You must work to improve it.'

'I'm sorry my script is so poor. I'll practise it, I promise,' she said, before giving him a cheeky grin. 'Please do read it, though. I think you'll find it a thrilling tale.'

Master Aubrey glanced at the paper. 'A suicide at the crossroads?' He rubbed his hands together. 'Good, good. Ghosts, spirits, desperate souls. Although murder would be better. After all—'

'Everyone loves a good murder!' Lucy and Lach joined in on the familiar phrase. They all looked at each other and laughed, a funny moment of camaraderie summing up everything they'd been through together these last two years.

'Truth be told, I think there's a question about whether this was indeed a suicide,' Lucy said when their chuckles had subsided. 'I witnessed something odd—'

'Of course you did!' Lach interrupted. 'Hasn't anyone ever asked you why you're around when so many strange deaths occur? Why is that, Lucy?'

Lucy frowned. She *had* encountered more than her share of suspicious deaths and murders these last few years. None sadder, though, than the death of Bessie, a merry soul who had been her most beloved friend. So much had passed since

42

then – Lucy was hardly the girl she'd once been, in those days before she'd been touched by evil. 'I don't know. It's not as if I cause them. I suppose I'm just—'

'Cursed!' Lach interrupted. He made the sign of the Devil, by putting his forefingers to his head like horns. 'There's no doubt about it.'

'Aw, get on with you, lad,' Master Aubrey said, rolling up Lucy's account in his hand and using it to swat his apprentice's head. 'Lucy's not cursed.'

'Of course not,' Lach said, making the sign again, this time when the master printer had turned away. *You are!* he mouthed at her and laughed when she stomped back to her bench to continue setting type.

'I'll read the rest of it later,' Master Aubrey promised. 'Right now, I need you to get to the work at hand.'

For the next hour, Lucy continued to set the type, her fingers flying as she placed each character backwards in neat rows. There was a rhythm associated with setting the print that was akin to playing a musical instrument, and interrupting the rhythm could result in mistakes. And Master Aubrey hated nothing more than adding an erratum to the end of a piece, especially when it was something that could easily have been avoided with a bit of care.

A rap at the printer's shop door caused them all to look up. Lucy was not the only one to recognize it.

'That's for you,' Master Aubrey said, nodding

at Lucy. 'Mind, we have a lot to do today, and I don't want you gallivanting about.'

'Maybe he's got news of another murder,' Lach said.

'Must you sound so gleeful?' Lucy asked over her shoulder as she opened the shop door.

As expected, Duncan stood there, ramrod straight, his soldierly bearing showing. Lucy could tell from his demeanour that he was there in an official capacity as he stepped into the room and nodded towards the master printer. 'Good morning. Master Aubrey, I need to speak to Lucy for a few moments, if you can spare her.'

Lach gave a whoop that was stifled by Aubrey. 'Hush,' he said to his apprentice. To Lucy he said, 'Be quick about it. Remember what I just said about not gallivanting.'

'Come in, Duncan,' Lucy said, taking his heavy woollen cloak from him. It must have been raining, because the cloth was wet to the touch. 'Pray, warm yourself by the hearth. Would you like some hot mead? Or perhaps some nourishing victuals?'

'No, thank you, Lucy,' Duncan said. 'I shan't stay long. I wanted to let you know that I just spoke with Doctor Larimer.'

'Oh?' Lucy asked, while both Master Aubrey and Lach stopped what they were doing, craning their necks to hear what Duncan had to say. They knew that the physician might take on a coroner's role to determine cause of death. 'What did you learn?'

'He and Doctor Sheridan have already completed their initial report. As you may have gleaned,

44

they are not convinced that the man killed himself. Doctor Larimer has called for a fuller investigation into the man's death, because they suspect foul play.'

'Foul play? Why? How could they know that? I mean, from what I overheard those men say, it seems that could be the case, but surely they would not draw conclusions in such a way.'

'No, their conclusions came from their own observations. First, his neck had been broken in a manner consistent with being forcibly hanged. Less consistent with suicide, though, unless the man had jumped off the branch, which might have resulted in the horrific break.'

'I see,' Lucy replied, trying to imagine the scene. 'So he would have had to climb on to the branch, wrap the rope around the tree, place the noose around his neck and then throw himself off.'

'Exactly,' Duncan replied.

'Then he wouldn't have needed the stool,' Lucy pointed out.

Duncan nodded. 'That is so. There's more. Doctor Sheridan told me that the man had recently suffered a great blow to the back of his head. They insisted that such a blow must have occurred when the man was alive. Judging from the wound, they believe that it occurred shortly before he was hanged. Quite unnatural. There is also a strong chance that his neck was broken *before* he was hanged, although they were less certain about this. Lastly, they concluded that the time of death was also consistent with when you discovered him.'

'His death must have happened just before I arrived.' She shivered. What would have happened if she had witnessed the event? Or perhaps she very nearly had.

'Lucy,' Duncan said. 'They also took into account what you had overheard the two men say about knocking over the stool. It sounds as if – as you suspected – the two men you saw may have at the very least helped the man to die, which is an offence punishable by law, and masked their involvement in his self-murder.' Seeing Lucy shiver, he touched her arm.

At his touch, Lucy stepped back, feeling a pang at the hurt expression that flitted across his face. Fortunately, something else came to her mind, returning them both to the issue at hand. 'I remember now that they called each other "Dev" and "Pike". Perhaps that will help.'

'Dev and Pike?'

'Yes, I think that's right.'

'All right,' Duncan said, making a notation in the small book he carried in his pocket. 'There's something else. I took it upon myself to further examine the man's clothes, wondering if we might learn anything about his identity or his death. It turns out that he was wearing a second pocket, hidden beneath his clothes.'

'Oh!' Lucy exclaimed. 'Doctor Sheridan must have missed it when he cut the clothes off the man's body with such haste. Did you find something?'

'Yes, but I don't know what it means.' Duncan opened up a pocket and withdrew a piece of paper that had been folded twice. 'I was thinking that

46

you might ask Master Hargrave if he can make head or tail of this. I most certainly cannot.'

Lucy took the paper from him, noting its coarse texture and greyish appearance. A very common type of paper, typically used for writing letters and records or keeping household accounts. Not usually what they used for printing. Unfolding it, she found it was about the size of a chapbook, just a few inches in all directions, a few hand-printed lines in the middle.

'What language is this?' she asked, squinting at the writing. It was clearly not English, and there were some unfamiliar symbols interspersed within the words as well. 'I've never seen such characters before.'

M YGHX HX YGC MIN ✝GP XCY YGC
& DWA
P LMJC GHL KCMB △Y ZT ZGC &
Y NFYM UNK ፡PYM L፡ZX UNK &Q
YKHV
Z △SYQRL JZ✝ LQR H□H. RIYH LQX
EZ ELI π

'I don't know,' Duncan replied, sounding frustrated. 'Doctor Larimer said it was no language he knew, although he thought one or two of the symbols were Greek. He suggested I might ask Master Hargrave about it, who has a very fine head for such things. Or his son.' He coughed. 'I would take it over to the Hargraves myself, but Hank broke up a tavern fight last night, and we've got several men cooling their heels in our cell.'

'Was there anything else in the pocket?'

'Nothing too useful. Just a few tradesmen's tokens. I'll visit the businesses later. Perhaps someone will be able to identify him.'

'I think you are right to see if either of the Hargraves can help us. They are quite knowledgeable.' Feeling the constable bristle slightly, she added hastily, 'Especially the magistrate, of course. Let me just copy the message so that you may keep the original.'

'No, I think it best that you show them the original.'

'Perhaps.' Taking a piece of paper and a quill, Lucy scrupulously copied every letter and symbol as faithfully as she could, before handing the copy to Duncan and carefully refolding the message and placing it in her own pocket. 'I shall ask Master Aubrey for leave to visit the Hargraves later. Perhaps he will allow me to go after I have completed my afternoon chores.'

Duncan studied her but did not reach out to touch her again. 'Thank you, Lucy. Please let me know anything you might learn from the magistrate.'

After the constable took his leave, Lucy stepped back inside to ask permission. While Aubrey's household was far less strict than most, she still could not come and go as she pleased. 'Master Aubrey, would it be all right if I—'

'Take a few hours to help Constable Duncan?' the master printer interrupted.

'Well, yes,' Lucy replied. 'I'd like to see the Hargraves tonight, if I may. The constable thought that they might shed some light on a few matters that have turned up in his investigation.'

Master Aubrey dramatically gestured heavenward. 'Why, Lord, am I so burdened with two halfwit apprentices?'

'I'll make all my deliveries and do extra ones. I'll also make the porridge every morning for a week,' she continued, adopting the playful wheedling tone that she reserved for such occasions. 'Besides, you don't have to pay me for the tract I just wrote.'

'Enough, enough,' Master Aubrey said. 'Let's just finish printing these broadsides. We must heed the time and get the order done.'

Five

Holding her small glass lantern high above her head, Lucy strode swiftly along Chancery Lane towards the Hargraves' home, trying to ignore how the tiny flame caused long ominous shadows all around her. The regulations against lanterns and open flames in effect over the past year had finally been relaxed by the City's authorities, so she was grateful for the small light that the lantern provided. She would have preferred to have left Master Aubrey's when it was less dark and there were more people around. Still, she was glad that he had let her go at all.

The fog had grown thicker as she walked, muffling the sounds of distant church bells tolling eight o'clock, distancing her from the world around her. The stillness reminded her how few people were out and about at this hour. Most only ventured into the streets when absolutely necessary, especially when the fog was as thick and impenetrable as it was tonight. Many had grown used to the evening curfew which, like the regulations concerning lanterns, had been recently relaxed.

She turned down the walk to the Hargraves' home. She hoped the magistrate and Adam had long finished their supper and were not entertaining any guests this evening. Although the windows were shuttered, she could see the soft glow of candles gleaming in Master Hargrave's study. Going around to the back, she knocked at the kitchen entrance.

'Who's making deliveries at this hour?' Cook grumbled as she slid open the lock. Then, when she threw open the door, her grumpy expression changed as she realized who was standing there. 'Oh, Lucy! It's you! Well, come on in, lass. Don't let the chill in.'

Giving a little squeal, Annie jumped up from the wooden table, nearly knocking over her cup of hot mead and earning her a scowl from Cook. Laughing, Lucy allowed herself to be caught in the servant's scrawny arms. Cook's husband, John, gave her a friendly smile but stayed silent in his customary taciturn way. Standing together with them caused a wave of nostalgia to flood over Lucy. Cook and John had watched over her like parents for the several years she'd served the Hargraves, and when Annie came along, she felt she had gained a little sister. *I miss them terribly*, she realized. *I'm also envious that they still live here, with the Hargraves. Sometimes I wish I did, too.* That last fleeting thought passed quickly, however. She was grateful to have found work that she loved with Master Aubrey. Nothing could match the beauty of creating and selling books.

'What brings you here so late?' Cook asked. 'You cannot be here for one of your games of chess with the master.'

'Do not fear, nothing is amiss,' she said. She gave an exaggerated sniff, taking in the delicious aroma of Cook's stew which still lingered in the

51

air. 'Perhaps I'm just here to have a second supper.'

'Oh, of course, sit down!' Cook cried and began to bustle about. 'Annie, get a hunk of that rye bread. John, hand me a bowl. Lucy's looking too thin. I'll just warm the stew—'

Lucy threw up her hands. 'Nay, Cook. I was just teasing. I am indeed quite full from supper. To be truthful, I'm here to see the Hargraves about an important issue. Alas, it has naught to do with chess.'

'I see,' Cook said, sitting down opposite her, while Annie sat close beside her. John remained standing, leaning against the wall. 'Did Master Hargrave invite you? Or perhaps it was the young master? He's recently returned from the New World.'

'I did know. I've already seen Adam – Master Adam, I mean. He came to see me at Master Aubrey's yesterday.'

Lucy caught Cook and John exchanging a glance, causing her cheeks to flame as hotly as the kitchen hearth. While they may not have known the details of what had gone on between her and Adam, she sensed they knew something of what his feelings had been. They'd never discussed any of this, and Lucy could not discern what they thought of her relationship with either of the men interested in courting her. She'd never dared ask their opinion, although it would not have surprised her if they had favoured the constable as a more suitable match.

Casting about for a different topic, Lucy pulled out *The Cook's True Delight* that she and Lach

52

had been working on that morning and slid it across the table.

'For me?' Cook beamed, examining it, always happy to get new recipes to try. Then her brow furrowed as she looked more closely at the woodcut. 'Why is there a witch here? I'm not making a witch's brew. Not for the magistrate! This is a godly household!'

'Yes, of course,' Lucy said, trying to soothe her feelings. *A pox upon Lach!* 'Oh no! Don't throw it away!'

Unfortunately, she was too late. Cook had already crumpled up the broadside and thrown it on the fire. It blackened for a second and then was gone.

'I'll bring you a recipe for a godlier stew next time,' Lucy said, feeling a bit chagrined. 'May I go see Master Hargrave now?'

Cook shooed her away. 'Get along with you now!' Then, less gruffly, added, 'Stop back before you leave, Lucy. I'll send you back with some jars of stew.'

As she walked down the corridor, though, she was stopped by Annie tugging on her sleeve. 'Have you seen that wretch Sid recently?' she whispered. 'I never see him much at church and he hasn't stopped by for victuals in a long time. Stupid rascal.'

Lucy hid a smile. She didn't know how Annie had developed such a soft spot for the lad. 'I'll ask Duncan,' she promised. 'He usually keeps up to date on Sid's doings.' *Especially when those doings meant sending him to the stocks.*

Looking satisfied, Annie danced back to the

53

kitchen, and Lucy sighed, hoping that the young woman's affections had not been misplaced.

Hearing Master Hargrave's assent to her quiet knock, Lucy walked into her former employer's study. The Hargraves had moved here after the fire, and she'd only lived in this house a few days before taking up residence at Master Aubrey's. Still, there was a comforting familiarity to the room, being among his books and maps and great tasks. It smelled of burned tallow, spilled ink and the musty aroma of old books – very much as parts of Master Aubrey's shop smelled as well.

'Ah, Lucy,' the magistrate said, standing up when she walked in. The respectful demeanour he bore towards her was one of her old master's most endearing traits. Even when she'd served in his household, he'd always been gracious and kind, never beating his servants as other men would to correct their mistakes and maintain order. 'I've been expecting you.'

'You have?' Lucy asked, feeling pleased but confused. 'We had no appointment, as I recall. Pray, forgive me if we did.'

'No, no. You've done nothing amiss. Adam said you'd probably stop by.' Here he chuckled. 'You were certainly right, son.'

Lucy swivelled to find Adam standing before a cushioned chair in the corner, smiling slightly.

'Did the constable tell you I'd be coming?' she asked.

'No,' Adam said, his smile fading. 'I just had a feeling you'd want to discuss your latest quest with Father.' He picked up a quill off the desk

54

and set it back down in the same place. 'Why did the constable think you'd be coming here? Did you speak to him today?'

Lucy turned to Master Hargrave. 'A new mystery has emerged, sir! I thought you could help us solve it.'

'Us?' Adam asked.

The magistrate darted a look at his son. 'Sit, please, Lucy,' he said, gesturing to the red embroidered chair next to Adam. 'I should very much like to hear how I can help you. First, tell me about yesterday's exciting news. Adam told me some of what transpired, but naturally I'd much prefer to hear it from you.'

Instead of seating herself, Lucy clapped her hands loudly as if standing before a crowd. 'Good people! I have today the tale of a most astonishing event, right out of St Giles-in-the-Fields, on Drury Lane. Whereby I did see, with mine own eyes, the startling sight of a corpse dangling from the old hanging tree, where witches, murderers and suicides might find themselves hanged . . .' With this opening statement, which caused both men to start and then laugh, Lucy launched into the story of what had transpired the day before. Her experience selling broadsides and true accounts from atop a wooden box had taught her how to spin a good tale. She began to dramatically re-enact how she'd discovered the body and hid from the two men, using her whole body, voice and words to tell the tale. She also embellished the details, adding more to her reactions, and telling more of the ghosts of bodies hidden at the crossroads.

Throughout, Adam and Master Hargrave wore amused expressions on their faces, applauding heartily when she concluded. 'So ends the first part of *The Corpse at the Crossroads*,' she said, offering a deep curtsy before sitting down, exhausted.

'Brava, brava! Wonderful, Lucy,' Master Hargrave exclaimed, clapping heartily. 'A remarkable tale, to be sure. Shall we soon have the pleasure of reading this *True Account*?' He laughed. 'Although, to my mind, five ghosts drifting in and out of Drury Lane may have been a few too many. Nevertheless, we shall be sure to buy several copies when it is printed.'

Lucy grinned. Although she knew that Master Hargrave did not put much stock in the more fanciful elements of the tale, she was touched that he'd shown such a keen interest in her first attempts at writing.

'The first part?' Adam commented. 'What, then, is the second part? You mentioned a new mystery when you arrived.'

'Constable Duncan stopped by to tell me that a message was found on the corpse, and he would very much like your thoughts.'

'Indeed?' the magistrate asked. Both he and Adam looked intrigued.

'Yes, apparently they found it in a second pocket that the man had kept tied beneath his clothes. They were hoping for something else that might help identify him.' She extracted the bit of vellum from her pocket and handed it to the magistrate. 'Doctor Larimer said one of you might understand what this message means.'

Adam leaned over his father's shoulder so they could study the paper together. Both men frowned at the same moment, their blue eyes looking almost identical. While the magistrate's hair had thinned considerably and whitened over the last few years, Adam's was still thick with a slight wave.

'This is not a different language,' Adam declared. 'This message is in cipher.'

'So odd,' the magistrate agreed, holding it up to the light. 'Could be a simple substitution cipher, or one that relies on the recipient knowing a specific key. Very strange indeed.'

'Do you think that this message has something to do with the man's death?' Lucy asked. 'I know that Doctor Larimer has suspicions about whether the man actually killed himself. He and Doctor Sheridan said they thought he'd been struck on the back of the head before he was hanged. They also believe there is a good chance that his neck was broken beforehand, although their findings are not conclusive.'

'Is that so?' Adam asked. 'That would require a level of premeditation, then, to hang a dead or nearly dead body. They'd have to bring along rope and the stool, at the very least. It is possible that they simply waited for the man to arrive, unless they lured him there in some fashion.'

'Perhaps the message tells him to come to the crossroads, where he met his fate.' Lucy swallowed. 'We've seen that before.' Unexpectedly, a tear pricked her eye. Years ago, before the plague and the Great Fire, her fellow servant and good friend Bessie had received such an invitation and ended up meeting death instead.

'Ah, Bessie,' the magistrate said, having followed her thoughts. 'She was a good lass.'

'Indeed,' Adam added. They were all quiet, thinking of the lively girl Bessie had been. Then he cleared his throat. 'It is possible, as you say, that the message told him to come to the crossroads. It is also quite possible that he was killed for the message itself. Or to keep him from delivering it. Either might make sense, if you think about it, given that the message was hidden upon his person.'

'So, it may have been more about the message than the man? Who would kill the messenger?' Lucy asked. 'And in such a manner?'

'"No man delights in the bearer of bad news,"' the magistrate replied. 'Sophocles had it right. Just because a man brings bad news does not mean that he should be killed.'

Lucy nodded. There were laws against town criers being killed for sharing bad news from King or Parliament. Even she'd been on the other end of some wrath for singing the news of the day, particularly when such news was disturbing or troublesome.

'Perhaps he was a spy? Or a traitor?' Lucy asked.

The magistrate clucked his tongue. 'Perhaps. Although he'd be thrown in jail if a traitor to England and tried as a spy. I have heard of many men who encrypt their correspondence as a matter of course. Some tradesmen, merchants, bankers – occupations like that.'

Lucy nodded. 'Constable Duncan said the man appeared to be in trade. He found a few trader's tokens that he was going to investigate.'

'Sometimes such secret messages are more playful, sent between friends or lovers,' Adam added. 'I knew some scholars at Cambridge who corresponded in such fashion with women with whom they were infatuated.'

'So he may have been a courier. Between merchants? Lovers? Traitors?' Lucy pondered. 'How can we know?'

'We are still just surmising, as we do not know in fact if this man was a messenger. Certainly, as you yourself just pointed out, Lucy,' Adam said, 'what a fantastic method of murder. To hang a man at a crossroads, in broad daylight, when anyone might come along. Such a cold and purposeful act.'

'It does make me wonder about the ring,' Lucy said. *Maybe we should ask a jeweller about it,* she thought. *It shouldn't be too hard to convince Duncan.* There was such a man on the Strand who had a good reputation for being knowledge-able and fair. Maybe he'd have some thoughts on who had made the piece. 'That might help,' she murmured.

'What might help?' Adam asked.

'Oh, nothing,' she replied, watching as he took another piece of paper and began to rapidly copy the characters and symbols using one of his father's finely cut quill pens. He clearly was following her same instinct from earlier.

The magistrate held the original under his flea glass. 'Some of this does indeed seem to be Greek

59

characters. Although I do not believe this to be a mathematical equation, a good acquaintance of mine might be pressed to weigh in on the matter. I am thinking of the mathematician Neville Wallace, who we might seek out for his good counsel in this matter.'

'Wallace?' Adam asked, his brow crinkling a bit. 'I remember meeting him once or twice. If I recall correctly, he advised Parliament on various ciphers and messages over the years, before King Charles was restored to the throne. He was quite good at it, too, from what I understand.'

'Indeed,' his father replied. 'He's a member of the Royal Society, recently returned from Cambridge. The King, I've heard, wanted him nearby when he learned of his keen mathematical skills.' He rubbed his hands together. 'I believe we just might entice Mr Wallace with hearty fare and a good puzzle. I shall invite him and his wife to dine this week.'

Six

After Lucy had spent the morning sweating over *The True Tale of a Most Monstrous Cat*, she was finally able to slip over to the jail and tell Duncan what she had learned from the Hargraves. But neither the constable nor Hank was on hand when she arrived, and in their stead she found a Welshman by the name of Gruffyd keeping watch at the jail. She didn't know Gruffyd very well and had a hard time understanding him because his accent was so thick. Finally, after much pantomiming, she understood that Duncan and Hank were down at the stocks a half mile away.

Lucy hurried down Fleet Street towards the pillory at the other end. There she saw the constable and Hank next to a man bent over at the stocks. She stopped short when she saw his face, her hand flying to her mouth. *Speak of the Devil and the Devil shall appear*, she could almost hear her mother say. It was Sid, the pickpocket who Annie had just asked about the night before.

Duncan was standing beside the stocks, his arms crossed as he kept a stern watch on the hecklers who had gathered. A few boys came along, hefting raw eggs and tomatoes in front of the pickpocket, threatening to toss them on his face. Sid exchanged good-natured barbs with them. Just another merriment to pass the time.

'Oh, Sid,' she said, moving to stand in front of the lanky young man, just as a pulpy tomato was plopped on to his mop of brown hair. 'Whatever did you do this time?'

'Hey, Lucy,' Sid said, craning as best he could to look up at her. 'Why don't you guess? I'll let you give me a kiss if you get it right.'

'Not a chance,' Lucy replied, at the same time stopping Duncan as he reached out to swat Sid across the back of his head. She took out a small handkerchief from her outer pocket to wipe some of the egg yolk and tomato pulp off Sid's forehead and cheeks, ignoring the taunts and jeers of the spectators for breaking up their sport.

Hank spoke up then. 'Why bother, miss? This one will never learn. How many times have you been in the stocks just this month, Sid?'

'Five, I think,' Sid replied, giving a cheeky grin.

She shook her head at him. 'You need to change your ways, Sid. You can't keep pickpocketing and this kind of petty theft.'

'I should stop getting caught, you mean,' Sid replied. Hearing him, some of the boys around them guffawed.

'Isn't there something else you want to do? Is there a profession you want to pursue? Can you not try to make a livelihood for yourself?'

Sid smiled. 'Are you trying to make an honest man of me, Lucy? Are you asking me to settle down? I'd be happy to live off your earnings as a bookseller. I'll look after our children while you follow that noble profession!'

Beside her, Duncan stiffened while the crowd

around them laughed. Some of them began to jeer now at Lucy, and she straightened up. 'I don't intend on marrying anyone soon,' she said.

'I think it's best if you leave, Lucy,' Duncan said. 'Besides, there's something I'd like to talk to you about.'

'I have something to tell you, too,' she replied. 'Just let me say one more thing to Sid.'

Leaning down, she whispered in Sid's ear, 'Annie was asking about you, when I went to the Hargraves' last night. What do you think that I should say to her? Do you think she'd be pleased to know you've been in the stocks five times this month already? Oh, Sid.'

Sid's face changed. 'Annie – asked about me?'

Lucy stood back up without responding, allowing Duncan to lead her away.

'You went to see the Hargraves?' he asked when they were out of earshot of the hecklers. 'Did you show them the message? What did they say? Could they read it?'

Taking his sleeve, Lucy pulled the constable over to the side of the street where relatively few people were selling, buying or otherwise meandering about. 'Yes, I showed the note to them. They did not recognize the language. Indeed, they said it was more likely written in a secret language, a cipher of some sort.'

'A cipher?' Duncan whistled. 'I wonder what that means.'

'Adam – I mean, Mister Hargrave – said that such ciphers were often used among tradesmen, and, of course, to send political and military secrets. He said it was also not so uncommon

63

among his set to send such coded messages to acquaintances and friends. Both the sender and the recipient would just need to have a key. He said it was a type of a game for some.'

'I see. Coded messages to hide military and state secrets make sense. I've never heard of them being used by tradesmen, or just between individuals for merrymaking.' Duncan fell silent, apparently thinking. 'Would they usually use a messenger or pass the message directly?'

'That I don't know,' Lucy replied. 'I think there is usually someone who plays the role of messenger. At least when they are sending these ciphers as games.' *Had Adam ever sent anyone such cryptic messages?* Perhaps in those more carefree days before the plague and Great Fire had torn their worlds apart. 'They told me that they were determined to solve the puzzle, although it might not be possible without the key. However, Master Hargrave was going to reach out to a scholar of mathematics that he knows from Cambridge and ask if he might be able to decipher the message.'

'I see. That would be helpful.' From the stiffness of his reply, Lucy could tell that he hated to ask the Hargraves for such assistance.

She touched his sleeve. 'Duncan, there is a jeweller on the Strand who might be able to answer some questions about the ring. Who crafted it, who might have bought it – that sort of thing.'

'That is a good idea,' Duncan replied. 'When would you be able to visit the jeweller? Are you free now, perchance?'

Looking up at the sun, Lucy tried to determine the time. 'Is it about two o'clock? I have another hour or two of selling to do before Master Aubrey might expect my return.' She glanced at her dress, which was looking rather worn. 'However, I'm thinking that I might change my dress before we go.'

'You look sprightly enough to me.'

'I should look better for a trip to the jeweller's, to ensure he takes me well,' Lucy said, before continuing. 'If you can retrieve the ring from the jail, you can meet me over on the Strand in about thirty minutes. I'll be in front of the Red Lion. With any luck, I can sell a few pieces from my pack to offer Master Aubrey as some fruitful proof of my labours.'

'Pardon me, sir,' Lucy called a short while later to the costermonger, whose handcart full of old cabbages, carrots and other withered-looking vegetables was blocking her path. This time of year, fresh vegetables and other produce were getting scarce, even though the new greenhouses had started to help ensure that people had something other than root vegetables. 'I should very much like to get around your cart.'

The vegetable man scowled at her. 'Well, you're a pert miss,' he said. 'Can't you see my wheel is broken?'

Looking down, she could see that the wheel had indeed cracked in half, making it likely unmovable. Right now, she'd have to squeeze between two stands, and the cart looked well lodged into place. The man was still trying to

65

pick up some of the vegetables that had dropped on to the ground, brushing the dirt off one by one and placing them back into the cart. She was just helping the man tug the handcart to the side of the path when Duncan's voice came booming behind her. 'Mind the way! Constable's business,' he called. 'Move this cart along.'

Although he growled a muffled oath, the vegetable seller nevertheless moved his cart out of the way with great difficulty.

'You brought the ring?' Lucy asked the constable. 'Let us be quick, then.'

They walked quickly, not speaking. Duncan appeared to be lost in thought. Finally, he spoke up. 'Lucy, there is something I have been wanting to ask you, and now seems to be as good a time as any.'

'What is it?'

Duncan hesitated again. 'Had you known that Adam had planned to return?'

Has he been writing to you? Lucy could almost hear the underlying doubt in his question. She swallowed. 'He hadn't told me, no. I do know that his father was most satisfied to see him returned, hale and in good spirits.'

'In good spirits,' Duncan repeated, guiding Lucy gently around some steaming manure. 'Do you know why he returned?' Then, before she could answer, he added more questions. '*Is* he planning to stay? I thought he was assisting with the development of a new law code in the colonies. Could they be done with that already?'

'I don't know,' Lucy replied, suddenly desperate

to change the subject. 'There's the jeweller's shop, just ahead.'

To her surprise, Duncan handed Lucy the ring as they reached the shop. 'I think it would be better if the questions came from you, rather than me. It is not uncommon for people to distrust men of the law like myself, even when they have nothing to hide. I will just play the role of your protector, and let you do the talking.'

'As you say,' Lucy said, passing into the shop.

A quick glance around revealed the shop to be empty of customers, which Lucy was grateful to note. She thought it would be harder to ask about the ring if others were about. The walls were lined with wooden cabinets with glass doors, behind which displays of sparkling bracelets, rings, earrings and hairpieces could be seen. No cheap jewellery for the masses – this is what bankers, lawyers and merchants might buy their wives and daughters.

For a moment, Lucy stood in awe by one gorgeous display. Gold posy rings were laid carefully upon red velvet. Above the rings were even more fantastic items. Rings with sculptures of tiny houses and figures set on top or inlaid into the circlet. Elaborate pendants depicting tiny marble statues akin to what the Greeks and Romans had created in a bygone era. Beautifully crafted elephants and camels and parrots carved into brooches, inlaid with rubies, amethysts and other precious gems. 'How marvellous,' Lucy said, reaching out to gently touch one of the rings.

'No touching!' a man barked from the corner, causing her to flinch and drop her offending hand.

Beside her, Duncan stiffened, though he did not say anything, as the man stepped towards them, staring down at them in a menacing way. He looked as if he could knock the constable down in one blow. Obviously, he was there to protect the merchandise and jeweller from thieves and harm.

Looking around, Lucy spied a man with greying brown hair standing at a table in the corner, appearing to be fixing the clasp on a bracelet. Smoothing down her dress, she approached the jeweller, glad that she had bothered to change into one of her finer Sunday dresses. She did not wish to look as if she'd been sent by her mistress to make inquiries, but rather that she was there of her own accord. 'Pardon me, sir,' she said.

'Yes, miss?' the jeweller asked, his eyes flitting between her and Duncan, before returning to Lucy. 'Do you wish to purchase a pendant? Or something for your hair? I can see that you are of a simple nature.'

'What? Oh no,' she said, quickly pulling the ring from her pocket, laying it in front of him on the table. 'We do have a question about this piece. I was wondering if you might be able to tell us anything about it. Who made it? Who might have bought it?'

The jeweller glanced at Lucy speculatively before picking up a brass flea glass off the table and holding it over the ring to examine it more closely. 'Intriguing,' he said, studying the inscription and peering at the ring's two faces. Then, after a few minutes, he set the ring and flea glass down, and gave Lucy a questioning look. 'First, I need you to tell me how it came into your possession.' He frowned at the constable. 'Did you give it to her?'

'The lady found it,' Duncan said, gesturing to Lucy. 'We'd like to learn more about where it came from.'

'Found it?' the man in the corner scoffed. 'That's a tale we've not heard.'

'I didn't steal it,' Lucy protested, feeling mortified as an image of Sid rose in her thoughts, as she'd seen him earlier, his head and hands locked inside the pillory, being pelted with rotten vegetables. How he'd laugh if he'd known that she'd be accused of theft herself just a short while after she'd advised him to change his ways. Her cheeks burned a bit. 'I didn't.'

The jeweller held up his hands. 'That's not what I was suggesting, although, of course, I will not engage in the trade of stolen goods. Rather, I simply meant that this is not a ring that I would want my own daughter, who is likely around your age, to give or receive.'

'Why do you say that?' Lucy asked, exchanging a glance with Duncan.

'I suspect that this *memento mori* was created to remind the wearer that life is fleeting. That one moment you are full of life and rosy-cheeked like this cherub' – he tapped the cherub's face, before turning it over to expose the skull – 'while the next moment you are dead. There is nothing between that moment of life and death. Not very cheery, of course, but there you have it.'

'That's what Adam said,' Lucy murmured to Duncan.

'Moreover, I've seen these *memento mori* worn by individuals who are seeking to warn others that they should not be trifled with,' the jeweller added. 'They serve as a type of warning to those around them. As a gift, I could see it meant to be viewed as a reminder of the imminence of death, or perhaps even as a warning.' The jeweller continued to stare at the ring. 'I must say,' he said, 'these dual faces are very unusual. Most often, you see just a skull. Like these.'

He pointed to a collection of jewellery in one of the cloth-covered trays. Lucy and Duncan leaned in, examining the intricate pieces crafted from silver and gold, depicting skulls or entire skeletons in coffins. 'This contrast seems more thoughtful,' he said, still studying the piece. 'Perhaps it was specially commissioned by the patron. Or the artist simply designed the piece this way.'

'Do you know who crafted this ring?' Lucy asked.

'I'm not familiar with the specific artisan, no. However, I've seen similar work in the Netherlands and other parts of the Continent.'

Lucy glanced at Duncan. They probably had all the answers they could get out of the jeweller. 'I need to be heading back,' she whispered. 'Thank you, sir.'

As they turned to go, the jeweller stood up. 'I'd spare a few coins to purchase this ring from you, as the quality of the craftsmanship is quite good, but I fear that it would bring ill upon my shop. A piece like this can be troublesome to have around.'

'Why is that?' Duncan asked.

'There are some who consider such objects to be unnatural, magicked, cursed. I do not believe such foolish nonsense myself, but I do know that is why some jewellery merchants will not carry such objects, nor will they even trade with those who do.' He coughed. 'Do you happen to have the other one?'

'Other one?' Lucy asked. 'What do you mean?'

'Such rings are usually sold in pairs,' the jeweller replied.

'There was no other ring, as far as I know,' Lucy said thoughtfully, as she allowed Duncan to lead her out of the shop and back on to the busy street. A sudden gale blew and caused Lucy to hug her cloak more closely to her body. 'Why was he wearing that ring?' she asked, hating being thwarted. 'I just want some answers.'

'I know,' he replied. 'I want answers, too. At the same time, there's something disturbing about this ring. Do you not feel it, Lucy?'

'I do not believe the ring to be a magicked object, but I imagine that others might.' When she picked up her pace, Duncan easily matched her stride. 'All of this is very strange indeed. A man hanged by someone else at the crossroads. A secret message in his pocket. A ring warning about death. What can we make of it all?' She sighed. 'Perhaps when we decipher the message, we'll get the answers we seek.'

Seven

'I've read your piece, Lucy,' Master Aubrey said later that evening, wiping up the last bit of beef and carrot stew with some hard bread. 'Have you learned anything about the man's identity?'

'What man?' Will asked, draining his cup of ale before peering into the pot to see if anything was left. Her brother had grown so much taller than her these last few years and was far wider in girth and muscle. His work as a blacksmith was long and hard, and sometimes it seemed as if his appetite was never sated.

Lach snickered. 'Lucy found another dead body – hasn't your sister told you about it yet?'

Will smacked his hand to his forehead. 'Oh, Lucy. Tell me you've not got yourself involved in another odd tale.'

'I haven't had a chance to tell you,' Lucy said, beginning to stack the shallow tin plates. Once again, she was left completing some of Lach's evening tasks. Why she'd allowed this to happen, she didn't know. Especially when the apprentice would gloat and point to crumbs she had missed when wiping down the table. 'Indeed, I witnessed something quite strange the other day when I was out peddling my tracts. Perhaps if you did not spend so much time with your lady love, you would not be the last to know now.' She cuffed her brother lightly on the ear.

Will stretched, grinning widely. 'That is so. I can hardly tell my Lina to stop being so enticing, now, can I?'

Lucy was about to retort when they heard a sharp rapping at the shop door. Master Aubrey pointed at Lach. 'Tell them we're closed.'

A moment later, Lucy heard a surprised greeting from Lach and a familiar voice. Adam appeared inside the shop, his hat in his hand.

Will stood up and heartily clapped Adam on his back. 'Good evening, friend! When did you arrive back in London? I did not know of your return.' Here he threw Lucy a meaningful look. 'I fear my sister told me nothing of it.'

'Don't blame Lucy, Will,' Adam replied. 'She knew naught of my return.'

'What brings you here this evening, young Master Hargrave?' Master Aubrey said. 'We're honoured to see you twice in two days. That in itself is quite unusual to be sure, particularly since I believe you have yet to buy any of my more recent pieces.'

Adam bowed his head, acknowledging his words. 'I will most certainly do so,' he said. 'Right now, I have a matter to discuss with Lucy.'

'Oh,' Lucy replied, stepping back. Master Aubrey grunted, and Lach guffawed. They all looked at each other as Adam drew Lucy aside.

'My father has invited the mathematician Neville Wallace to dine with us tomorrow night. When my father mentioned the cipher to him, he was easily enticed.' He paused. 'Lucy, we'd like you to join us.'

Will and Master Aubrey both swivelled to stare at her, while Lach let out a surprised whoop.

73

'What?' Lucy asked, swallowing. She could feel a faint flush creep over her neck. *How could she attend the supper as their guest?* Such an invitation was unexpected to say the least.

'To serve the family's dinner?' Master Aubrey asked. 'Is Annie unwell? Or Cook?'

Adam straightened up even more. 'No, sir. My father and I are inviting Lucy to join us for supper. As our guest. We would like her to meet Professor Wallace and his wife. He may have some answers for us about that message that was found, and I wanted – I mean, my father and I wanted – Lucy to be on hand for the discussion. She might have some questions that neither Father nor I might think to ask.'

Her heart began to flutter, causing her to miss what Will said to Adam next. Although she'd eaten with the Hargraves before, she'd never been invited as a guest when other visitors would be present. Adam's next words brought her back.

'I can promise you, Lucy, Mrs Wallace is quite kind. To be sure, Professor Wallace would spend the evening discussing the latest treatise on mathematics if left unchecked, but he may be able to provide us with valuable information about that cipher.'

'Everything about that man's death does seem to hinge on us deciphering that message,' Lucy agreed. 'Also' – she grinned – 'I do miss Cook's food.'

At her words, Adam's brow cleared slightly. *He was worried I wouldn't want to come*, she realized.

'Then you must accept,' he said, chuckling.

'I'm certain that Cook will make your favourite dishes – just say the word.'

'That is very kind of you,' she replied, trying to keep from twisting her skirts.

To everyone's surprise, Lach jumped in then. 'Sir,' he said to Master Aubrey, 'we just traded with that old bookseller Richardson for some scientific pieces. Some were on optics. Lots of formulas. Perhaps Lucy could bring a few along, for the mathematician to see.'

Adam rapped his knuckles on the table, looking pleased. 'By all means, Lucy, you must bring those tracts along. Lach here is completely right. Professor Wallace would enjoy them.'

'It's settled, Lucy,' Master Aubrey said firmly, after seeing her try to protest. 'She will be there promptly at seven o'clock. Lucy, please see Master Adam to the door if you would. We must begin readying ourselves for tomorrow.'

Lucy accompanied Adam to the front of the shop. The others had remained in the room, although they were likely all eavesdropping.

'Thank you for the invitation,' she said, twisting at her skirts.

Adam seemed to have something else on his mind. 'Did you visit the jeweller today?'

'Yes, I did,' she started. 'Hey, wait! How did you know I visited the jeweller?'

He grinned. 'Lucy, it was not so hard to follow your thoughts last night. Tell me, what did you learn?'

She filled him in on what the jeweller had said, including how some people viewed such rings as magicked objects.

'I see,' he replied. 'There are many strange things here. I hope Professor Wallace can help us with this. And I look forward to seeing you.'

Lucy hung her cloak on one of the hooks in the magistrate's kitchen. She'd arrived at seven o'clock as requested but was at a loss to know what to do next.

'The master will be pleased to see you in the late mistress's dress,' Cook said, glancing at her while scraping dough into a pan. 'It was one of his favourites.'

'Oh, dear. I didn't realize it was a favourite of his.' Nervously, Lucy ran her hands down the woven blue silk dress, a fine garment that had once belonged to the magistrate's late wife. When she'd left his employment, Master Hargrave had graciously given her this dress and several others. She hadn't wanted to accept them at first, but he had insisted. 'For your dowry,' he had told her. 'Or sell them to provide the apprentice fee for Master Aubrey. Or simply wear them, if you like. These are yours, Lucy, to keep or sell as you please.' She had been loath to part with this particular one.

'No need to fret,' Cook replied, wiping her flour-covered hands on her skirts. To her surprise, Lucy found herself enfolded in a meaty hug. 'You do us all proud. Indeed, you honour Mistress Hargrave's memory by wearing this dress so well.'

Even as Lucy smiled at the compliment, she could almost hear her mother whispering in her ear, admonishing her not to gaze too long into a looking glass. *No need to invite the Devil in,* she'd say.

Annie stepped into the kitchen then. 'The Wallaces have already arrived. I just poured out the sherry,' she said. 'Oh, Lucy! You look so bonny. Shall I bring you in? I'll say it all fancy-like, won't I just?'

Taking in their eager faces, Lucy began to breathe faster. *What am I doing here in Mistress Hargrave's old dress? I was once their servant! Have I forgotten my station?* For a moment, she wanted to turn around and head back to Master Aubrey's and tell them it had all been a mistake. That she hadn't been expected to dine with them at all. That she should be back in the kitchen with the other servants. Then she thought of Master Hargrave, sending her the invitation. Of Adam bringing it to her. She straightened her back and nodded to Annie. 'Lead the way, if you would. Pray, just don't overdo it.'

Sombrely, Annie led her down the corridor and opened the door to the drawing room where the others awaited. 'Miss Lucy Campion,' she announced, as if introducing Lucy to a royal court.

Oh, the airs Annie is putting on, Lucy thought, feeling a bit chagrined. *Whatever will they think of me?*

Both the Hargraves were looking at her warmly. The magistrate's smile widened when he recognized the blue dress. She relaxed a bit when she saw how pleased he appeared. 'Welcome, Lucy,' he said, extending his hand. 'Allow me to introduce you to my old friend and his wife, Professor and Mrs Neville Wallace.' He spoke easily as if it were common practice to introduce his former servant to his invited guests. When she inclined her head, he continued. 'This is Lucy Campion, who is another family friend. She works for Master Aubrey, printer and bookseller, and I believe she has brought some tracts for you that you might wish to peruse after supper. Is that correct, Lucy?'

She nodded, murmuring a pleasantry. Master Hargrave then poured her a glass of sherry, although there was a fatherly warning in his eye as he handed it to her. *Take care to not overly imbibe*, she could almost hear him say. She smiled and nodded back at him, taking just a small sip to show she understood. The fearsome introductions done, Lucy was now able to steal glances at the Hargraves' guests.

Professor Wallace looked to have at least fifteen years on his wife, maybe more, with a distinguished face and upright though slightly stout figure. She looked to be about thirty, with reddened cheeks and curly brown hair messily pulled into an unruly bun. *Did she not have a lady's maid?* Lucy could not help but wonder. Even though she'd never styled hair with ease, she would have been mortified if she'd let Mistress Hargrave or Sarah out with such unkempt hair.

At the same time, seeing that Mrs Wallace was not perfectly coiffed helped Lucy to feel more at ease in the setting. Professor Wallace also looked as if he lacked a manservant, for his clothes were all a bit rumpled, and there might even have been

78

a hole under one arm. Indeed, he looked as if he was hardly paying attention to what was going on around him, appearing deep in thought. *Perhaps that's how mathematicians are*, Lucy thought.

'I'm sure my husband will appreciate the chance to review new tracts, although I'm rather afraid we will lose him entirely if we give them to him now.' Mrs Wallace smiled conspiratorially at Lucy.

'It is Lucy,' Adam added, 'who has brought the puzzle for you to examine.'

Professor Wallace blinked. 'Ah, so. Looking forward to it, my dear lass.'

Mrs Wallace gave her a bright glance. 'I simply cannot wait to hear this story.'

'Lucy excels at telling stories,' Adam said, his unexpected fervour making Lucy blush.

'Is that so?' Mrs Wallace said, looking from one to the other.

When Annie called them to supper and Adam seated Lucy next to himself, Mrs Wallace's speculation grew even more thoughtful.

'Have you known one another long?' she asked.

Annie, who'd been ladling leek soup into each bowl, giggled. Lucy gave her a warning glance. 'A good while,' she replied, not sure what else to say. She changed the subject. 'Have you lived in London long? I understand you used to live in Cambridge.'

'Not for some time, although I do miss my scholar's life,' Professor Wallace said. 'I lived in Cambridge many years before I met my wife; she but a few. King Charles asked me to return,

79

so that he might seek my counsel on matters of state from time to time.' Spoken by another man, his statement would have been the words of a braggart, but he uttered them with a matter-of-fact explanatory air. 'I don't know if it was a blessing or a curse that we moved back to the city after the plague had already passed, but before the fire.'

'Thankfully, the fire never reached our residence,' Mrs Wallace said, clasping her hands together. 'We were out on the Thames watching the blaze, ready to pay the oarsmen a hefty sum to take us over to Southwark. Then the great miracle occurred, and the flames turned back in on themselves, praise be the Lord.' She looked around at everyone and smiled. 'Although some neighbours fled and others returned, we've made a home here since. Neville has forged a circle of scholars and tutors to amuse him. Musicians, scientists, poets – those sorts. Every so often, they join us for some good cheer and lively discourse, those ideas that are not readily consumed by others.' She looked eagerly at the Hargraves. 'You must join us one evening. I am sure you will be diverted.'

Master Hargrave and Adam both inclined their heads graciously at the offer. Mrs Wallace's eyes flicked over to Lucy. 'You would all be very welcome.'

Lucy bowed her head, hiding her surprise at the generous invitation. She took the tiniest sip of her wine, enjoying the warmth and patter of the conversation around her. For a short time, the Wallaces and the Hargraves chatted about different topics. An amusing observation by Sam Pepys. The planned rebuilding of London. Some news of King and Court. The latest theatrical productions at the Swan and Globe.

All the while, Lucy toyed with the pocket resting on her lap, thinking about the cipher inside. She wished she could pull it out and ask Professor Wallace to decipher it then and there. But instead they all engaged in everyday, mundane chatter. *There's a murderer on the loose*, she wanted to shout, but instead she smiled and occasionally murmured a pleasantry.

As the initial conversations began to wane, Mrs Wallace turned to Master Hargrave. 'Tell us, Thomas. How does Sarah fare?' she asked, setting down her spoon. 'I had hoped to meet your lovely daughter this evening. My husband mentioned her, but could provide few of the details that we women so adore to hear, of course. Is she with relatives? Don't tell me she's abroad this time of year?'

The magistrate's smile faded slightly, and Adam leapt in to answer. His response was direct and unvarnished. 'My sister Sarah is pursuing her conviction and faith in the Lord, in the Quaker way. She is in the Massachusetts Bay Colony now, following the Inner Light.'

He set his fork down, regarding the Wallaces steadily. If they were stunned that the magistrate's only daughter had turned Quaker, they hid it well.

'I see,' Mrs Wallace murmured, while Professor Wallace took another bite of the braised pork dish that Cook had so carefully prepared.

'I am of the mindset that following one's

81

conscience in matters of religion is a good thing,' Professor Wallace replied, 'so long as it does not bring about unnecessary disorder. I do not like the chaos that such radicals have wrought.'

'Indeed,' Master Hargrave replied. Lucy could see that his knuckles had whitened slightly. Only someone who knew the magistrate well would know that he was upset by the professor's comment.

'Perhaps, Professor,' Adam said, turning to their guests, 'you might enlighten us on the subject of secret writing.'

'That topic, I fear, may take us all the way into dessert,' Mrs Wallace said, giving her husband a tender smile. 'My husband is likely to talk until told to stop.'

'Such a fascinating topic,' Professor Wallace said, setting down his fork. 'In the ancient world, the Romans and Greeks had wondrous methods to cover their writing. They might write their plans on cloth or wood and then cover them with wax. Later, the recipient would simply scrape the wax off, allowing them to read the message.'

'Seems dangerous – so easily discovered,' Master Hargrave commented.

'I agree. However, they also had many more ingenious methods, those ancients,' Professor Wallace said. 'Herodotus tells us of a king who shaved a courier's head to ink a message. They waited until his hair grew back, and then the courier was sent through enemy territory with the hidden message intact! Suffice it to say, most secret communications would suffer under such a prolonged test of time.'

Master Hargrave clucked his tongue. 'Indeed.'

'Tell them about the ink from plants, dear,' Mrs Wallace said. To Lucy she added, 'I'm sure you'll be intrigued.'

'Ah, the inks!' Professor Wallace said, then took a deep swallow of his Rhenish wine. 'Certain plants contain juices that allow writing to be made virtually invisible until gently warmed. Pliny the Elder would use the milk-like liquid of the Tithymalus plant to write messages, because it dried clear.

'Difficult to use on a printing press,' Lucy murmured to herself, thinking of the way the ink was spread across the type. 'It would never hold.'

Catching her comment, Professor Wallace chuckled. 'Nay, this ink would only be used with a quill, of that much I'm certain. Although I'm fascinated by the idea of an entire pamphlet printed in secret ink! Everyone would think they are purchasing plain paper!'

'Didn't della Porta, the Italian scientist, also have a form of secret writing?' Adam asked. 'As I recall, it was quite fantastical.'

'Fantastical indeed,' Professor Wallace replied, rubbing his hands together. 'Yes, della Porta somehow discovered that one might pen a message using a mixture of alum and vinegar, on to the shell of a hard-boiled egg. The ink, invisible to our eye, would permeate the shell. Only when the egg was cracked and the shell removed would the message be revealed upon the boiled egg's albumen.'

'That is truly amazing,' Master Hargrave said.

'We have very much advanced our understanding of hidden writing over time. Now it is no longer just a question of steganography, which is what we call concealed writing. Now we think more about cryptography, or scrambled writing,' Professor Wallace said, bringing his goblet to his lips but not taking a sip. 'Many of them have a pure mathematical solution. Those are indeed the most elegant, the most beautiful.'

Mrs Wallace smiled indulgently at her husband before looking around at the others. 'As you can see, my husband has been in love with all things mathematical since he was exposed to the late William Oughtred's *Clavis Mathematicae* as a young man.'

Beside her, Adam murmured in Lucy's ear, '*The Key to Mathematics*.'

'The art of deciphering is more than just the beauty of a mathematical solution,' Professor Wallace said. 'Recall, if you will, the case of Mary Queen of Scots. In an earlier age, the cipher she used to communicate with that traitor Anthony Babington might not have been broken in time. Babington's rebellion might well have been successful. We could have had a damned Papist on the throne today!'

Lucy's eyes widened. Her knowledge of history was a bit scant, particularly since it was still frowned upon to speak so much of the doomed Scottish queen, though her great-grandson Charles II currently occupied the throne.

'Indeed,' Master Hargrave murmured. 'I recall something of these details. The Scottish queen and Babington had been communicating in secret,

84

trying to incite a rebellion against Queen Elizabeth. When the plot was discovered, he and his fellow plotters were drawn and quartered. Mary denied any knowledge of the plot until the secrets of their correspondence were exposed, and she was executed as well.'

'The cipher was simple, but their use of it was truly careless,' Professor Wallace said, with a slight sniff. 'They brought about their own misfortune.'

Lucy glanced at the professor curiously. He almost sounded disappointed that the cipher had been broken. Perhaps recognizing how his words sounded, Professor Wallace continued, 'They had too much confidence in themselves and in their cipher.' He shook his head. 'The plotters wrote out their plans in detail, overly secure in their belief that the cipher could not be cracked. They might have, for example, done a double substitution or used transposition. Although I suppose such a thing was not truly understood until Vigenère published his *Treatise on Secret Writing* a short time later.'

'My understanding of the case was that they called in a linguist to decipher the messages,' Master Hargrave said.

'Yes, that is so. Those treacherous plotters completely underestimated the skill of Phelippes, who apparently cracked the cipher very quickly.'

'As I recall, Mary was not implicated in the plot, at least not at first,' Adam said.

Professor Wallace nodded. 'That is so. It was Lord Walsingham, Elizabeth's spymaster, who advised that they wait to move on the plotters until they had evidence that Mary knew about and endorsed the plot to kill Queen Elizabeth.' He shook his head. 'Foolish woman. Overly confident and no doubt desperate, she confirmed the assassination, ending her message with the sign of the gallows. Her complicity in the plot was confirmed, which, of course, confirmed *her* fate with the henchman.' He raised his glass. 'Let us drink, then, to the intelligence of Phelippes, the mathematician who stopped a revolution!'

Eight

Professor Wallace pushed aside his plate with a satisfied sigh. Master Hargrave nodded at Annie who'd been waiting to serve more apple pie and cheese, should anyone want a second helping. 'Please clear the dishes, Annie. We shall stay in here for a while.'

Out of habit, Lucy almost stood up to help Annie clear the table and take the dirty dishes to the kitchen. Adam caught her hand under the table, effectively keeping her seated. In his smile, she remembered that she was there as the Hargraves' guest. 'Would you like to show them the cipher you discovered, Lucy?' he asked.

'Yes, indeed. Let us see this cipher,' Professor Wallace said, rubbing his hands together.

Lucy withdrew the original vellum message from her pocket, and the magistrate handed his friend the flea glass. Professor Wallace moved to seat himself next to a lamp so that he could see the characters and symbols better.

As her husband studied the paper, Mrs Wallace turned to Lucy. 'Tell us more about how you came upon this odd thing.'

At Master Hargrave's nod, Lucy offered a shortened but still vivid version of the story with which she had regaled the magistrate and Adam. She left out some key details, though, including her encounter with the two grave robbers. Experience with investigations and loyalty to the constable kept her from spilling everything.

'How extraordinary that the constable would just leave this in your possession,' Mrs Wallace commented, as her husband continued to study the paper under the flea glass.

'Constable Duncan knows that I am well acquainted with the Hargraves,' Lucy explained. 'He does not have too many other scholars in his acquaintance. Neither Doctor Larimer nor Doctor Sheridan could shed any light on it, and they suggested I bring it to the Hargraves. We made a copy, of course, which I left with him.'

'We in turn determined it best to bring it to Professor Wallace,' Adam added, inclining his head in respect. 'Given his noted authority in the field.'

'I see,' Mrs Wallace said. 'That does indeed make sense.'

Breathlessly, everyone watched Professor Wallace as he examined the paper, holding it first at length and then closer to the lamp. *We are watching him as if he were a street performer*, Lucy thought. *What magical trick will he perform?* Indeed, he only needed a cap for coins before him to make the illusion complete.

Finally, after studying the paper for a few minutes, he looked up. They all leaned forward.

'Alas, I cannot decipher it,' Professor Wallace said, glancing at his wife who looked disappointed. 'The regular frequencies of common letters do not apply, at least not outwardly so. If we have the cipher key, then, of course, we should determine the message very rapidly. The sheer number of possible combinations is unfathomable, even if it can be derived mathematically.' He tapped on the paper. 'Despite the poor hand, I believe this cipher was devised by someone with a keen mathematical mind.'

'Why do you say that?' Adam asked.

Professor Wallace pointed at several of the odd characters they'd noted before. 'Because of these. These may indicate nulls and doubleths, which those with less experience with ciphers would be unlikely to include.'

'What are nulls and doubleths?' Lucy asked, tasting the unfamiliar words with her tongue.

'A doubleth is often used to suggest a repeated letter, such as the letter "t" in the word "letter",' the scholar replied.

'This sounds like setting type,' Lucy said, imagining the typeface. 'We have blocks for double t's and double l's to save time, double n's and double e's as well. We use spacers to separate the word.'

Professor Wallace nodded. 'I agree. There is a similarity there, if you think of each character as a distinct entity to decipher, similar to how you would set each piece of a tract separately.'

'So that makes it harder for someone to decipher a message if frequency is removed,' Adam said, responding to the professor's earlier remark.

'Exactly,' Professor Wallace replied. 'Such techniques are used by cryptographers to confuse their readers and to keep the cipher from being readily broken.' He pointed to one of the symbols. 'This, I suspect, is a "null". A null means no character. Such symbols may be used to hide breaks between words. Others might be symbols outside the alphabet that indicate coded words, perhaps ones that are more standard, such as "the", "and", "to" and "from". They could even be given names.'

'Oh, that is also the same,' Lucy said. 'Instead of writing out the word "and", we might use an ampersand. Except,' she added, 'we set all type backwards.'

'It is possible that this cipher is also backwards,' Professor Wallace said. 'We cannot know just by perusing it in this way.'

'So, it sounds as if we need the key to the cipher,' Lucy said. 'If there's no way to work out the cipher for ourselves?'

'Yes—' The mathematician broke off, frowning. 'Wait a minute. There is something familiar about this particular symbol.' He pointed the last character on the page – π. 'Obviously, it is the mathematical symbol for *pi*, first used by the Greeks. I have seen it in a cipher before.'

'Do you recall what it means?' his wife asked eagerly.

'Yes.' He handed the flea glass to the magistrate. 'It is the sign of the gallows, which Babington also used in his cipher.'

Mrs Wallace clapped her hand to her mouth. 'The body was found at the gallows! Surely that cannot be a coincidence.'

Lucy clasped her hands together in excitement. *Maybe they'd be able to decipher the message, after all.* Suddenly, she felt one step closer to finding out what had happened to that man, a thought that was oddly satisfying to contemplate.

'Could the rest of it be written in Babington's code? Could it be as simple as that?' Master Hargrave asked, sitting forward in his chair. 'Surely you have a copy in your own home?'

'Yes, I certainly do so,' Professor Wallace murmured, still studying the paper. 'I believe, however, that there is something else familiar . . .' Once again, he closed his eyes and leaned back in his chair. Then, as they silently watched him, something of his demeanour changed. He was no longer as excited as he'd been the moment before. He seemed softer, weaker somehow. 'Oh. That's it.'

'You remember?' the magistrate asked eagerly. Although he always seemed so calm and logical, Lucy could almost see him as a young boy watching a puppeteer, sitting forward in rapt excitement. 'Where have you encountered this cipher before?'

'I believe this cipher may have been created by a former pupil of mine.' He glanced at his wife, and she set down her cup abruptly on the table. 'The hand that wrote this message was so ill – I didn't realize.'

'What's his name?' Adam asked. 'Your pupil?'

'Er, not a man at all,' Professor Wallace said, wiping his forehead. Inexplicably, a dull red rose in his sallow cheeks. 'That is to say—' He broke off again, looking helplessly at his wife.

'Lucretia?' she asked, a faint look of consternation appearing on her face as well.

When the mathematician didn't reply, Master Hargrave prompted Mrs Wallace. '"Lucretia", you said. Pray tell, who may she be?'

91

Mrs Wallace raised her chin. 'Miss Lucretia de Witte, the only daughter of the late Sir Benedict de Witte. Amsterdam-born, distant relations to the House of Orange. For a time, one of my husband's pupils here in London. A favourite at that.'

A long, heavy pause followed. When the Wallaces looked pointedly away from one another, the magistrate shifted uncomfortably in his seat, and Lucy and Adam exchanged a glance.

Professor Wallace pulled at the neck of his shirt, as if suddenly finding it hard to draw a breath. 'She had a fine grasp of mathematics,' he explained quietly. 'So unusual for a woman.'

His wife looked at the others, a slight smile returning to her lips. She appeared to be trying to affect an amused air. 'The two of them exchanged a number of messages written in this cipher. A delightful pastime, it would seem.' Her lips tightened, belying the sense of light-heartedness she was trying to display. 'We've not seen Miss de Witte in a very long time, have we, my dear? Or at least *I* have not seen her.'

'N–no, dear,' her husband replied. 'We haven't seen Miss de Witte in quite some time. Truly, dear, I have not seen her.'

Thankfully, Master Hargrave broke into the Wallaces' uncomfortable exchange. 'Just so I understand, Neville,' he said, 'you believe that this message is written using the cipher that Miss de Witte created?'

'Yes, I believe so. Perhaps. I'm not certain. This is not Miss de Witte's hand. Just something about the symbols seems familiar. Although, as

I said, it seems to derive in part from Babington's cipher as well. Of course, I shared that cipher with Miss de Witte at the time, so she may well have incorporated that into her own communications—' Professor Wallace dropped off again with another hasty glance at his wife. He began to mop at his brow more earnestly. 'It is rather hot in here, don't you think?'

'Is there anything else you can tell us about this cipher?' Master Hargrave pressed. His tone was cordial but firm, and even without his robes, he was taking on his probing magisterial demeanour. 'Neville, please. It is important. If the man who bore this message was murdered, as I am beginning to believe he was, we must learn all we can.'

Professor Wallace gestured vaguely to the first symbol. 'If I recall, Miss de Witte created a cipher where the very first symbol would tell the recipient how to decipher it. She was quite devious and skilled in that regard. She had two codes, each needing to be derived in terms of the other. One as a function of the other.'

'It should not be so hard to decipher, then, if you have the key?' Adam pressed.

Mrs Wallace stood up then, tears welling in her eyes. 'I'm afraid I asked my husband to discard her papers when the lessons concluded. They were taking up too much space in the house.' She looked as if she was about to burst into tears.

Lucy half stood up, wanting to throw her arms around the woman to comfort her. Indeed, if it had been Cook or Annie or Sarah, she would have done so. But it would be wholly improper, and she gripped the arms of her chair instead.

Professor Wallace shifted in his seat, a profound look of regret and shame on his features. Lucy could hardly bear to look at him. 'Indeed. That is so. I'm sorry I cannot help you.'

'Could you look at the message again,' Master Hargrave asked. 'Perhaps you'd remember the cipher—'

Neville Wallace stood up and moved next to his wife, drawing her to him. 'No, I'm sorry, it was a long time ago. It was all a mistake. I cannot remember. I'm sorry. I think it is best that we take our leave, my dear.' He looked at Master Hargrave. 'Please have our carriage brought around.'

'I should like to visit the privy first,' Mrs Wallace said in a small voice.

'Let me show you where it is,' Lucy offered. 'This way, Mrs Wallace.'

As they walked down the hallway, Mrs Wallace touched Lucy's arm. 'Lucy, you must think I'm a ninny. It's just that—' Tears looked as if they were about to well up in her eyes again.

'You don't need to explain,' Lucy said hurriedly. Indeed, she did not. 'I'm so sorry that this turned out to be an upsetting evening for you. I did enjoy the conversation, though.'

To her surprise, Mrs Wallace grasped her hands and smiled at her. 'It was truly a pleasure, Lucy, to meet you. What a lively storyteller you are! If you ever have any new mathematical tracts, I am certain that Neville would greatly appreciate receiving them. For myself, I should very much

94

like to learn more about the bookselling trade. You are welcome to call any time you are free.' She sighed. 'Some days, I'd welcome any diversion, so, truly, please do not hesitate to call.'

'I shall see you home, Lucy,' Adam said, after they had said their farewells to the Wallaces. He reached for one of the brass lanterns that the Hargraves kept by the front door, opening the tiny glass door to light the wick inside. Although the lantern was designed to keep the candle from blowing out, he pocketed some flint just in case. 'A bit windy tonight.'

'Yes,' Lucy agreed, wrapping her cloak more tightly around her body. 'There's been a bite of late. The almanacs are predicting a particularly chilly winter. The Thames may even freeze over again, though likely not until January or February, I imagine.' She was aware that she was chattering, and she wasn't sure if he was paying attention.

'Shall we?' he asked, extending his arm.

Hesitating, she curled her fingers around the crook of his elbow, feeling the rough-hewn wool. This was not the fine-cut cloth he had once worn. Perhaps his finances had become straitened during his time in the New World. The passage alone must have been a tidy sum.

The fog swirled around them gently, softening the sounds of night. He held the lantern up above them so that she could see. The moon was obscured above by the fog that hovered over the city, except for a strange bright patch in the sky that gave them some evidence of the celestial's body serene existence.

'So, we may have learned something,' Lucy commented, thinking through the evening's conversation, trying to keep her mind off their unexpected closeness. It had been a long time since they had walked together like this, and she wasn't quite sure what to do. 'The cipher may have been created by Lucretia de Witte. Who is she, I wonder?' she mused. 'The mention of her name caused quite a response from both Wallaces.'

'That is certainly so.' Adam held the lantern higher, so that their shadows on the dark streets grew longer. In the distance, she heard some dogs barking and she shivered. She'd recently sold some tracts that told of a true tale of a woman beset and killed by a pack of wild dogs. In Southwark, but it may just as well have been in the midst of London proper.

'I think that Miss de Witte and Professor Wallace . . .' She hesitated. As a servant, she had long learned not to speak ill of her betters.

Adam had no such qualms, accurately finishing her thought. 'Were guilty of adultery? That would be my assumption, given the exchange between the Wallaces.' He clicked his tongue in annoyance.

'It is unfortunate that they threw away the cipher,' Lucy said. 'Although understandable. No woman would want to be taunted by her husband's infidelity.'

'Just so. It is indeed unfortunate. However, we did learn something important about how we might undertake deciphering the message,' Adam said. 'If Miss de Witte did indeed create the cipher, perhaps she still has the key. If so, we should be able to decipher it easily enough.'

Lucy stopped and looked up at him. 'How do you know that Miss de Witte was not herself involved? Maybe she sent it? Or maybe she was supposed to get it?'

Adam hit his forehead. 'Of course, Lucy! You are quite correct. We do not know if Miss de Witte was involved,' he replied. 'Other than being the creator of the cipher. We cannot simply ask her to supply the code without rousing her suspicion. We must proceed with care.'

'Perhaps we could try to find out in a more roundabout way. Maybe there is a way to discover who else might have used the cipher she created,' Lucy said. 'Perhaps she shared it with someone else.'

'That is so,' Adam said.

'Also, I did not quite understand everything Professor Wallace said about how such ciphers work,' she said. For some reason, she did not feel embarrassed to admit her own ignorance to Adam. 'Would the person who sent it have to be particularly skilled in mathematics? Would the person who receives it? I wasn't certain what Professor Wallace meant by different codes.'

'My understanding is that one simply needed the key. The first symbol would tell the recipient which part of the cipher to use. Truly, it seems that we just need to acquire the key.'

'I will tell the constable tomorrow,' she said. 'He should know what to do next.'

Adam gave her a rueful look. 'What will Duncan do? Just march up to Miss de Witte's door and

97

ask for the key? Ask her to translate the message for him? Ask for the people of her acquaintance with whom she might have shared the cipher and key? Do you think she will even be "at home" when he comes by?'

Lucy stopped short, hurt by his unexpectedly harsh tone. It was true that Duncan would not have easy access to Miss de Witte, but she felt hurt that Adam would be so blunt. 'I don't know how he'd approach her. He's not an idiot, even if he doesn't have a scholar's education.'

She started to pull open the door, tears rising in her eyes. An insult to Duncan felt like an insult to her.

'Lucy! That's not what I meant! Please—'

'He can certainly tell her about the man's death. Perhaps she knows who he is, if he's been serving as a messenger.'

'That's true. Duncan can do that. Just think about it, Lucy. What will she say then?'

Lucy brushed away a tear. 'She'd say . . .' *What would she say if Duncan asked her such a thing?* She sighed. 'She'd say, "Why did you come to me? Why do you think that I would know this man?" and Duncan would have to say that a message had been found and Professor Wallace had named her.' She looked away, grudgingly continuing. 'He'd be giving away his hand to do so. If she's somehow involved with that man's death, such a pronouncement would tip her off. Then everything could be lost.'

'That's right, Lucy. Believe me, it pains me to say this to you.'

Lucy stared up at him, searching his face. 'Why do you care about this, Adam?'

'I care because you do, Lucy. I know that you are determined to bring about justice. Indeed, I feel the same way.'

His intensity caught her by surprise. She remembered once how he had intervened at a dog-baiting spectacle, even though he had received a beating for his troubles. 'This is not for you to do. This is the work of Constable Duncan.'

'I could say the same to you, Lucy.' He straightened up then and moved away.

Nine

'You received my message,' Lucy said to Duncan, who had just stepped into the printer's shop. She had asked Will to slip a note under the constable's door at dawn's first light, on his way to the blacksmith's shop where he had been working for the last four years. Her brother was generally reliable unless he was under the spell of his latest lady love, and then what he might remember of his responsibilities was anyone's guess.

'I did. Took me a few hours before I could make it here. I was continuing my investigation and I have some news as well,' he said, looking at the piece she was carefully laying out on the worktable. 'What's this? Another monstrous tale?'

Lucy laughed. '*True News from Southwark*,' she said. 'The most unusual story of how a two-headed dog caught two rats at once.'

He made a face. 'Some things are not worth knowing.'

'It'll sell quickly, though – just you wait. Especially now that we have found this most compelling woodcut to accompany it.' She tapped on the small picture plate. The image was a witch and her familiar, which was the closest they had been able to find. 'Master Aubrey should see if he can swap some woodcuts with other printers,' she said, more to herself than to

Duncan. 'It would be a good thing to switch the images we use.'

'So you met with the mathematician last night? At the Hargraves',' Duncan said, his smile fading as he pulled out the note that she'd sent him.

'Yes,' she replied and filled him in on what Professor Wallace had told her about secret writing. He perked up when she mentioned that the mathematician believed that Lucretia de Witte might have created the code. 'You can't assume, of course, that she had anything to do with this message. Perhaps if we could learn who else knew the cipher, then that might give us a point to explore further.'

'That is very helpful, Lucy; thank you for your efforts.'

Lucy frowned as the previous night's conversation with Adam arose in her thoughts. 'I'm afraid that Master Adam thinks you won't be able to speak to Miss de Witte directly.'

Duncan laughed, a lightness stealing back over his features. 'You sound surprised. Sometimes, Lucy, I think you are the only one who does not remember my station.' He chuckled again. 'I cannot simply walk up to her door and inquire about a cipher that she created, and which may have been connected with a murder. Adam is quite correct in this regard. Such a thing will only result in a door slammed in my face and being ushered off the premises.'

'That isn't right,' Lucy said hotly.

'No. It isn't.'

'Something else occurred to me last night,' she

101

said. 'I thought I might speak to Professor Wallace's wife again. So odd to say, but I do believe that Mrs Wallace showed a true interest in me. If you can imagine, she invited me to call on her. Any time, she said. I do believe she may be lonely.'

'It is not odd that she has a true interest in you, Lucy,' Duncan replied, shuffling his feet. 'Not odd to me at all.'

Lucy hurried on. 'I was thinking that I should ask her again about the cipher. Maybe Professor Wallace didn't actually get rid of it. It's possible the cipher and key are still among his papers. It is worth asking her to check again, I believe, even if it will be painful for her to consider.'

Duncan rubbed his jaw. 'That may be so. It may lead somewhere fruitful. I hope you will be careful.'

'You said you had some news for me as well? What is it?'

'We identified the corpse,' Duncan replied. 'Name's Paul Corbyn. A mercer of brass and iron, as far as I can tell. Mostly in the form of household goods, such as pots and pans. Other kitchen tools.'

'Truly?' Lucy asked, impressed. 'How did you discover his identity?'

'I followed up on the tradesman's tokens that were in the deceased's second pocket, which had been found tied around his waist, hidden from view. They were mostly from the same blacksmith's shop.' Duncan rubbed his hands together. 'Hank and I made a few inquiries there and found that one of their regular customers, a mercer, hadn't been seen for a few days. Turns out the missing man matched the deceased's description.' He sighed. 'That man had a few enemies, judging from what the blacksmith told us. Customers who were waiting on his goods. Thought they'd been swindled when he didn't show up.'

'I see.'

'The blacksmith then directed me to Corbyn's street. After asking around a bit, I found my way to his house.'

'What happened then?'

'The servant said straight away that the master was missing and hadn't been home in some days. He hadn't packed a valise or any such thing,' Duncan said. 'Moreover, when I asked her what her employer looked like, the description matched that of our corpse. Dark hair, slim build, clean face, sea serpent tattoo on his arm.'

'What did his wife say? Had he been very melancholic?'

'That is the odd part. When I met Mrs Corbyn, she insisted that the dead body could not be that of her husband.'

'That's not so surprising, is it?' Lucy asked. 'I should think that many women would not wish to believe their husbands were dead.'

'That is so. Still, I could see beneath her angry and dismissive words that she was worried and distraught. After some persuasion, she agreed to accompany me to Doctor Larimer's to view the corpse.' Seeing him grimace, Lucy patted the constable's forearm. Without a doubt, serving as Death's messenger was the hardest part of his job. He continued. 'Doctor Sheridan let that poor woman peer upon her husband's face without very much compassion, I'm afraid. The poor woman passed right out and had to be revived by a pungent scent that the physician had on hand. She did confirm then that the dead man was her husband, Paul Corbyn.'

'What did you say of his death? Did you tell her how he'd been found hanged at the cross-roads? What did she say about that?'

Duncan nodded. 'I wanted to see what she'd say first about the idea that he had committed self-murder. I asked her about her husband's state of mind, to see if she thought he'd been melancholic or in a desperate state.' He paused. 'At first she claimed that there had been nothing to note. That although he was phlegmful and tended towards black bile, he was not unduly despondent.'

'I see,' Lucy replied. 'Did you ask her about the crossroads? Do they live near there?'

'Not so close,' Duncan replied. 'Certainly, there are closer crossroads to his home. She did not know what he might have been doing at that crossroads. She was quite distraught, as you can imagine. Her faith is quite strong, it seems. I could see she was devastated when she realized that her husband cannot be buried on hallowed ground without a dispensation from the Church, due to being a suicide.'

'You must have told her then what the physicians said? That he might have been murdered? She must have been relieved – well, to the extent that one can be with such news.'

'No, she was not. Quite the opposite. She was quite insistent that he had no enemies who would wish to harm him.'

'I see,' Lucy said. 'Did she ask about the ring?'

Duncan shook his head. 'No, she asked about the money he might have had on him, but not about the ring. She just said it was common practice for him to wear two pockets. The outer one in which he'd carry his timepiece and a few coins—'

'The one that was stolen by those two men I saw,' Lucy said. Her heart beat faster as she recalled the encounter. 'Pike and Dev.'

'Exactly,' Duncan replied. 'However, I asked her if there was any other missing jewellery. She said he did not like to wear a ring because his fingers would swell, and he was otherwise not up for adornment. I must say, her response to this seemed genuine. My sense is, if she was being truthful, she knew nothing of the ring discovered around his neck.'

'What about the message – did you ask her why he might be carrying a coded message?'

He shook his head. 'No, I could not think of a way to ask without unduly raising her suspicions or causing her more distress.'

'Did you ask her if she knew anyone named Pike or Dev?'

'I did ask her, and she claimed to have never heard of either of the names.'

'Did you believe her?'

'You know, Lucy, I'm not sure I did. She seemed wary throughout our whole conversation. Truth be told, I couldn't tell you *what*

105

she might have been lying about, but I know that she was lying about something. That bothers me and I'm not certain how to proceed.'

'I am not certain either,' Lucy replied. 'For now, I shall call on Mrs Wallace tomorrow. Maybe soon we can finally get some answers about Miss de Witte and the coded message, if not about Mr Corbyn's murder.'

The Wallaces' home was located to the west, in an area that was steadily drawing the wealthier sort, particularly those who'd been displaced by the fire. The air was a bit cleaner here, being upwind from both the Thames and the River Fleet, as well as the polluted and sickly areas to the east. The streets here were much wider, too – enough so that even two carriages could pass without getting stuck or causing a collision.

Lucy approached the residence with some trepidation, her sack full of all the mathematical and scientific tracts she could find in Master Aubrey's stores. Several had been bound with hard leather covers, which were heavier and harder on her shoulder than the simple collection of papers she usually carried. The previous afternoon, she'd been surprised how readily the master printer had permitted her to make the trip, even helping her to fill the bag. 'Good,' he'd said, rubbing his hands together. 'Rich scholars always want more. We'll buy books with him in mind, in the future. Mind you hook him well, Lucy.'

'Lucy? Is that you?' she heard someone call. 'Come here, if you would.'

Looking into the small courtyard, she could see Mrs Wallace seated on a low stone bench, a small leather-bound book in her lap. The woman was staring at her with keen interest.

She gave her a little wave and walked over. 'Good afternoon, Mrs Wallace.'

'Come here,' Mrs Wallace replied. Her lips and cheeks looked faintly bluish, as if she'd been outside for a spell. 'Tell me, what brings you to my doorstep this fine Saturday? After the other night's startling conversation, I must admit that I was rather hoping to see you again, although I did not dare hope it would be quite so soon.'

Smiling, Lucy gestured to her pack. 'Thank you, Mrs Wallace. As you may recall, I work for Master Aubrey, helping to make and sell books. I had mentioned your husband's interest in procuring mathematical and scientific treatises, and Master Aubrey sent me here with a variety of books that he thought might be of interest to Professor Wallace.' *That is all true,* she thought, *even if it was not the real purpose in coming here today.*

'Is that so? How kind of Master Aubrey,' Mrs Wallace replied. 'I should rather like some new books of my own.'

'What are you reading?' Lucy asked, gesturing to the book she had set down.

Mrs Wallace caressed the leather cover. 'One of Will Shakespeare's plays. *Othello.* Do you know it? I find myself utterly absorbed.'

Lucy nodded. 'I've heard of it, but not yet read it or seen it performed.' While Master Aubrey did have a few of Shakespeare's longer plays, they were harder to sell and it was rare that they would try to sell them outside the shop. Lucy had very little time to indulge in reading anything other than the tracts she was creating or selling on any given day, although she read as much of the Bard as she could lay her hands on.

'We do not get to the plays as often as I would like either,' Mrs Wallace said with a sigh. 'I thought things would be different when we moved to London. That is what I get for marrying to please my father before he died. He was keen to see me settled and thought it best for me to wed someone more established. It's only been five years and I am much like an abandoned widow or spinster. Oh, do not look forlorn! I speak in jest.'

'Perhaps he will take you if you divert him with some of these works of natural philosophy,' Lucy said, trying to keep the pity from her voice. So few women had the choice of marrying for love. Most were expected to help their families or improve their own lot. 'I had hoped I might see you first. Some wives like to purchase such items for their husbands.'

Mrs Wallace patted the bench. 'Sit beside me. I'm afraid I would not know which texts he already has, or which might be of interest. However, I'm very happy to look at them. Perhaps you can guide my decision.'

Lucy perched on the end of the small bench. 'I think that several of these are new products. We traded them with some booksellers in Cambridge, so they may not have been well circulated among scholars yet.'

'I see,' Mrs Wallace said, a slight shadow crossing her face. 'My husband is one of several scholars who helped found the Royal Society a few years ago. He's been invited to give lectures about natural philosophy at Paris and Wittenberg. I know he is particularly eager to keep abreast of new discoveries and principles.'

'He still tutors, you mentioned.'

'Yes, the sons of certain noble families, though mostly that tutelage is the lesser subjects, to prepare them for Oxford or Cambridge. No notable minds among them, he's mentioned very sadly more than once.'

'Some of his pupils have been women?' Lucy asked. 'You mentioned Lucretia de Witte—'

'Oh, that woman!' At Lucy's raised eyebrows, Mrs Wallace gave a short mirthless chuckle. 'My apologies, Lucy. That woman pursued my husband for months after he tutored her, sending him all sorts of ciphers. Can you imagine? I am not a woman lacking in either compassion or kindness, let me assure you, but this woman sorely tried my patience. For some reason, she found in my husband a willing target for her misplaced affections.'

Mrs Wallace's voice dropped considerably, and she leaned closer to Lucy's ear. 'She had it in her head that dear Neville would leave me for her! What a harlot!'

'How did you know that?' Lucy asked, even though she felt deeply uncomfortable with the direction of the conversation. 'Did you read the messages yourself?'

'Heavens, no!' Mrs Wallace cried. 'He told me

so himself. The poor man! He had no idea about her intentions, thinking they were just engaging in a clever pastime.' She smoothed down her skirts. 'He swore to me over and over that he had in no way encouraged these untoward intentions. The poor man – I've never seen him in such a state! Since that time, he has refocused his energies on mathematics and formulas, working of late to extend Cavalieri's law of quadrature.' A small smile tugged at his mouth. 'I have forgiven him his trespass against me. As for Miss de Witte – I found her to be too calculating through and through, and I believe her intentions were always suspect.'

'I see,' Lucy replied.

'I've shocked you.'

'I was just wondering why she continued to pursue him with no encouragement from your husband.' Then, hearing her words out in the open, Lucy grew flustered. 'Pardon me,' she said, standing up and bowing her head. 'I meant no offence.'

'Lucy, you've caused me no offence. I've wondered this many a time myself. He told me there was nothing to it. He said they were just riddles, jests between them, using that code she created. Neville was delighted to finally have someone to indulge him in these games. I suppose I was lacking in this regard. She became besotted with him. Such a foolish, unstable woman.' She shifted uncomfortably. 'He assured me her love was unrequited.'

'Oh. Of course.'

Mrs Wallace touched Lucy's arm. 'Let us not

110

speak of her. Let me ask you something, while you are here. I admit to being quite curious,' she said. 'The other night, the Hargraves treated you as one of the family. Pray, tell me, how did you become such an old family friend, as Thomas has called you? I hope you will forgive me, but I do not think you came upon your current station by birth.'

'I served in Master Hargrave's household for several years,' Lucy replied, her chin still high. 'He took me on when I was a young girl, and his family always treated me kindly, for which I will always be grateful. There are many of my station whom fortune did not favour so well.'

Lucy paused, half expecting Mrs Wallace to ring for a servant and have her cast from the premises. Not everyone of Mrs Wallace's sort would willingly converse with a former servant. When she did not, Lucy continued. 'I then became the late Mistress Hargrave's lady's maid before she succumbed to the plague.'

'Ah, the plague – such a misery. God rest those many departed souls.'

Like Mrs Wallace, Lucy clasped her hands and muttered a quick prayer.

'Pray, continue, Lucy. How did you come into your current occupation?'

'Well, after my mistress died,' Lucy said, wringing her hands slightly, 'I began to realize that I no longer occupied a clear place in the magistrate's household. By then the great devastation had occurred, and it became clear that there might be other opportunities that had never been open before. The magistrate, with his generous spirit, bestowed upon me some wealth from his wife's belongings, since his only daughter had become a Quaker and eschewed most frivolities.'

'You accepted the frivolities, I take it,' Mrs Wallace said, her tone kind, not judgemental.

'Certainly. With those garments, I was able to procure a place for myself and my brother Will above Master Aubrey's shop. Will works at the blacksmith's and is making a good living. I am not a true apprentice, since I have not been accepted into the guild, but Master Aubrey has been teaching me much in exchange for the tasks that I do.' She giggled. 'He says I have a very good talent for selling – perhaps a bit more than his actual apprentice, Lach. How he would shout and rant if he ever heard the master say such a thing!'

'You did not wish to wed?' Mrs Wallace asked. 'Surely a comely lass such as yourself must have suitors.'

'I am content right now to remain unwed,' she said, crossing her arms. 'I am still but two and twenty. I have a few more years before I am a spinster in the eyes of the world. Besides, there is more I should like to learn from Master Aubrey. He has said that ever since the Guild Hall has burned down, and all records and contracts, the stationers' guild has been quite lax. More women have been taking on their husband's and father's businesses after the combined disasters of the plague and fire, and so it is not quite as uncommon as it once was.'

'Indeed,' Mrs Wallace said. 'I helped my own

father, also a Cambridge scholar, keep track of his records. He was one who studied botany and the natural law. I would have continued with such work, were we still living there. I'd like to help Neville more. Sometimes his papers can get quite muddled.'

'You said that you had thrown away the work of Miss de Witte,' Lucy said, trying to sound casual. The whole time the two had been conversing, she'd been trying to think of how to bring it back around to Miss de Witte and the cipher. 'Are you quite sure of that?'

'It is interesting that you ask me that,' Mrs Wallace said, giving her a curious look. 'I don't know why, but I feel I can trust you. Maybe because the Hargraves hold you in such high regard.' She made a rueful sound. 'I did not expect to tell you this, given that we have just met, but what I said the other night was not the entire truth. I feel I can tell you now. I feel I can trust you. *Can* I trust you?'

'Yes,' Lucy whispered.

She gave a little laugh. 'This whole time, I've been calling you Lucy. Perhaps you can call me Joanna in return. Then I shall feel more at ease in what I am about to reveal.'

'Yes . . . Joanna.' The name fell awkwardly from her lips, her skin itching a bit at such unexpected familiarity. It went against everything she'd learned as a servant. *Perhaps I should unlearn such things*, Lucy thought.

'Come with me,' Mrs Wallace said, oblivious to Lucy's discomfort. Standing up, she extended her hand to Lucy and led her inside the house.

'Neville is in his study working; we can stop by later. I wish to give you something first. Come with me.'

After leading her up the stairs, Mrs Wallace drew Lucy into a small parlour that opened into a bedchamber area. The lingering smell of perfumed talcums and scents reminded Lucy of how Mistress Hargrave's chamber used to smell. Although she breathed the aroma in happily enough, she was still twisting her hands. *What is it that Mrs Wallace wishes to give me?* She hadn't come expecting a gift and she did not know what to say.

'You look concerned, Lucy,' Mrs Wallace said, correctly interpreting her expression. 'Oh, I understand. Do not fret. The gift is not as you think.' She smiled sadly. 'I did indeed keep the messages that Neville exchanged with that woman, even though I told you they'd been destroyed. I wish to give them to you.'

Lucy stared at her. 'Why did you keep them?' *And why did you say they were destroyed?*

'I must seem so pathetic,' Mrs Wallace said, giving a rueful smile. 'What woman would keep such a thing? The truth of the matter is, the moment I asked Neville to discard the messages, I regretted it. The brilliance of his mind . . .' She looked off in the distance. 'How odd this must all seem to you. I was worried, you understand, that they might contain something important. A thought that would be forever lost. I knew that I would never forgive myself if I had done anything to damage his work.' She

114

sighed. 'He threw them in the hearth after I scolded him. When he stalked away, I grabbed the poker and retrieved them before they all burned up.' Opening a large chest that rested at the end of the bed, Mrs Wallace knelt down to extract a smaller wooden box. 'Neville never looks through my things. A fortuitous trait, to be sure.'

Lucy knelt beside her as Mrs Wallace withdrew several sheets of rumpled parchment, which appeared to have been burned in parts, and laid them on the bed. 'This decision is not easy, you must understand. I wrestle with the notion that I am betraying my husband by passing them on to you. At the same time, they represent a betrayal of marriage and they hurt me so. I despise them.' Tears shone in her eyes. 'I could tell from his countenance that he suspected that message you brought had been written in the same cipher. Perhaps they will help you make sense of it.' She bit her lip. 'If they help you decipher the message, then I feel that a good deed will have come out of that painful matter. Please don't share them with others. I have never deciphered them and I—'

Lucy patted her hand. 'I promise to treat them with care.' She began to look over the messages. Like the message found on the body, they were all in the same coded rows of mixed-up letters and symbols, although the paper was far finer and the writing far more elegant.

'They'd send them back and forth to each other,' Mrs Wallace explained, her face growing flushed. She tapped on one of the messages.

'This line was written by my husband. That script' – she tapped the other – 'was penned by *that* woman.'

'Is one of these the cipher?' Lucy asked, looking at all the pages.

'Alas, no. I did not find it when I searched the hearth,' Mrs Wallace replied. She sighed. 'I suppose it is good that I never had the key, for the Devil would surely have tempted me to decipher their exchanges. My heart would have been injured, far more than it has already been.' She stood up, wiping her eyes. 'Let us visit my husband now. I'm sure he shall be delighted with the selections you have brought.'

Before they left the chamber, Mrs Wallace gripped her arm. 'Pray, do not mention what we discussed or bring that woman's name up. She caused quite a rift in our marriage that has only come to be mended over time. I should not like to see the fabric of our union pulled apart by the threads again.' She stared into Lucy's eyes. 'You saw how he pretended not to recognize the cipher. Perhaps he was initially deluded because it was not in her hand, but there was an excitement there as well. I sometimes think his feelings for her are hiding just below the surface.' Tears filled her eyes. 'I sometimes worry that if she were so inclined, she could seduce him again.'

Lucy's heart lurched. *How awful to feel so uncertain in love! But had she not experienced such discomfiting sentiments herself?* 'I will not say anything to him,' she said, following Mrs Wallace out of the room.

* * *

'My dear, we have a visitor,' Mrs Wallace called, after knocking several times on the door of the study.

'Go away,' they could hear his muffled reply.

'He's a bit cranky,' Mrs Wallace said. 'When he's in this state, he'll only come out for luncheon.'

'I have brought some tracts for you,' Lucy called, not deterred. She began to read off one of the titles, which was all in Latin. She knew she was butchering it by the way Mrs Wallace was grinning and holding her ears.

At that, Professor Wallace stuck his head out. 'I am trying to think!' he nearly shouted at his wife. Then, recognizing Lucy, he stopped short. 'You! What are you doing here?'

'I was hoping to trade some of these for the Babington tract.' His brow cleared and they proceeded to negotiate for a while, with Lucy getting the best of it. She would have conceded on a few prices, but Professor Wallace was not used to haggling. Even the Babington tract cost her very little.

When they were done, Mrs Wallace walked her out of the house. 'Come back any time, Lucy. You have provided an unexpected bright spot to my day. Please do keep an eye out for tracts that Professor Wallace might enjoy.'

She pressed Mrs Wallace's hand. 'Thank you, Mrs Wallace – Joanna. I will certainly do that. And what you've given me should be helpful.' With that, Lucy walked quickly home, hoping she could get through her mountain of chores quickly and start trying to decipher the message.

Ten

Later that night, once Lucy had mopped the floors and cleaned the supper dishes, she retreated to her bedchamber where she could at last review the writings she'd received from Joanna Wallace. There were six pieces in all, each having been written on the same fine parchment, although it was different from what had been discovered on the body of the corpse. She began to smooth the sheets out, laying them side by side so she could view them all at once.

Upon first glance she could see that they contained rows of letters and symbols, all neatly printed by hand, not printed on a printing press. The messages appeared to have been written by two people, with two different pens. The first hand was Professor Wallace's elegant and precise script, while Miss de Witte's handwriting seemed less practised and consistent.

She picked up one of the shorter messages, in which Professor Wallace had written: E C XKVJT RBI BIANR AJT LGIAPI RBI IZI. RI **:** HI XBAR C AH EZ AJT EZ. The second part was shorter still and contained Miss de Witte's response. *L UANYX +.*

'What does this mean?' she wondered aloud. 'Is there truly a rhyme or reason to these?'

She pulled out the Babington tract and began to read through it. The first part was hard going, containing lengthy and complex discussions of mathematical symbols and formulas that she did not understand. She started to flip through the tract in dismay, feeling disappointed that she could not make sense of it for herself. Then, towards the end, she found an excerpt of the key to the Babington cipher. Excitedly, she began to check all of the characters and symbols on each of the messages against the key. A number of the symbols had to do with royal doings and army manoeuvres.

'There's the sign of the gallows that Professor Wallace had mentioned,' Lucy said, looking at the π symbol.

She continued to pour over the key, comparing it to all the symbols. She was just beginning to give up hope when she found a match. She sucked in her breath. The symbol stood for the word 'Devil'. It appeared three times, once on each of the first three lines. She sat back. *What could it mean?* No answer presented itself. She kept checking and double-checking the messages against the Babington tract, to no avail. There were no other matches to be found.

Retrieving some sheets of paper from a small box she kept on her table, she dipped one of her newly sharpened quills into a jar of black ink. Slowly, tediously, she began to copy each of the messages on to fresh pieces of paper, double-checking as she went to make sure she did not make a mistake. She spread them out so that the ink could dry without getting smudged.

Finally, hearing the church bells distantly

chiming eleven o'clock, she reluctantly blew out her candle and crawled into bed.

'Look, this message talks about the Devil,' Lucy said, trying to get the others interested in what she had figured out the night before. Although it was just past eight o'clock, everyone was still looking a bit bleary as they began to ready themselves for church.

'Not so loud, would you, sister?' Will said, rubbing his forehead. 'I had rather a late night last night.'

Lach nudged him. 'Out too late with the ladies, eh?'

'You could say that,' Will replied, giving them all a cheeky grin.

'I don't believe I even heard you come in last night,' Master Aubrey commented, and Will's grin grew wider. 'Who's to say I did?'

Lucy flicked her finger at him. 'I'm trying to tell you something important,' she said.

'That the message you found is about the Devil? That seems far-fetched, don't you think? Hardly a subject while we prepare our countenances for church and absolution,' Will said, adopting the serious tones of a priest.

Lucy rolled her eyes. 'I wasn't saying it was *about* the Devil.'

'What's it about, then?' Lach asked.

'I don't know yet,' she replied, suddenly feeling a bit foolish. 'Still, it means something that the word was repeated, I just know it.'

None of the others were impressed. 'You should

wait till you figure out more of the message before you start crowing,' Lach said.

'I wasn't crowing,' Lucy said hotly. She wanted to tell Duncan, and Adam for that matter, about what she had learned. Yet it did seem as if she was making too much of her discovery. *Well, then, perhaps I'll wait to say anything about it. Although,* she thought, *there's no reason I couldn't mention it when I see Duncan at church.*

'I'll only be a minute,' Master Aubrey said as the congregation roamed out of the hallowed doors of St Dunstan-in-the-West and into the dusty road after the morning service. 'I just need a word with the good priest before we leave.'

'He wants the priest to know he was there today,' Lach muttered to Will, and they all laughed. It was no small secret that Master Aubrey would much rather be in a tavern or in his own bed than a pew, but the priest had begun to take note of his absences on recent Sundays. Later, he was supposed to instruct his servants and apprentice in the Bible, as befitting a godly master of the household, but it was more likely he'd head to a friend's house to play some cards.

'Hope it doesn't take too long! We've got some broth and bread prepared for our noon meal,' Lucy said. Given that they weren't supposed to toil on the Lord's Day, their meals today would be simple but hearty. *I wonder if I can look at the ciphers today, rather than read the Bible,* she thought, immediately feeling guilty. *Not exactly the Lord's work. Although the good Lord would*

121

hardly wish a murderer to go free, she supposed. Of course, it's unlikely that Master Aubrey would mind her efforts, as long as her efforts were not known to others and thus reflect badly on him.

As they waited for the master printer to return, Lucy looked around for Duncan. She'd not seen him earlier during the service and she still wanted to tell him about the little thing she had discovered. For some time, they'd been attending the same service, though by design or by simple coincidence she could not say.

Almost as if she had conjured him, he appeared at the church gate and strode over to her. 'Lucy! I thought I'd find you here,' he said. 'Do you have a moment?'

'Good morning, Constable Duncan,' she replied. She glanced over at Master Aubrey, who was still waiting to speak to the priest. 'I have a few minutes still.'

'What do you need with Lucy *now*, Constable?' Will asked.

'Is she doing *all* your investigations?' Lach chimed in.

Ignoring the others, he said in a low tone. 'Paul Corbyn should have been buried today,' he said. 'As we suspected, the church has refused to bury him or give him a proper funeral, because they believe him to be a suicide.'

'But he wasn't,' Lucy said.

'I was over at St Clement's just now, on a hunch it might have been attended by the Corbyns. Sure enough, I saw Mrs Corbyn pleading with the priest to bury her husband, but he refused to do so. She was distraught.'

122

'Why did she not have Doctor Larimer send an official declaration to this effect? Surely he would have done so.'

'I agree. I was surprised, too. In fact, I very nearly intervened, because she continued to plead for mercy on her husband's behalf as a suicide.'

'How odd,' Lucy replied. 'Does she not understand what you were telling her?'

'I'm not sure what she understands,' Duncan replied. 'I was thinking that we might speak to her together. I am certain she is hiding something.'

'Why do you need Lucy to come with you?' Lach asked again.

Lucy scratched her elbow, waiting for Duncan to reply. His answer was glib, almost as if he had practised it. 'Mrs Corbyn may be willing to talk if another woman is there. It is just a hunch. I believe that Hank and I might have distressed her when we last spoke to her. I am hoping that Lucy's presence may be more calming and help us acquire the answers we seek.'

Lucy sighed. While it was true that the rawness of death had likely damaged the woman's resolve, she wished that they did not have to enquire after the truth in such a fashion. 'All right, here's Master Aubrey,' she said, seeing the printer on his way back. 'I'll ask his leave.'

'I'm ready for my noon meal,' Master Aubrey said, smacking his lips. 'Duncan, would you care to join us?'

The constable smiled. 'No, sir. Thank you, I cannot. I have some official business to attend to.'

Master Aubrey jabbed his finger at Lucy playfully. 'Why do I feel as if you won't be around either? How am I expected to instruct your foolish mind with the teachings of the Bible?' He continued to grumble as he walked away, still shaking his head. 'Yet I'm the one who comes to grief with the priest. How is that fair?'

Eleven

Lucy shifted the straw basket in her hands as she and Duncan walked down the street where the Corbyns lived. She'd stopped back at Aubrey's to grab one of the jars of stew that Cook had given to her the other day, thinking it best to bring along victuals when visiting someone in mourning. Seeing this, Duncan offered up a small leek and chicken pie as well. 'I was planning to have that for my noonday meal,' he said regretfully.

'Did you make it yourself?' she asked, sniffing it appreciatively. 'I didn't know you had such skill.'

'No, no, someone brought it by for me.'

Lucy gave Duncan a sidelong glance which he did not return. She knew from time to time there were ladies in the area who hoped to make a match with the constable, but so far none of them had come close.

Walking down the street, it was quickly evident which was the Corbyns' home. Rushes had been laid in the street to soften the sound of horses' hooves and rattling carriage wheels, and they could see that the unshuttered windows had been draped in black crêpe, suggesting the house was in mourning for a man of means.

'Mr Corbyn must have been successful in his trade,' Lucy whispered, peering about curiously.

'I suppose. For all the good it did him,' Duncan replied as he knocked on the front door.

A servant opened the door, her eyes clear of tears. 'What do you want?' she asked, recognizing Duncan.

'We're here to see your mistress,' he said pleasantly. 'We should very much like to pay our respects.'

'Is that so?' she asked, her eyes narrowing.

What an odd servant, Lucy thought. *So disrespectful. She'd never have lasted a minute at the Hargraves' or Larimers'. Or even at Master Aubrey's, for that matter, and he was the least observant of his godly duties of the lot.*

'Yes,' Duncan said, more firmly.

The servant shrugged. 'Mrs Corbyn is in the drawing room. If you would follow me.'

As the servant led them down the long corridor, Lucy peered all around. The place appeared fancy and elegant but not particularly well kept. It looked as if it hadn't been thoroughly cleaned in a long time, and there was dust, cobwebs and fur everywhere. Even some dried leaves left over from autumn foliage. *Not many servants must work here*, Lucy thought. Or they are very poor indeed. It said something about the state of the household to see such disrepair.

'Have there been many other mourners?' Lucy asked.

'No,' the servant replied, sounding smug. 'A dreadful thing, to be sure. Self-murder is a shameful act. Although he was not even particularly melancholic, to my mind.'

Behind her, Lucy and Duncan exchanged a

126

bemused glance. Lucy grabbed his arm so that he would slow down. 'Why would she tell the servant that it was suicide? You already told her the physicians thought otherwise?' she whispered.

Before they could ask anything else, the servant threw open the doors of the drawing room. There were no mourners there, Lucy noted as they walked in. No trenchers of food had been laid out either, as if Mrs Corbyn had not expected any visitors. The only sign of mourning here was the black crêpe draped across a pair of mirrors on the side wall.

Mrs Corbyn looked at them. 'Oh, Constable Duncan' she said, appearing fatigued. Was there a touch of fear there as well? 'What are you doing here? Is there something else I can do for you?' She looked at her servant. 'Bertha, you may be excused.'

The servant left the room, but Lucy had the feeling she was probably lingering on the other side of the door, her ear pressed to the wood. Such was the way of servants, keeping tabs on the doings of the household.

Lucy looked around the room in curiosity. There were stately paintings adorning the walls, mostly portraits of stern-looking men and barely smiling women. Someone had pasted penny pieces next to them. Most of the cheaper pieces appeared to be of a religious nature – sermons, notices of miracles and other true accounts focusing on the glory of God. It was not uncommon to post such pieces, but usually that was something that poorer people did – those who could not afford framed art and leather-bound books – not those of the merchant's superior sort.

She gestured wearily at Lucy. 'Who's she?'

Lucy stepped forward, holding out the basket 'I brought these for you. Just a meal—'

'Why would you give that to me? Do you know me?'

'Well, no. I'm an acquaintance of the constable and I heard about what happened and—'

Mrs Corbyn interrupted her with an unpleasant sound. 'I don't need anything from the likes of you.'

Lucy stepped back. The woman sounded more like a fishmonger's wife than the widow of a well-to-do merchant.

Duncan coughed. 'As I already informed you, Mrs Corbyn, your husband's death was most certainly *not* a suicide. The physician has confirmed this beyond doubt.' He lowered his voice, probably also aware that the servant was listening at the door. 'Have you had any more thoughts about his death? Did he have enemies? Anyone who might have wanted him dead?'

Tears welled up in her eyes. 'Constable Duncan, I know that he died of his own hand, as much as it pains me to say. He'll get a suicide's death, buried in unhallowed ground, with no funeral service. The priest assured me of that today.' She gulped, fighting back tears. 'There's nothing we can do for him now, and I'll thank you to keep your mouth shut.'

She picked up a small silver bell from the table, and the door opened almost instantly at its tinkling sound.

'Bertha, these *guests* are leaving now. Please show them out.'

'Yes, madam,' the servant said, sounding more defiant than meek.

To Lucy's surprise, Mrs Corbyn did not comment on the seeming insubordination of her servant, choosing to ignore it instead. 'I'm going to my room to rest. Suddenly, I've got quite a headache. You can bring me a tisane later.'

Without another look towards Duncan and Lucy, Mrs Corbyn swept out of the room. With that movement, for the first time her actions seemed befitting of a wealthy merchant's wife.

Bertha raised her eyebrows. 'This way, if you would,' she said, leading them unceremoniously out.

'I don't think she was telling the truth, do you?' Lucy asked Duncan after they had moved down the street. The whole exchange with Mrs Corbyn had been puzzling. 'The way her servant treated her! That would never have happened at the Hargraves'. Or at Aubrey's, for that matter.'

'No, there's something odd going on,' Duncan agreed. 'In my experience, family members will do anything they can to convince authorities, both church and court alike, that their loved one's suicide was accidental or stemmed from natural causes. When pressed, they might even claim a suicide to be murder, since the stigma around self-murder can be brutal. Why, then, is Mrs Corbyn persisting in her claim that her husband killed himself, when it causes her such distress?'

'I've been thinking about that, too,' Lucy replied. 'She seemed eager to convince *us* that he *did* kill himself. Does she not care that her husband will be buried in unconsecrated ground? Did you see all the sermons and godly works that had been pasted to the walls? I think she has a deep faith and she cares deeply.'

'Why was she so eager to let us believe that his death was a suicide? Why not seize on the idea that he had been murdered?' Duncan asked. 'It just doesn't make sense.'

'He might have been involved with something troublesome, and she knew it. Maybe she knows who murdered him and is too afraid to say,' Lucy said. 'Perhaps she's afraid that they will come after her, too.'

'So stubborn!' Duncan replied. 'We might be able to help her.'

'Unless exposing her secret will do her more harm than good.' Then another thought occurred to her. 'Maybe she had something to do with his death and doesn't want us to investigate!'

They stared at each other. 'I will find out where she was at the time of his death,' Duncan replied, looking a bit chagrined. 'I should have done so already! After all, when a man is murdered, it is almost always by his wife.'

'Here you go, brother,' Lucy said, setting a second bowl of stew in front of Will, before scraping out the last bit for herself. The rest of the day had passed easily enough. When Lucy had returned home, she continued to pore over the Babington tract, to see if there were any more clues to be found. Alas, nothing new had emerged.

Will grunted his thanks. 'What's the latest? Figured out who the murderer is yet?'

'No, but the dead's man wife, Mrs Corbyn, was quite insistent that her husband *had* committed suicide. Even though she'd been quite tearful at the prospect of him being buried in unconsecrated ground. He'll be buried in a potter's field, for certain, with none but her own prayers said for his soul.'

Master Aubrey sopped some bread into his stew before stuffing it in his mouth. 'You said before that the physicians are fairly certain that it was not self-murder,' he said as he chewed.

'Yes, that is so. She's choosing not to accept that fact.' Lucy set down her own spoon and looked around the table eagerly. 'You know what else is odd?'

'Even more odd than someone insisting someone's death was suicide when it was murder?' Lach asked. 'Besides an odd ring around his neck? Besides a coded message being found on his body? Besides being hanged when he may already have been dead? Tell us, Lucy, what *else* is odd?'

'Oh, Lach,' Lucy said, clapping her hands. 'You've been paying attention.'

'Out with it,' the apprentice said, nearly growling. 'You've told us everything else. Don't hold back now.'

'Adam thought the corpse looked familiar,' Lucy said. 'When we viewed it earlier in the week. He was quite troubled by it.'

'You viewed the corpse?' Lach's face took on a pinched look, making his freckles stand out. 'Why in heaven's name did you do that?'

'You said he was a merchant,' Master Aubrey said, swatting absent-mindedly at Lach. 'I assume Master Adam would have met him through trade.'

'Mr Corbyn was a mercer of household objects. Pots, pans and the like. Adam said he hasn't bought anything of that nature,' Lucy replied. 'However, Doctor Larimer showed us a tattoo on the man's upper left arm. It was the image of a sea serpent. Quite fanciful and ornate, if you ask me.'

'A sea serpent?' Will dropped his spoon into his bowl. 'No! It can't be.'

Lucy stared at him. 'Will, what is it? What's wrong?'

Will's face had nearly drained of colour. 'Dark curly hair, you say?' he asked, his tone suddenly hoarse. 'Slim, wiry build? A misshapen nose?'

'Yes,' Lucy whispered. 'That's right. Will, what's wrong? Who was this man?'

Everyone stared at her brother, waiting for him to explain. His cheeks had started to regain their usual ruddy colour, although there was something pained in his expression. Moreover, his body was starting to shake.

'I think . . .' Will stopped and started again. 'I think he may have been a guard at Newgate Prison.' He stood up, abruptly pushing his chair back, near toppling it to the floor. 'Pardon me, I need some air.' Her brother lurched away, and she could hear him being sick outside the shop in the dark recesses of the street.

132

'A Newgate guard?' Lucy repeated, as a groggy, sickly sensation came over her. Just thinking about the dreadful prison might have made him unwell. She remembered, when her brother had been imprisoned, how anxious she had been, how sickly the sights she'd witnessed. The rats, the rotting corpses, the hopelessness of the men there. It was only by the grace of God, and Adam's help, that her brother had been freed from near certain death.

No wonder Adam had recognized the man but couldn't place him. Like the others, he'd probably tried to push images of that godforsaken place from his mind.

A few minutes later, Will stepped back inside. Wordlessly, Lucy poured him some mead from the pitcher on the table, which he drank quickly.

'Fetch the lad some ale, Lucy,' Master Aubrey said, clapping Will on the back. 'You'll be all right, lad. That's your past. None of that can harm you now.'

Lucy ran to pour her brother some ale, putting it in front of him. They all watched him as he took a few gulps. Finally, he wiped his mouth against the back of his hand. 'Usually, the guard's tattoo was covered, of course,' he muttered, staring down at the cup. 'There was this one day, though, when someone threw a pot of piss on him, and he tore off his shirt. That's when I saw it.' He took another sip. 'I've wondered sometimes what happened to all the inmates and guards of Newgate Prison during the fire. I guess some fled.'

Lucy nodded. She'd wondered herself. She'd

133

heard some prisoners had been evacuated as the fire had spread and sent to other jails. There'd been no stories that they'd succumbed to the flames. Quite the opposite, in fact. The miracle of the Great Fire was that only a handful of people had died in the blaze outright. The fire had moved slowly over three days, before turning back on itself, and most inhabitants had been able to flee with whatever movables they could carry. 'What did you say the man's name was?'

'Paul Corbyn.'

'I don't remember any guard with that name.'

'He must have changed it,' Master Aubrey supplied.

Lucy snapped her fingers. 'He didn't just give himself a new name. He stole the merchant's identity. He and his wife.'

Certainly, after the Great Fire there were many who forged new identities, many through less than legal means. There were cases of servants who had stolen their deceased master's trades and tools, and effectively their livelihoods.

'Being a merchant has to be much better than a Newgate guard,' Lach commented.

'So how would that happen?' Lucy continued to ponder, as she tore apart a bit of bread into increasingly smaller pieces. She glanced over at her brother. Thankfully, Will seemed to have returned to his usual colour, and his appetite, she was glad to see, once again appeared hearty. She placed the crust of bread on his plate. 'Eat.' She turned back to the others. 'How could he have taken the merchant's identity and no one be any the wiser?'

'Perhaps he managed to find the original merchant's papers. Maybe he didn't bother – so many records and papers were lost during the fire. Easy enough to forge a new life for yourself, given the upheaval all around.' Master Aubrey took a deep swallow of his ale and then continued. 'Those days, just after the fire. So many of us had lost so much. During the plague, so many people died. People I've known for years, gone with a single stroke of the good Lord's judgement.'

His last words were spoken with a notable bitterness. Not for the first time, Lucy wondered who Master Aubrey may have lost in those terrible years of plague and fire. She suspected sometimes that was why he was rather lax about his godly duty to his apprentice and household. She knew he never sang with the rest of the congregation during the service, and only muttered the occasional response when the preacher might be looking at him. Not a heretic or an apostate certainly, but not a man who exalted in the presence of the Lord.

'He would have had to know that the Corbyns were gone and their house was empty,' Lach said. 'Or had to ensure it was available.' Here he wagged his red eyebrows in an exaggerated way.

'Just so,' Lucy mused. 'What about servants?' She remembered the unpleasant woman who'd opened the door and led her to the dead man's widow. 'I only saw one woman, although I suppose others might have been tending the kitchen or laundry.'

'Maybe the others died,' Will said. 'Or maybe the Corbyns bullied them.'

135

Lucy nodded. The servant she'd seen had not seemed particularly grief-stricken, or even slightly moved by her late master's passing. If anything, she'd been insubordinate. Which made sense if she had something on the Corbyns, assuming she knew that they were not who they claimed to be.

What could have happened to the real Corbyns? Why would the servant allow someone to live in her master's home? Or, perhaps, she had also taken the opportunity that the plague and fire had provided. Perhaps she'd never been a member of the Corbyn household either.

She thought about the portraits on the walls – how someone had pasted the penny press alongside them. She'd never seen any among the Hargraves' acquaintance do such a thing. *That's what it would look like if you moved into someone else's home, and their movables and furnishings were still intact.* She remembered too how Mrs Corbyn had sounded. 'I remember thinking she was like a fishmonger's wife,' Lucy said. 'Not the wife of a rich merchant.' She frowned. 'So why kill a Newgate guard at the hanging tree at a crossroads? What does that mean?'

'The real question is,' Master Aubrey said, rubbing his hands together, 'was Corbyn's murderer someone from his past or someone from his present?'

Twelve

'You again,' Mrs Corbyn said, glaring at Duncan and Lucy, standing at her front door, positioned as if to physically bar them from her home. Like yesterday, the house was silent, forlorn and empty of mourners. The rushes had been removed from the street, and the black crêpe had been taken down from the windows. 'I've told you everything I need to about my husband's suicide. Please leave me to mourn in peace. It's time to let the dead rest.'

'Is the real Paul Corbyn resting in peace somewhere?' Lucy blurted out before she could restrain herself.

Mrs Corbyn stared at her, her face draining of all colour. 'W–what do you mean?'

'Your husband was not born Paul Corbyn, was he? He was, in fact, born with a different name, and had a different occupation before the Great Fire – is that not so?' Duncan asked, taking a step closer. 'Indeed, was he not a guard at Newgate Prison, and not a mercer at all?'

Mrs Corbyn stared at her. 'Why would you say that?' she whispered, glancing around, no doubt to see if the servant was listening. She stepped out of the house, shutting the door behind her. 'Who told you this fanciful tale?'

Duncan waved his hand. 'Never mind how we know it. Don't bother denying it, either. We know it to be true. Why don't you simply tell us about it?'

The widow pursed her lips tightly shut.

'Well, at the moment I cannot press you to explain; that is so,' he stated. 'However, I can certainly arrest you for stealing someone's identity. Then you can tell me all about it, in your jail cell.'

Mrs Corbyn swayed a bit on her feet but steadied herself against the wall. 'I knew this day would come,' she whispered, tears gathering in her eyes. 'I knew that there'd be a reckoning.'

'Can you tell us about it?' Lucy asked. As the woman fell into a defiant and stony silence, she pressed more. 'Is that why you clung to the lie, claiming his death was a suicide? Because if you acknowledged his death to be a murder, you were afraid that it would not take long for the authorities to realize that you two were not who you claimed to be, and you'd see everything taken away?' Hearing Mrs Corbyn moan, Lucy pressed on. 'Don't you want your husband's murderer caught and brought to justice? Don't you want your husband buried in hallowed ground?'

'Too late for that! I'll lose everything.'

'You'll lose everything anyway if the relatives of the real Corbyns come forward.'

'Small chance of that. They're all dead.'

'Tell us.'

'You have to understand that my husband was a good God-fearing man. He worked every day at that hell-hole at Newgate, dealing with halfwits and other lowlifes. Every day, he'd come home with stories of the terrible things he'd

138

witnessed and heard. Until he stopped. I could tell it was all eating away at his soul. He wasn't like those other guards. Those terrible men.'

'What was your husband's given name?' Duncan asked. 'We know he was not Paul Corbyn, which was the identity he stole. Tell me now, and I may not arrest you today for theft.'

'Jack Campbell,' she whispered. 'I'm Mariah.' A brief smile flittered over her face, and her eyes glistened with tears. 'I have not been able to call him by his given name for over a year. It is indeed quite tragic that he will not be buried in a proper grave with a proper headstone. May the good Lord forgive us both for this lie.'

'Could you tell us what happened?' Lucy pressed.

'Jack led those men out of the Newgate Prison during the Great Fire. The mayor had said to abandon them, but he couldn't. He unlocked them and led them out. His intention was to bring them to one of the other jails, but in the chaos he was not sure where to go. He told me that they pleaded with him to be set free. So, God bless him, he did. He let those men free. Cut-throat murderers all.' Mrs Corbyn sat down, disregarding her fine skirts.

After exchanging a quick glance, Lucy and Duncan sank down beside her, crouching on either side of the woman who was now weeping into her hands. 'What's going to become of me?' she wailed. She was no longer the haughty woman she'd been.

'I will let the magistrate know that you have

cooperated with this investigation,' Duncan replied. 'Assuming, of course, that you continue to answer our questions. How did you come upon this particular identity?'

Mrs Corbyn sniffed. 'We saw what happened after the fire. We knew the merchant who lived here had died during the plague, and even after the fire, it was still vacant. So it was not so hard for him to unearth the merchant's records. At first his customers were suspicious of the change, but he just claimed to be a cousin of Mr Corbyn. Over time, he just started using Mr Corbyn's given name as well. Then we were able to take everything over.'

'What about your servant? Did she know that her employers were frauds?' Duncan asked.

'Bertha is a servant we picked up after the fire. As far as I know, she never knew the Corbyns personally, although I believe at some point she figured out our deception. She became less loyal after that, and she clearly felt she had something on us.' She began to weep softly. 'Every day, I was so fearful of being discovered. I pleaded with Jack to leave, start a new life again, but as the Campbells we once were. He wouldn't have it. Said that he enjoyed being a mercer, enjoyed being in trade.'

'Mrs Corbyn,' Lucy said, leaning forward. 'As Constable Duncan said the other day, your husband did not kill himself. Surely you know that to be true. Why do you persist in saying that he did?'

Mrs Corbyn murmured a small prayer and began to rock back and forth. She suddenly looked desperate and alone. 'It's the reckoning. We have to pay.'

A shiver ran up and down Lucy's spine. 'Do you know who killed your husband?' Lucy prodded. 'Please, if you do, say something. Could it have been someone who knew the true Paul Corbyn? Someone who resented that you'd taken over his identity and trade? Now's the time to tell us what you know. Let justice be done.'

Mrs Corbyn muttered something that Lucy didn't quite catch. 'What was that?' Lucy asked. 'I didn't hear you.'

This time the woman spoke louder. 'No good deed goes unpunished.' Tears began to slip down her cheeks and her words turned into a wail. 'No good deed goes unpunished!'

Before Lucy or Duncan could say anything else, Mrs Corbyn ducked back into the house, slamming the door behind her. They could hear the key turn in the lock, so there was no following her back inside. Beyond the wood door, they could hear the woman's rising hysterical tears. When Lucy glanced back, she could see the servant standing at the glass window, staring with a knowing smile on her face.

The sun disappeared into the rising fog, and Lucy shivered. She tugged on Duncan's sleeve. 'What are you going to do about Mrs Corbyn?'

He sighed. 'To be honest, Lucy, I truly do not know. I think these cases are everywhere. She should be arrested and brought to trial. Imprisoned for this deed of impersonating the Corbyns. I know that to be true. Yet such cases have been hard to prove, unless one of the Corbyns' relatives learns of this and sues them. It sounds as if they are all dead. It would be different, of course, if it turns out she was involved in the murder.'

'Do you think that likely?'

'No. It is my opinion that all of Mrs Corbyn's lies stem from her fear of being discovered. She was scared witless, that one – despite her defiance. She's a rabbit living like a lion.'

'You know what I've been wondering?' Lucy asked, stepping around a woman carrying a heavy basket of soaps on her head. 'Which men did Mr Corbyn lead out of Newgate Prison?'

Duncan rubbed his jaw. 'Well, since he was recognized by Will and Adam, he was probably working in the wing where—' he paused.

'Men were on trial for murder,' Lucy finished his thought. Mrs Corbyn's words came back to her then. '*No good deed goes unpunished*,' she murmured.

'What?'

'It's what Mrs Corbyn said. I wonder if letting those men go free was the good deed she was referring to.' She straightened her shoulders. 'We *must* decipher that message. We must find a way to speak with Miss de Witte. Get that cipher once and for all.'

'I don't think I can simply demand that she hand it over. My authority does not extend that far.'

'I know. We have to go through Mrs Wallace, to arrange an introduction. I know there's bad blood between the two women, but there's no time to lose. Maybe if I talk to her, I can get her to give it to me.'

'To get that introduction, are you going to ask the Hargraves for help?' The word *again* was almost tacked on to the end of Duncan's question.

Lucy shook her head. 'I shall call on Mrs Wallace tomorrow. I don't know why, but I have a good feeling about her. I believe she will help us, despite her personal distaste for Miss de Witte.'

Thirteen

'Mrs Wallace,' Lucy called over the hedge, seeing the mathematician's wife digging listlessly in the near-frozen ground. 'I'm rather afraid you are cutting up some of the more useful herbs. The essence of that one is in the roots, and it will not regrow, being removed in such fashion.'

'Oh, Lucy,' Mrs Wallace replied, looking up. 'Cook has the afternoon off. We have guests coming soon and I was hoping to dig up some nice roots.' She looked around the garden with a mournful air. 'I'm afraid I'm rather hopeless at this sort of thing.'

Lucy regarded the little herb garden with a mournful air. The Wallaces' cook might be unhappy if she saw the mess that her mistress had made of her preciously tended garden, especially as they moved into the coldest time of the year. 'I would be happy to bring you some of our older tracts on the growing and preserving of herbs.'

'Thank you, Lucy,' Mrs Wallace replied, straightening up, making a grimace as she did so. It was clear that she spent very little time on tasks such as these. 'What brings you here today?'

'I was just passing by,' she lied. 'Tell me, how did Professor Wallace find the tracts I brought the other day? Are there others he might like me to procure?'

Mrs Wallace smiled. 'I think Professor Wallace would always appreciate the newest learning in science and mathematics. Music, too. In fact, we have some scholars coming here tonight. They can be quite raucous in their gatherings, which, between you and me, is why I like to have such gatherings when Cook is not present.' She looked at Lucy, a slight smile on her lips. 'I thought perhaps you wanted some more assistance with the cipher. Did you learn anything in those messages I gave you? Did the Babington tract help?'

Lucy shook her head. 'I just learned a word, I think. Devil.'

'Devil? How odd. What did you make of that?'

'Nothing, I'm afraid.'

Mrs Wallace looked at her sharply. 'Tell me the truth, now, Lucy. Is that why you came back? I believe that I have provided everything that the dastardly woman sent my husband.'

Being direct seemed to be the best answer here. 'Yes, it's true,' Lucy replied. 'I'm sorry I was not honest with you at the start. It's really important that we decipher the message, and it seems only your husband and Miss de Witte may know how to do so. Could we not just . . .' She hesitated. 'Could we ask your husband for the key? Surely, he must have had a copy to read Miss de Witte's messages. Or perhaps as a mathematician he could figure it out again.'

Mrs Wallace's face flushed to a dark and unpleasant shade of red. 'We most certainly cannot ask him.' Then her tone softened. 'For a year we had not spoken that woman's name until it came

145

up at Master Hargrave's the other night. I do not wish to have him remember her words, her embraces—'

'Embraces?' Lucy exclaimed. The flirtation must have been more serious than she assumed.

'Yes,' Mrs Wallace said, blowing her nose. 'Theirs was no simple flirtation, I know it. It humiliates me to speak of it, to think of it! He swore that it was just a love affair of the mind, but I knew better.' She shook her head. 'All that is neither here nor there,' she said, clearly trying to collect herself. 'Let me strive to be more noble of heart. I shall take my lead in this from you, Lucy, dear. I shall set my grievance aside, so that we may speak to her directly.'

Lucy stared at her. 'Speak to her directly? Why in good heaven would you do that? Speak to your husband's—' She stopped herself before she could utter words that would surely be hurtful. 'Why, pray tell, would you subject yourself to such an encounter?'

'To be honest, Lucy, it hurts me to think of my husband enamoured of her and she with him. At the same time, I believe it is petty and unworthy of me to let my emotions, such as they are, interfere with a more noble pursuit of justice. Perhaps she will produce the cipher for you. Perhaps, then, justice for that poor man may be served.'

Lucy could see that she was trembling. 'There must be a better way,' she said.

Mrs Wallace gave a delicate shrug. 'I have decided to set my pride aside for the greater good.' Her eyes travelled doubtfully over Lucy's serviceable dress. 'I had thought you might accompany me as my companion. You *do* have nicer clothes, do you not? I was quite struck by the lovely attire that you wore to the Hargraves' the other night. I should never have suspected that you were once their servant. Oh!' she added hurriedly. 'Your face! Lucy, I did not intend to offend.'

'I am not offended,' Lucy said, relaxing from her rigid pose. 'I am proud to have served the Hargraves – they are honourable people, and my experience with them was a good one. If my face conveyed anything, I was thinking that you are quite right. I have no fine clothes other than the dress I wore the other night, which would not do for an afternoon call. I am not of her level and she'd see through me instantly. I think it would be better if I come with you as your attendant.'

Mrs Wallace looked her over, a thoughtful expression on her face. 'Lucretia might know that I do not keep a lady's maid. Besides, I do not want to incur the Hargraves' wrath if they hear of me treating you as a servant, even one in the manner of a lady's maid. I think, perhaps, Adam in particular would like you to be viewed as one of his kind.'

Lucy started to demur, but Mrs Wallace waved away her comments. 'You know, I had thought to have you wear one of my older dresses, but I think they would hang ill on you. Let us be forthright. I will introduce you as the woman you are, a printer's apprentice and bookseller. If the Hargraves invite you to dine, then you are

147

fit to call on Miss de Witte as well.' She looked towards the sun. 'Let us go now. There is no time to lose.'

Within the half hour, Professor Wallace had summoned a carriage and they were on their way to Miss de Witte's home. If he'd been surprised or confused by Lucy accompanying his wife on what appeared to be a social call, he did not show it. He did raise his eyebrow when his wife told him where they were going, but he gave the address to the driver with no comment.

Lucretia de Witte's home was grand and elegant, and it was clear that she was quite well-to-do. When her servant opened the door, Mrs Wallace and Lucy were ushered into the drawing room. 'Miss de Witte will be with you soon.'

As they waited, Lucy looked around the room. Above the hearth was a portrait of a young man, perhaps in his early twenties, wearing the robes of a scholar. There was a black scarf tied across the top of it, but it was not shrouded completely. The subject was likely dead, but his death was not recent.

'That's her brother,' Mrs Wallace whispered, coming to stand behind Lucy. 'He died last year. She was quite distraught and had this portrait commissioned from memory.'

'I see,' Lucy said, still studying the man's face. He looked gentle, scholarly. At his elbow, a brown leather-bound book with gold-leaf edges had been placed, a yellow cord wrapped around it, keeping it shut. A piece of paper was sticking out of one end of the book.

Stepping back, Lucy continued to peruse the painting. The subject was holding a piece of rolled-up leather in his left hand, and she could just see a ring on his forefinger. Her mouth went dry. *It can't be!* Startled, Lucy stepped closer to examine the ring, which appeared to have two faces – a cherub looking out at the viewer and a side angle of a skull facing the man. 'Is that the same ring?' she whispered.

'The same ring?' Mrs Wallace asked. 'What do you mean?'

'Oh, nothing,' Lucy said, continuing to study the portrait. It was then she noted the direction of the seated man's finger. He appeared to be pointing at the book resting at his elbow. No, that wasn't quite right. The man was actually pointing at the exposed edge of the paper that was poking out of the book. She could see now there was some faint writing on the scrap of paper. Was the writing a cipher? She rubbed her eyes.

'You're not the first woman to be enraptured by my brother Hammett,' a woman said from behind her. 'It is unfortunate that he is no longer with us to enjoy the fruits of such admiration.'

Lucy spun around. A beautiful woman, her blonde hair elegantly swept up, stood before her, dressed in a violet brocade gown that had an overlay of silk. Her green eyes commanded their attention. 'Good afternoon, Mrs Wallace,' she said, the chill in her tone unmistakable. 'What brings you and your acquaintance to my home? I have not seen you in over a year, not since your parting words made it clear that I was no longer welcome in your lives.'

'You were no longer welcome because—' Mrs Wallace stopped her own speech abruptly, then began again. '*Lucretia*,' she said, stressing the woman's name, 'do allow me to introduce my acquaintance, Lucy Campion. She works for Master Aubrey, a printer and bookseller over on Fleet Street. She is an apprentice.'

Miss de Witte's eyes flicked over at Lucy, but she did not say a word.

'I brought her here today because she is able to procure all kinds of interesting tracts and books. She has brought along a few mathematical tracts, which I thought you might wish to review.'

'Why would you do that?' The chill in Miss de Witte's voice was still stark.

'My husband told me that he did not return your affections and that nothing untoward had happened between you.' Mrs Wallace looked toward the portrait, apparently trying to compose herself. Having turned, she did not catch the way that Miss de Witte arched her brow and looked amused, but Lucy saw it. *They did commit adultery*, she thought, feeling sad.

'I know that your brother passed away soon after,' Mrs Wallace continued, oblivious to what Miss de Witte's expression had revealed. 'I was not able to provide you with solace, even though we'd once been friends. For that absence, I wish to make amends with you now.'

Lucy stepped forward, opening her pack. 'I have a few mathematical tracts, which I thought might be of interest to you. We booksellers trade with many people, and I have all sorts of offerings. If there are other titles you desire, I may be able to procure them for you.'

Miss de Witte looked thoughtful. 'You say you are an apprentice? So unusual for a woman.'

'That is so,' Lucy replied, thinking a dose of truth might be appropriate here. 'However, while I do work for Master Aubrey and have learned many aspects of the trade – setting the type, running the press and selling the pieces – alas, I am not a true apprentice to Master Aubrey.'

'No?' Both women said at once. She could tell that she had surprised Mrs Wallace as well.

She hastened to explain. 'Master Aubrey has written to the stationers' guild about my application, and accepted the fee, which Master Hargrave provided for me when I left his household. It is unusual, as you say, for a woman to become an apprentice in any guild, and usually only in very specific circumstances, such as taking over for a father or a brother who had died. It is true that the stationers' guild has only admitted a handful of women that I'm aware of. However, since the fire—'

'Since the fire, the world has changed,' Miss de Witte said, waving away Lucy's words. 'That is something that does not need to be explained. I very much hope that you will be granted access to the guild, as the clothmakers' company and the drapers' guild have both seen fit to do for their young women serving as apprentices.' She gave a tinkly little laugh. 'Just as I should have been allowed to study at Cambridge like my brother,

151

although certainly the private tutelage I received stood me in good stead.'

Beside her, Mrs Wallace shifted uncomfortably, but Lucy nodded. There were times like these when she wondered why women were denied from pursuing livelihoods and education that men partook in so easily. She'd read some tracts and pamphlets these last few years that had pondered this question, and she'd never seen a response that truly explained it. 'I have heard many Quakers, both men and women, say the same. They speak of spiritual equality between the sexes in ways that I seldom hear others do. Husbands and wives are helpmeets, and women are allowed to express their thoughts and conscience as they are so moved.'

Both women looked at her in surprise. 'You seem to have thought about this,' Mrs Wallace said.

Lucy felt a flush rising in her cheeks. Perhaps she was speaking above her station. Still, she could not refrain from replying. 'I do read many of the tracts I sell, even if my understanding is not as superior as some. My knowledge is scant, but I have spent some time among Quakers. I know something about their beliefs and the manner in which they treat one another.'

Miss de Witte looked thoughtful, and her smile seemed genuine for the first time. 'Let us have tea. I believe there is much we can discuss here, and I admit to being highly intrigued by your occupation.'

She waved a bell and the servant who had opened the front door appeared. 'Mavis, bring us tea to the study, if you would.' She turned back to the other two women. 'There are some pieces I should like to get my hands on. Pray, come with me.'

Miss de Witte opened a small door off the drawing room and beckoned them to enter. Lucy looked around in wonder. On the shelves were a number of the fine leather-clad volumes that were hand-stitched by the most skilled book-makers. Around the rooms there were also pouches of neatly stacked tracts, broadsides and pamphlets.

'So many books,' Lucy exclaimed, touching the spine of one book with a careful finger. 'Even more than the Hargraves, I'd wager.'

'Please, feel free to look at them more closely,' Miss de Witte said. 'You can see that I've been quite the collector, but I will not pretend to have read them all myself. Many, but certainly not all. A great number of them, of course, belonged to my father and brother, who were both Cambridge scholars.' She turned back to Lucy. 'It is through them that I met Professor Wallace.'

She smiled slightly when Mrs Wallace stiffened. 'Let that be all bygones,' she said, waving her hand. 'Water under the bridge, isn't that so?'

'Yes, indeed,' Mrs Wallace said through clenched teeth. Lucy touched her arm in a friendly gesture of support, and Mrs Wallace's smile became more genuine.

'I am told that you created an entire cipher that you used to write messages,' Lucy said carefully.

Miss de Witte looked startled. 'You told her about that?' she asked Mrs Wallace.

In response, Mrs Wallace gave a delicate shrug. 'While I was not fond of your communicating with my husband in such a manner, I do believe it was a peculiar indicator of your particular form of genius.'

'My particular form of genius,' Miss de Witte repeated, looking thoughtful. 'I should not have thought of it that way. It just seemed the most pleasant and elegant way to communicate my thoughts. From one like mind to another.'

'Indeed,' Mrs Wallace said tightly.

Lucy jumped in, thinking that Mrs Wallace was about to crack like an egg. 'I should very much like to know how you went about building a cipher. Did you have a key?'

'Oh, yes, of course there was a key!' Miss de Witte said. 'There's no way even the most brilliant of souls could hold my cipher in his mind, so detailed and complex it was.'

'Perchance, could you show it to me?' Lucy asked. 'I should very much like to see it.'

Miss de Witte made a funny twist of her lips. 'Alas, I threw it all away some time ago. Such a cipher caused too much heartbreak.' All three women fell silent. The servant entered then with mugs of tea and sweet cakes. 'You two eat,' Miss de Witte said, pulling out a quill, ink and a piece of paper. 'I shall begin to make a list of books that I should like Lucy to procure.'

Lucy and Mrs Wallace each took one of the cups and a sweet cake. As Miss de Witte scribbled out authors and titles, Lucy mentioned a few

154

pieces that she could remember. 'I am not so versed in such scholarly pieces,' she admitted. 'For they are not ones I will sing about in the market or at the festivals.'

'I should say not,' Miss de Witte replied, and then, to Lucy's surprise, a full smile crossed her face before she laughed. 'To sing about Euclid. Or Pythagoras! Imagine! The absurdity makes my sides ache to think about.' Her smile transformed her beautifully. She no longer appeared so sallow and stern; now she looked like any other happy young woman.

As Miss de Witte continued to write down names, she would chuckle out loud from time to time. 'I wonder how Kepler's *Observations* would sound set to tune. What is a popular tune?'

'"Where is my love?"' Lucy said, and hummed a few bars. 'We use that one a lot when we are setting the murder ballads, particularly when it is about a husband accused of killing his beloved.' This brought an amused tittering from the women, although not the raucous guffaws of the usual audience, who heartily appreciated the joke.

Miss de Witte suddenly seemed tired, her mirth and humour quenched. 'My brother would have enjoyed many of these books,' she said, more subdued. 'His death is a loss that I will never forget, nor forgive.'

Lucy glanced at Mrs Wallace. Perhaps it was time to go. Mrs Wallace took the hint. 'Lucretia, my dear, let us get together again soon, perhaps when Lucy has a few new pieces for you. Right now, we shall take our leave.'

Miss de Witte barely nodded, her earlier gaiety

155

completely dissipated. Languidly, she rang a little bell before sinking back into a large overstuffed chair. She seemed completely exhausted. 'Mavis will show you out.'

As the carriage returned them to the Wallace household, Lucy turned to Mrs Wallace. 'How did her brother die, do you know?' she asked. She'd been struck by something Miss de Witte had said. 'Did he succumb to the plague or some other malady?'

'No,' Mrs Wallace replied. 'Neville told me that Lucretia's brother had been murdered. In a tavern. A little way out of London. Hertfordshire, I believe. Hoddesdon, perhaps. Or maybe it was Broxbourne. I do not recall. I know that he was travelling back to London from Cambridge, and had stopped at a coaching inn there.'

'Murdered? How awful!' Lucy exclaimed, her thoughts beginning to whirl. *What a coincidence!* Miss de Witte's brother had been murdered. What about the portrait? Hammett de Witte had been depicted wearing a ring that very much resembled the ring found around Paul Corbyn's neck. Moreover, that Paul Corbyn, formerly Jack Campbell, was a Newgate guard who'd let several prisoners go free during the fire. A sense of a tenuous connection began to be forged. 'When did his murder occur, do you know?'

'I'm not sure exactly. Sometime last summer. The great plague had mostly passed, because I know that travellers with health certificates were allowed in and out of the city again, but before the Great Fire.' She sighed. 'It was at this

156

time that Lucretia began to send Neville those coded messages. I did not understand at the time the nature of her travails. The pain, the sadness, the turmoil she must have been experiencing. She did not confide such thoughts with me, and I did not understand. I only saw a beautiful woman turning to my husband, though I see now that her flirtation brought a necessary diversion to a very deep pain.'

Lucy felt a sharp pang in her own chest. The pain of a loved one's death, especially at the wilful hands of another, could not be readily understood by others.

'I could only see how she encroached on my rather hapless husband, who became enamoured of her intellect as well as her beauty,' Mrs Wallace whispered, beginning to weep in earnest. 'I felt that she was trying to trap him, to steal him from me.'

Lucy patted her hand, the gesture feeling woefully inadequate. 'Miss de Witte was deeply pained by her brother's untimely demise – that is certain. It also sounds as if she sought to transgress the fidelity of marriage, which is a torment that she has no right to inflict.'

Mrs Wallace sniffed. 'That is most certainly so.' She looked back at Lucy. 'What interested you about her brother's murder, may I ask? You seemed entranced by his portrait.'

'It was the ring he was wearing. So unusual,' Lucy said. Hearing the church bells in the distance, she seized Mrs Wallace's hands. 'I must hurry back to Master Aubrey's now. He will be glad of this order from Miss de Witte, and I thank you. I know that it was not easy for you to speak with her and—'

Mrs Wallace raised her hand. 'Not another word about it, if you would. I am very much hoping that this will all stay in the past where it belongs.'

Fourteen

'Say, Master Aubrey,' Lucy said as she began to clear the bowls from their evening meal. 'Do you recall the murder of a Cambridge scholar in Hertfordshire? Maybe in Broxbourne or Hoddesdon? I don't remember ever seeing any true news about it or any ballads. I heard tell of it today and I was curious. It would have happened before I started working with you.'

Master Aubrey scratched his ear. 'Doesn't ring a bell,' he said. 'Have you checked with Duncan? He may have heard about it.'

'I stopped by the jail, but he wasn't there,' Lucy said. 'I was thinking that I might check your stores after supper. It's possible someone wrote about it. I've never seen any mention of it, though.'

'While you're looking for it, why don't you pull out some *Strange News* and *Monstrous Accounts*. I have a mind to go to Southwark in the morning, visit the Globe and the Clink. That is what everyone clamours for there.'

'Yes, sir,' Lucy said, hurrying to finish washing and drying their dishes. As soon as she was done, she took a lantern into the back room to look at the different piles of penny press that Master Aubrey tended to collect. Currently, they were in loose piles, separated by type: astrological predictions, true accounts of monsters come to life, strange robberies and thefts, recipes for health, collections of merriments, political transgressions, petitions and, of course, many stacks related to murder – a favourite pursuit of Master Aubrey. Fortunately, he was rather diligent about trading with other booksellers, and so there was always new stock to sell.

After more than hour had passed, Lucy could not find anything related to the murder of Miss de Witte's brother. Plenty of murders set in taverns, but none that seemed to describe the circumstances of Hammett de Witte's death.

'I couldn't find anything here. Still, there must be an official record of Mr de Witte's death,' Lucy said to Master Aubrey, who was still seated at the kitchen table, reading. She handed him the collection of *Monstrous Accounts* that he had requested. 'Maybe I could ask Adam to look through the rolls.'

Master Aubrey chuckled as he looked through the selection she'd just given him. 'A monstrous account of a woman with two heads. Ah, that's a good one!' He looked up at Lucy. 'Keep in mind that the Great Fire burned so many important records. A true account of what happened may not exist.'

'That's true,' Lucy said, sighing. The conflagration had caused so much havoc, and they were all still dealing with the long-protracted aftermath. 'I should probably see the Hargraves, let them know what I learned.'

Master Aubrey swatted at her. 'Enough of your coy entreaties, lass! You can run over there right now, as long as you're back by nine o'clock.'

* * *
160

After throwing on her cloak and grabbing her lantern, Lucy walked quickly to the Hargraves'. It was colder and foggier than she expected, and the winter winds were certainly picking up.

When she entered the kitchen, she was surprised to find Sid sitting there, enjoying some apple pie with Cook, John and Annie. 'Out of the pillory, I see,' she said to the pickpocket. 'Whatever are you doing here?'

'I could ask you the same thing,' Sid teased.

Annie nudged him with her elbow. 'She's here to see the magistrate, silly.'

'Master Hargrave, of course,' he replied, still grinning.

'I *am* here to see the Hargraves,' she said to Cook and John. 'Are they finished dining? It should take but a minute. Indeed, Master Aubrey has only given me an hour's leave.' She hesitated. 'Are they alone? I should not like to embarrass them by calling on them in this fashion.'

'They do not have visitors,' Cook replied. 'They are in the study.'

'Oh, don't get up,' Lucy said. 'I can show myself in.'

As she walked down the corridor, she could hear Adam talking. 'I spoke to Sam Pepys today. He told me of a new street that is to be made from Guild Hall down to Cheapside, with enough ground on either side for houses to be built. Lucy!' he exclaimed when he saw her in the doorway.

'Welcome, Lucy! Pray, enter,' the magistrate called. 'What brought you out on a night such as this?'

'I have some news,' she said. Spying the familiar cipher on the table, she asked, 'Have you made any sense of the message that was found on the body?'

The Hargraves both shook their heads at the same time, father and son looking once again remarkably similar in their expression despite the decades between them. 'It is a tricky code, to be sure,' Master Hargrave said. 'It is no wonder that even Professor Wallace, with his acuity and prowess with numbers and equations, cannot recall it from memory. I believe we must go to the source, Miss de Witte.'

'Er,' Lucy hesitated.

Father and son exchanged a glance, and Adam raised an eyebrow. 'Out with it, Lucy,' he said. 'We know you are thinking about something.'

How well they know me, she thought. 'I was indeed thinking about something. I met Lucretia de Witte today and—'

'What?' Adam exclaimed, banging his fist down on the table, still holding his fork.

More controlled, Master Hargrave took a deep breath. 'Lucy, why ever did you see her?'

'I thought it would be helpful to meet her. I went over with Mrs Wallace, who is quite kind indeed. I thought maybe I could find the key in Miss de Witte's house and—'

Master Hargrave shook his head. 'I will pretend that I did not hear you speak of stealing property from someone's home.'

Chagrined, Lucy gulped. 'I'm sorry, sir.' She paused. 'Actually, it ended up coming up in my conversation with Miss de Witte today. She claims to have thrown it all away and did not recall it any longer. I'm not quite sure I believe her, but I would not know where she would hide such a thing even if she still had it on hand.'

Master Hargrave nodded his head. 'Well, we have shown our hand now, so there may not be a chance to get it out of her. That is unfortunate.'

Both the Hargraves seemed a bit disappointed in her, making Lucy feel disappointed in herself. Then another thought struck her. 'I did learn something interesting. Lucretia de Witte's brother was murdered, in a coaching inn just outside of London. Hertfordshire. Perhaps Hoddesdon or Broxbourne. Apparently, he was killed last summer, well before the fire.'

'Intriguing,' Master Hargrave said. 'Are you thinking there is some connection here?'

'Yes, I am. I saw a portrait of this brother hanging in Miss de Witte's house, and you'll never believe this: he was wearing a ring that was either the same or an exact replica of the ring found around Paul Corbyn's neck!' Lucy exclaimed, feeling pleased when both men looked thunderstruck.

'Preposterous! Are you certain?' Master Hargrave asked.

'Quite! Mrs Wallace told me it was around the time of her brother's death that Miss de Witte started sending Professor Wallace all those coded messages, although Mrs Wallace had not known anything about the brother's death. She told her to stop sending messages to her husband, though, because they were committing—'

Infidelity. She couldn't quite bring herself to

163

say the word, remembering how flighty the late Mistress Hargrave had been before she died. Glancing at Adam, she could see the sadness etched in his face, and she hurried to end the awkward moment. 'I came here because I was hoping that you might be able to check the rolls, although I know quite a few records were destroyed during the fire. I was thinking that someone might have written a penny piece about it. I've already checked through Master Aubrey's collection. There are a few murders that happened near taverns, but none that seems quite right.'

'Out of Hoddesdon or Broxbourne, I would say Hoddesdon is more likely,' Adam said. 'There are quite a few coaching inns there, and it would have been likely enough for a Cambridge scholar to stop there before arriving in London.' He glanced at his father. 'Do you agree, sir?'

Master Hargrave nodded. 'Hoddesdon, yes. I do concur.'

'There are other booksellers who might have some pieces about the crime,' Lucy replied. 'I thought I'd visit a few shops tomorrow. They may be aware of the story.'

'Let us go to Hoddesdon and speak to people there directly,' Adam replied. 'Easy enough to do.'

'Oh,' Lucy said, the flush again rising in her cheeks. She was not sure about the propriety of travelling unaccompanied with Adam in such a way. It would be at least an hour's journey, perhaps a little longer depending on the weather and the state of the roads. 'I must first speak with Master Aubrey. Maybe, when he learns that I have a list of books that both the Wallaces and Miss de Witte seek, he will let me bargain with the scholarly booksellers there. I do not know if he will permit me otherwise.'

'Then I will join you,' Master Hargrave said. Adam and Lucy looked at him in surprise.

'Father?' Adam asked.

'The old master of my Cambridge college moved to Hoddesdon some time back, as I recall. He called on me recently and I could easily arrange to return the visit.' He pulled out a piece of paper. 'Let me write a note to Master Aubrey. I should think he'd be pleased that we are helping him acquire the books he needs for London customers at no cost to himself, other than the loss of his apprentice for the day.' He began to pen a note to the master printer in his elegant script.

'Thank you, sir,' Lucy said, touched by the magistrate's understanding of her situation.

'Then it is settled,' the magistrate replied. 'Let us say the morning after next. We shall pick you up in the carriage at eight o'clock.'

Fifteen

On Thursday morning, just after eight o'clock, the hired carriage came rattling down Fleet Street, stopping in front of Master Aubrey's shop. Lucy, with the printer's help, had packed her bag with many favourite pieces that were easy to sell. A selection of recipes, true accounts, sermons and, of course, murder ballads that she would trade. She had also brought along a small selection of nicer bound books that she might sell to the scholars' shop that Master Aubrey had told her about. Peeking in her pocket, she also made sure that she had a few extra coins, because she was not sure how many of the books desired by Professor Wallace and Miss de Witte might be available for purchase. Lastly, she checked that she had brought along Master Aubrey's special printed seal to ensure that booksellers knew that she was authentic. 'Do not lose that,' he said sternly.

When the carriage pulled up, Adam hopped out to help her in. They sat together facing Master Hargrave, who held up a bound legal tract. 'I've been looking forward to reading the legal opinions of Sir Timothy Littleton for some time now. A longish journey to Hoddesdon will be just the trick. Or it will help me sleep along the journey.'

Within the half hour, they had left the confines of London and were moving into more open spaces along the well-travelled road. At first, Lucy looked excitedly through the window, as this was not a direction she had journeyed before, but after a while the terrain became less varied. Tall leafless trees, animals foraging for food, the occasional pocket of homes and farms, a church or two. There were also many graves – the head-stones a keen reminder of how far the plague had stretched in that dreadful godless year. She shivered at the memory.

'Are you cold, Lucy?' Adam asked. He pulled out some blankets from a box and, without waiting for her assent, tucked one around her. 'The driver said the route can get chilly this time of year.'

Lucy pulled the blanket around her. It smelled slightly of horses, but she was grateful for the additional warmth. As they jolted along, Master Hargrave put aside the treatise and rested his head back, soon lolling to sleep. Lucy pulled out the messages that Mistress Wallace had given her – exchanges between her husband and Miss de Witte – as well as the Babington cipher.

'See this mark, and this one here?' she said, pointing to a couple of the symbols. 'I believe that this one is the sign of the gallows, and this one is the sign of the Devil.'

'Yes, I concur,' Adam said, after carefully comparing the symbols. He glanced at Lucy. 'You have been so dogged in your pursuit of this truth. Is that the constable's influence on you?'

'You have been dogged as well. Agreeing to accompany me to Hoddesdon,' she said. Then, more hurriedly, she added. 'The idea that a murderer could go free, when we might have a clue to his identity, is not something that I can easily swallow.'

Adam looked as if he was about to say something more when the carriage began to slow.

'Hoddesdon, just ahead!' the driver called. 'We'll change horses at the coaching inn.'

When the driver stopped on High Street in Hoddesdon a few minutes later, Adam opened the door and stepped on to the street before the driver had a chance to climb down from his perch. Not waiting for the portable steps, Adam raised his hand to Lucy to help her down. Clasping his hand lightly, she hopped down, eager to stretch her muscles.

Master Hargrave remained in the carriage. 'I believe my old friend lives on the edge of town, just before the coaching inns,' he said. He pointed to the church that could be seen just beyond the main road. 'Why don't we meet in front of St Katharine's in an hour and a half?' He then rapped on the side of the carriage, and the driver flicked his reins, causing the horses to amble off.

'Where shall we go first?' Adam asked.

Lucy looked around, trying to get her bearings. 'Master Aubrey told me he thought there were two bookseller's shops.' She pointed at the row of shops. 'Look, isn't that the sign of Cambridge? Master Aubrey told me that scholars go there to purchase their tomes. Perhaps the bookseller knows something of the crime.'

'Yes, I'm familiar with that shop,' Adam replied. 'Let us go.'

After crossing High Street, they entered the shop. Lucy looked around eagerly. It was very different from any bookseller's shop she'd ever seen. Rather than bags holding stacks of broadsides, pamphlets and other penny press, this shop reminded her more of Master Hargrave's study. There were shelves of leather-covered volumes with gold tooling, many with elegant gilded edges. Collectively, the books were quite beautiful and of a far superior quality to what Master Aubrey displayed at his shop. The bookseller clearly had set himself up well in this location.

'That's Master Barnaby, the owner of this shop,' Adam said, nudging her in the direction of a white-haired man with a neatly trimmed white beard. He was seated at a work bench in the corner and appeared to be repairing the clasps on the bindings of a leather-bound book.

Lucy pulled out the list of books requested by Professor Wallace and Lucretia de Witte. *Algebra Christophori Clavii Bambergensis e Societate Iesv* was at the top of the list, having been requested by each. She was about to approach him when a young man in scholarly robes came rushing into the shop, pushing against her as he went to stand before the bookseller. 'Master Barnaby! Sir!'

'Hey,' Adam called, looking indignant. He was about to say something about the man's loutish behaviour but Lucy put her finger to her lips. She wanted to see how the bookseller worked.

'I simply must procure Littleton's *Tenures in English* before my carriage leaves,' the scholar continued. His distress was so evident that it made Lucy wonder what truly transpired within the university's hallowed halls. 'I left my copy at home and I cannot rely on a Cambridge shop carrying this important piece. Please, I will pay anything!'

Anything? Lucy thought.

'Anything?' Master Barnaby asked at the same time, a clear note of disdain in his voice. 'Very good. I'll be right back, sir.'

As the scholar waited, he looked around the shop, his eyes passing over Lucy in a dismissive way. To Adam he said, 'I've got old Master Tinley this term. I don't want to cross that dragon by not having a copy of the book he recommended! I'd be tarred and feathered for certain.'

'A shame, to be sure,' Adam replied. Lucy could hear the slightly mocking tone, but the scholar did not, continuing to pace about.

Adam stretched his hand above Lucy's head, retrieving a book from the highest shelf. 'This is a recent favourite of mine,' he said, opening it up so that they could look at it together. 'John Dryden's *Annus Mirabilis.* The year of miracles.'

'Oh, I've seen this one, although in far plainer form,' she said, examining the fine binding. 'It is about the devastation England suffered these past years, is it not?'

'Yes, although I believe his point is that things could have been worse.'

The scholar tapped his foot. 'Where is he?' he asked.

The bookseller returned then, carefully wiping the dust off the mottled leather cover and

170

sprinkled edges. He named a sum that seemed five times the price that Master Aubrey had told her to expect. The scholar didn't even bother to barter. After paying out the sum to the bookseller, he pushed past Lucy and out the door. *So reckless with money. How fortunate to have such means.*

Since the shop was empty now, Lucy approached the bookseller, giving a little cough to get his attention. 'Pardon me, sir?'

Master Barnaby glanced at her but turned his attention back to the binding. 'Sir?' she repeated.

'What is it?' he asked, still not looking at her.

'I should like to know if you have any of these books,' she said, laying the list down in front of him, not even trying to pronounce the titles. Adam had hung back, continuing to read the Dryden piece.

The bookseller flicked his eyes over the list before straightening his spectacles and looking her over. 'This is quite a list. For your master, I assume.' Without waiting for her to reply, he said, 'I've got a few.' As before, he went into a back area to retrieve the texts, returning a few minutes later. He laid them out, before naming a ridiculous sum.

Lucy pulled out the printer's seal. 'Master Aubrey, the master printer I work for, instructed that I not pay more than one-third of what you just said.' He'd actually sent along enough money for about half that sum, but she decided to hold back on that.

Master Barnaby looked her up and down and named a new sum, lower this time.

171

'No,' Lucy said. 'We are not in a hurry. I should think we'll get them in Cambridge. Adam,' she called, 'I'm ready to leave.'

Hastily, the bookseller began to bargain with her and now she happily engaged. She'd learned to barter with merchants in the market, and she found that the bookseller was no different to a butcher haggling over the price of a cut of beef.

Adam stood back, watching her, looking pleased. 'You've really got a knack for this,' he whispered, as the bookseller wrapped the books up carefully in a wool bag. It was nearly time to leave, and Lucy still hadn't got any information.

'I heard tell of a murder in these parts,' she said. 'A Cambridge scholar?'

He grunted. 'I have no interest in that tale.'

'Was there perhaps a broadside or ballad about it, do you know?' Lucy pressed.

The bookseller turned taciturn. 'I don't know anything about that,' he said. 'You're better off at Master Johnson's. He sells that sort of stuff and nonsense.' He sat back down at his table, bending over the book he was repairing, clearly signalling the conversation was over.

'Master Johnson's place is over there,' Adam said, pointing to a shop with the sign of a printing press above the door. When they entered, Lucy felt a sense of familiarity and comfort. Unlike the last shop, there were no elegant hand-stitched and gilded books here. Instead, they were in stacks and pouches around the room, looking haphazard to the eye, but probably with their own system and order known only to the bookseller.

Even the bookseller himself reminded her of Master Aubrey, looking a bit creased and wrinkled. Master Johnson greeted them, and Lucy explained who she was, showing the seal. 'Ah Aubrey, certainly I know him. Glad I was when I learned he and his shop survived the fire intact. So many of our brethren did not see their stock spared. What can I do for you?'

She opened her sack, and the two began to trade. When they were done, she set her pack down. 'Master Johnson, I am looking for a specific piece about a murder that happened in this area. It happened at a tavern – summer of last year, I believe,' she said. 'The murder was of a Cambridge scholar named Hammett de Witte. Are you aware of such a piece?'

The bookseller snapped his fingers. 'Of course! That caused quite the stir when it happened.'

He led Lucy and Adam to the back of the shop. Like Master Aubrey, he had leather pouches hanging on hooks all over the walls, and in each were stuffed rolls of penny pieces. More pamphlets, broadsides, petitions, ballads and other true accounts were stacked on shelves, along with more specialized chapbooks, quartos and folios. 'As I recall, only a single piece was ever created. A ballad.'

He handed it to Lucy, who took it eagerly, with Adam peering closely over her shoulder. '*Love No More – the tragic tale of a scholar and a serving maid, with a brutal end to an untimely romance.*'

They read through the ballad eagerly, Lucy mouthing many of the words aloud. 'A gentleman

173

scholar, one Hammett de Witte of London, in his journeys to and from Cambridge, did seek to pass his time at the Two Doves, a coaching inn in Hoddesdon.'

'The Two Doves Inn?' Adam said. 'I know where that inn is. Very close by.'

'Yes, just a few buildings down on High Street,' Master Johnson confirmed.

Lucy continued to read. 'Though devoted to Latin, Mr de Witte sought to learn a new language and course of study taught by a winsome serving lass, Eleanor Browning, affectionately called Ellie by her friends. As their most dear acquaintanceship grew, on each occasion he stopped at the inn, another scholar from that same institution, one Philip Emerson, by all accounts a most angry and choleric man, did take note of their budding romance with anger in his heart.'

Adam clucked his teeth. 'I see. Go on.'

'Emerson, as it came to be understood, had fallen in love with that same servant, while she, unknowing, continued with her secret trysts with de Witte, ignorant all the while of the anger that was building in Emerson's heart.' Lucy gulped. 'Thus, when de Witte and his Ellie did seek to join hands, Emerson, acting upon his rage, did thus grab a carving knife from a table and ran it into de Witte through and through.'

'So not premeditated, it is clear,' Adam said. 'That might have mattered.'

Lucy continued to read, her finger moving under the words as she read each passage. 'Ellie then threw herself upon her lover's corpse, weeping and wailing all the while. When Emerson

174

entreated her to join him, she refused in such a heartfelt fashion that he knew he could never win her love, and he stabbed her, too. He then took the ring that de Witte had used to pledge his troth to the young maid, fleeing in the direction of London.'

'Hmm,' Adam mused. 'We still have some time before we said we would meet Father at the church. Let's go to the Two Doves. See if we can learn anything.'

Sixteen

Lucy and Adam walked into the Two Doves Inn, sidestepping a pair of drunken sots who were on their way out. Despite her protests, Adam had hefted the sack with the scholarly tomes on to his own shoulder.

'It's so dark in here,' Lucy murmured. Although the midday sun was streaking in through several windows, other windows were boarded over. Lanterns hung from the walls, their flickering glow adding more light in patches. She sniffed. A sour smell hung in the air, reeking of old cabbage and something musty.

Still, the place was full of people, mostly men, tippling, some staring sullenly into their cups, others in larger groups, in raucous laughter.

Adam carefully steered Lucy to a quieter corner towards the back. When they sat down, he beckoned to the tavern maid and looked around. 'I haven't been here in years,' he said to Lucy.

'Oh, you know this place?'

'Certainly. Everyone had to leave their coaches while the horses were rested and fed. This was as good a place to go as any on High Street.'

'What was it like to be a student at Cambridge?' Lucy asked, looking at one young man whose face was buried in a book. 'I imagine everyone was like him.'

He followed her gaze. 'Sometimes. Sometimes

more like *them*.' He pointed to the more bois-terous group on the other side of the room. She could tell the men were telling a bawdy story, trying to get the attention of the serving maid.

'I always imagined you spending your days and nights studying,' she teased. 'It's hard to imagine you cavorting about.'

'That's true enough – I was not one to, as you say, cavort. I will acknowledge, though, that life back then was not very complicated.' He smiled slightly. 'I studied at Trinity College before I studied law. The life of a scholar . . .' He shook his head. 'I can scarcely remember it now.'

'When you started your studies, I was still living with my mother in Southwark,' Lucy mused. 'I remember, when I first came to work for your parents, how Sarah would talk about you.'

Adam studied her face before replying. 'Is that so?'

'She was so proud of you. Of your accomplish-ments. Of course, she was a little more idle with her studies,' Lucy said with a fond laugh. 'Sometimes I think that she was of a differing measuring stick.'

'Luckily, the education provided to her by the tutors my father brought in was not entirely lost,' he said. 'I've heard tell how you'd listen to the lessons from behind the curtains.'

'Well, I was mostly cleaning and mending, not learning to argue in Latin.' She laughed again. 'I was certainly fortunate that your father treated me so well. My lot today would be far different if I had been sent to serve another master.'

'Lucy,' he said, covering her hand with his. The gaze of his blue eyes was intense, and she felt as if he could almost see right into her thoughts. 'I know that we come from different worlds. But I wish—'

She pulled her hand away as the serving maid appeared before them. Like most who worked in taverns, the young woman's bosom was half exposed, not covered by lace or cloth as other women working in a market or trade would. Her smile was friendly enough, however, and directed at both Lucy and Adam. 'A good day to you, friends. I'm Tabby. What is it you'd be liking today? A bit of meat and cheese and some ales?'

Adam glanced at Lucy who nodded. 'I'm sure Father will get a bite to eat with his friend. So, yes to all that, if you would, Tabby,' he replied, rolling a gold coin in his fingers.

'Certainly, sir,' the serving maid said, eyeing the coin. 'I'll be back straight away.'

When she walked away, Lucy pushed Adam's palm down on to the table, so that the coin could no longer be seen. 'No need to invite trouble,' she whispered.

Adam gave a wry smile. 'It may help when we ask her our questions. Maybe she knew Ellie. She might know something about the murders, too.'

When Tabby returned with their food, Adam slid the coin over to her. Seeing this, her eyes widened, looking as if she was about to swoon. 'Let me slice the cheese for you, sir,' she said, quickly tucking the coin away in her pocket.

'Have you worked here for a while?' Lucy

asked the woman, reaching to hand Adam a piece of cheese and hard bread herself.

'Oh, for a few years, I suppose,' Tabby replied, pausing to fan herself a bit. 'Glad you folks stopped in here. Everybody's been flocking to the Knight's Head these days. Lots who come in' – she gestured to the other scattered patrons – 'do a lot of drinking but don't always leave much for me.'

'You must have seen a lot during your time here,' Lucy said. 'Fights? Skirmishes?'

'Oh, those loud-mouthed louts always have something to say. Mostly harmless, mind you, but sometimes they've come to blows,' she said. 'Why, there was this first time I remember that—'

Lucy kicked Adam under the table. Taking the hint, he interrupted Tabby. 'We heard a murder even happened here?' he said, giving her his most charming smile.

Tabby snapped out of whatever spell she'd been under and frowned. 'Now, why'd you go and remind me of that terrible day? Bring back nightmares, it will! I only just started resting easy again!'

Lucy felt a pang at the woman's words. Hadn't she experienced the same after Bessie had died? There were still those nights when she'd reach for Bessie only to recall the dreadful fact of her death. 'Please,' she said, 'we truly would like to know.'

Tabby looked uncertainly back and forth. Adam slid another coin to her. 'Please. Tell us what happened.'

Gripping the back of a tall chair for support

179

with one hand, she pointed to a back corner with the other. 'I was standing just there,' she said. 'Never saw anything so terrible in my life. I hope never to see such a sight for the rest of my days! 'Twas my own dear friend Ellie who was murdered, struck down with her lover by a man whom she called a friend.' She cursed loudly. 'Philip Emerson! A despicable scoundrel who deserves to be hanged!'

She stopped then and looked around. 'How about you buy another drink for yourself and one for me, and I'll tell you all about it. Least you can do for dredging my pain up in such ways.'

Adam pushed over some coins. 'Please do. We're all ears.'

'I'll be right back,' she replied.

A few minutes later, she came back with a tray holding four tankards of ale and a turkey leg. She passed a new tankard each to Adam and Lucy and placed the other two in front of herself. Taking off her apron, she glanced at Adam. 'May as well take my meal now.'

'Of course,' Adam said courteously, and they watched as Tabby leaned back, putting her feet up on another chair. She then proceeded to down half a pint of ale before tearing off a huge bite of turkey with her teeth. 'As you were saying,' Adam said, prodding her gently, 'your friend was killed. How did that come to pass?'

'Yes, Ellie. Eleanor Browning, the younger sister of the innkeepers. She had the misfortune of catching the eye of two gowns. Hammett de Witte and Philip Emerson.' She waved towards some of the Cambridge scholars eating. 'They come in here sometimes, thinking they can have their way with us, just because we work here. Of course, there are some with fine manners and nice countenances that please us well.' She drained the first tankard and leaned towards Adam, whispering loudly. 'If you should like to ditch your sweetheart, there are some beds upstairs.'

'Thank you, I'm quite satisfied at the moment,' Adam said, again courteously, with a quick glance at Lucy.

An unpleasant sensation flashed through Lucy then. Annoyance? Jealousy? Anger? She curled her fingers in her lap, uncertain as to what she was feeling about the exchange. *I'm satisfied at the moment*, he had said. Did he only say that because she was there?

Tabby shrugged her shoulders. 'Suit yourself,' she said, before continuing her story. 'They fell in love. I believe it. Ellie was so besotted, and I believe the scholar Hammett was, too. He would write these beautiful letters to her – of course, neither of us could make head or tail of them.' Her face darkened. 'That was where the trouble began.'

'Trouble? What kind of trouble?' Lucy asked.

'She asked another scholar, Philip Emerson, to read those letters to her, so that she could hear her Hammett's words spoken out loud. I know now that must have tipped off a deep rage in Mr Emerson, when asked to read the words of a rival for Ellie's heart. The strange fellow must have been nursing a deep tenderness for her, unbeknownst to everyone! How could we have known?

181

Sometimes he'd sit with Mr de Witte, but most times he was off at a table by himself with his books and writings. A sullen chap, to be sure. His rage may have been growing for some time.'

'How did the murder come to pass?' Adam asked.

Tabby took a deep swallow of ale. 'Hammett gave Ellie a ring. She took it to be a promise of betrothal, but I was not so sure. She showed it to me in private, because she was scared to wear it publicly for all to see.'

'Why was that?' Lucy asked.

'Ellie didn't think her brothers would allow her to marry a poor scholar. Of course, as we learned later, Mr de Witte was a gentleman and man of means. He was absent-minded, not poor, and that was why he did not tend to his robes and clothes as he ought.' Her lips twitched nervously. 'It was an odd ring. I shouldn't like to have worn it myself. I told her it might fetch a pretty penny at the market, but she was intent on keeping it.'

'Odd? How so?' Lucy asked, glancing at Adam. 'What kind of ring was it? Can you describe it for me?'

'It had two faces. One had this red-cheeked cherub. The other had this wicked, grinning skull. Strange, I thought at the time. I said to her "Why give you a ring of death to pledge love and troth? It is odd, I tell you."'

'What did Ellie say?'

'She said that he had the way of a scholar,' she said, shrugging. 'His brilliance couldn't be understood by the likes of us, and other such things.

He told her that it meant only death would part their love.' She shivered. 'Poor Ellie. She didn't deserve what happened to her.'

'What did happen?' Lucy asked.

Here the excitement dropped from Tabby's voice. 'They planned to meet. She told me he said he was going to take her away from all this.' She paused to take a great bite of turkey, chewing while Lucy and Adam waited. Finally, she swallowed. 'I can still remember it as if it was yesterday.' She shivered, then took another bite of the turkey. 'Ellie and Hammett were standing there together. Over there.' She pointed to a front corner. 'She had consented to wear his ring and he had leaned down to embrace her. Mr Emerson walked in and, seeing them, grew enraged. I remember how he shouted, "You're wearing his ring?" Then—'

She shut her eyes as Lucy and Adam waited breathlessly, not daring to speak. Taking a deep breath, she continued. 'He seized a carving knife off the table there and thrust it into Mr de Witte's back. I'll never forget the sound Mr de Witte made as he sank to the floor. Then Eleanor began to shriek and scream – horrible, terrifying sounds – and threw herself on top of his dead body.'

She took a deep swallow of ale. 'It was not over, though. Mr Emerson stared down at her as she wept. "Come with me," he said, and she began to scream at him, saying she hated him and never wished to see him again. With that h–he' – she paused to wipe her eyes – 'he reached down, grabbed her by her hair, pulled her head back and slit her throat. Just like that.' Tabby closed her eyes. 'There was blood everywhere,' she whispered, pushing away the tin platter.

'No one stopped him? No one did anything?' Adam asked, his own voice sounding a bit hoarse. 'How could he murder two people like that? Why did no one try to wrest the knife away from him?'

'I cannot rightly say,' Tabby said, heaving a great sigh. 'It's as I told the court later. I don't know about everybody else, but I felt like a frozen block of ice. I couldn't move – I could only take in the horrors before me.' Guilt was etched into every twitch of her muscles.

'Then Mr Emerson fled?' Lucy asked, trying to imagine the scene.

'Yes, after he first pulled off the ring that Mr de Witte had given her and stuck it in his pocket. Then, in five steps, he lurched out of the door and into the street. It was only then we returned to our wits and determined to call the constable and a physician.' A tear appeared in her eye. 'It was obvious that there was nothing to be done. We just watched their lifeblood flow on to the floor. There.' She pointed to the floorboards. 'I had to scrub poor Ellie's blood from the wood. It took me weeks of cleaning every day. Finally, her brothers relented and paid for a new floor. I think it was hard for them to see the dark stain upon the inn. How her poor brothers lamented! I remember that Hammett's sister came as well! Laid right down on the floor while her acquaintance looked on—'

'What's this?' a stout middle-aged woman cried, setting a heavy pitcher of ale sloshing on to the table. 'Tabby Bell, how dare you sit and gossip in this way? I've a good mind to box your ears!'

'Oh, Mrs Browning!' Tabby said, her face growing ashen and her body starting to visibly tremble. 'I was just taking my dinner break and—'

'Gossiping about your betters and spreading lies with strangers!' Mrs Browning shouted. A few of the tavern's patrons turned around to see where the noise was coming from, but most did not look up. No one wanted to get involved with a skirmish in a pub. 'Get back to work before I bring the constable and have you thrown in jail for indolence!'

'Yes, madam,' Tabby said, picking up the half-full tankard and biting off another chunk of turkey. Without a further glance at Lucy or Adam, she scurried through a door on the side of the room, presumably heading back to the kitchen.

'I am sorry,' Adam said, turning on his full charm. 'We did not mean to gossip about your family. We are sorry for your loss – it *was* your sister-in-law who was murdered so cruelly? Right here, if I understood the girl correctly.'

'Ah, yes, poor Ellie. A silly, flighty girl, too caught up in the poetic words of a scholar. That love would have turned bitter, mark my words. At least she was spared that.' She blinked back a tear. 'Her poor brothers – one of whom is my own dear husband. They did not deserve to lose their merry girl. After their parents had died when they were still so young, it was she, with all her smiles and natural joy, who kept them from their

185

melancholy. It was that lightness that drew these scholars – both melancholic sombre sorts in their own way. Too much time reading, not enough time working – how could that be good for a man?'

'Did you know Mr Emerson very well?'

'Philip!' she spat on the ground. 'Such a scoundrel did not deserve to live. We thought it was all over after we suffered through the trial. He was caught in London, and so tried there, not returned to Cambridge. He ended up in Newgate where he was found guilty and sentenced to death by hanging.'

'Oh?' Lucy said, pulling at a thread in her skirt. 'When was he executed?'

'That's just it!' Mrs Browning cried. 'He never was. The good Lord in all his mystery saw fit to let him escape from Newgate.'

'Escape from Newgate? What do you mean?'

'We heard tell that as the Great Fire of London began to break out last September, someone saw fit to free the most desperate and wicked of God's creatures, without any thought to the terrible retribution that would be brought upon them.'

'Do you know who did such a terrible thing?' Lucy asked, trying not to show how excited she felt.

'We heard it was one of the guards, struck by a fit of conscience,' she said with a sniff. 'That Philip Emerson had no right to live on this earth. Should have been burned by the fire. Burn him of his sins. Then he might have been forgiven.' Her voice faded away, and for a moment she stood silent, her hands clenched together. Then, at the clatter of dishes on the other side of the inn, she seemed to recall herself. 'Are you having another drink? If not, it would be best to get on your way.'

Adam stood up, leaving some coins on the table. 'Thank you for the fine service, and for the company of your serving maid earlier. I hope that she will not be further punished because we sought to indulge our passing curiosity into the past. We did not wish to cause harm, and we'll be leaving shortly.' Adam turned to Lucy. 'I'll be back in a moment. Just need to use the privy. Meet you outside? I think there is a small roof to protect you from the rain.'

Seventeen

Lucy pressed against the stone wall of the Two Doves Inn, allowing the small overhanging roof to protect her from the cold rain that had started to fall. As she waited for Adam, she traced some of the knife marks on one of the beer barrels beside the wall. In warmer months, the business likely drifted outside the tavern walls, where people would stand at these barrels to drink and eat. In addition to regular marks made from cutting through meat and bread, there were a few words here and there that had been carved into the wood.

A tradesman glanced at her as he passed into the tavern, and then stopped. Her eyes locked with his for a moment.

Was there something familiar about him? she wondered, before looking away.

He continued on inside. *Why would I know anyone in Hoddesdon?* she thought. Out of curiosity, she moved closer to one of the open windows so she could watch what was going on inside.

The man who'd just entered called out to Mrs Browning. 'Hey there, wife,' he said. 'How do we fare?'

'We fare well. Some people were here asking about the murder. Tabby said they paid her well for a few questions.'

188

Mr Browning snorted, an angry sound. 'You don't say.'

'Dev, I'm telling you. We should charge every time someone wants to see the murder site.'

Dev? Lucy froze and stared at the innkeeper, a sudden fear coursing through her. He was definitely one of the two men she'd encountered at the crossroads. The clean-shaven one with the tattoo on his neck. She pushed herself away from the window, her back to the wall. Her heart began to pound.

'I don't want to make Ellie's death into a spectacle!' Dev Browning replied. 'Who was it? Are they still here? I'm going to knock them around a bit. Teach them not to make a mockery of death.'

'They were just here,' she heard Mrs Browning say. 'The man asked me where the privy was. She had a peddler's pack. A bookseller, I think.'

'A bookseller's pack? A woman?' His voice changed.

Oh no! Lucy clenched her fists. *He remembers me. What should I do? I need to get out of here!*

Adam appeared then, coming from behind the inn. Clutching her skirts, she raced towards him, her pack slung over her shoulder. His expression changed when he saw her. 'Lucy, what's wrong?'

'Run!' she shouted. 'We need to get out of here, now!'

'Give me your pack,' he instructed.

She grabbed his free hand. 'This way!'

Her hand still firmly clasped around Adam's, Lucy pulled him down a small passage between

189

two coaching inns so that they were running behind the buildings, weaving between outside hearths and laundered sheets on ropes, old chairs and other sundry items in the backs of the different inns and taverns. Mercifully, the rain had stopped as abruptly as it had begun.

'Lucy! What is going on?' Adam asked, panting heavily. 'We need to stop now! Tell me, what happened?'

'That man!' she managed to gasp. 'The innkeeper!'

Adam put his hands on her shoulders, trying to steady her. 'What is it? Did he hurt you?' He looked anxiously over her body.

'No, no! Yes!'

'What!' Adam roared, starting back in the direction of the Two Doves Inn. 'I'll kill him!'

'No, no, Adam,' Lucy cried, catching his arm. 'He didn't hurt me today. I meant that he was one of the two men who knocked me down that day on my way to the crossroads. The men who took the pocket and watch from Mr Corbyn's body.'

Adam stepped back, rubbing his jaw in disbelief. 'The innkeeper, Mr Browning? You saw him? You recognized him?'

'Yes, when I was standing in front of the Two Doves Inn, he looked at me as he passed inside. At the time I thought he looked familiar, but I couldn't place him. I heard Mrs Browning call him "Dev".' She crossed her arms. 'Then she told him that someone had been asking about his sister's murder. A female bookseller, she said. That she'd seen my pack. I could tell he remembered me then. That's why I ran.'

He stepped closer to her. 'You did right to run. If he was involved in Paul Corbyn's murder, then you might have been in danger.'

She looked up at him. 'What should we do? We need to get out of here. Hoddesdon is not so big. He might still see me.'

'Well, right now, let us head over to St Katharine's. Father may be waiting for us already. We can discuss it along the way.'

Lucy and Adam walked slowly to St Katharine's, still trying to catch their breath after their frantic run. Lucy kept looking around, hoping that Dev was not watching her. After some time, though, she began to feel better, taking in the beauty of the town as they strolled more comfortably along Spital Brook. They began to piece together everything they had just learned.

'So Hammett knew his murderer,' Lucy said. 'They were both Cambridge scholars, and it appears that they roomed together for a short spell.'

'Two men in love with the same woman,' Adam said. 'A time-honoured tale to be sure.'

Lucy glanced up at him, and then looked away. She couldn't read his tone. Disappointed? Resigned, perhaps. She hurried on. 'Tabby did say that he fled to London after the murder, but was arrested there. I wonder how that happened.'

'It was also interesting what she said about Emerson taking the ring off Ellie's hand before he left the inn. Surely not petty theft? Spite?'

'That ring is a mystery. Was it the same ring that Hammett was wearing in his portrait? If

Emerson took it, how did it come to be around Paul Corbyn's neck? What could that mean?' Lucy asked. 'Provided, of course, that it was the same ring. The jeweller said they often come in pairs.'

'*Memento mori*,' Adam mused. 'The words take on a new meaning if it was used as a betrothal ring.'

St Katharine's came into view. The magistrate was nowhere to be seen. 'Father could be waiting inside,' Adam said. 'Besides, it is chilly. Let us go in.'

A quick glance around showed that the magistrate had not arrived yet. A few other people were praying in scattered pews. 'Let us sit while we wait,' Adam said, sliding into one of the back pews and looking around.

Lucy wondered what he was thinking. *If we were in our regular house of worship*, Lucy thought, *the Hargrave household would have a much more prominent pew towards the front.* The back pews were usually allotted to lesser families and tradesmen.

Adam's mind was clearly on something far different. 'So let us think this through,' he whispered, his mouth close to her ear. 'Paul Corbyn was found hanged, with a ring around his neck that Hammett de Witte had once owned and given to Ellie Browning as a symbol of their troth. Philip Emerson plucked this ring straight from Ellie's hand after murdering her, and by all accounts had it on his person when he fled to London.'

'How did it end up around Mr Corbyn's neck,

then?' Lucy asked. 'Did Ellie's brothers – Dev and Pike – kill him at the crossroads? Had they discovered his identity? They must have. Except, why kill the guard and not Philip Emerson?'

'All good questions,' Adam said. Turning towards her, he reached over and took her hand in his. 'I do not like that he saw you at the inn. We don't know for certain that he recognized you, though.' His tone changed as he caught sight of something over her shoulder. 'Oh, here's Father.'

Lucy withdrew her hand from his swiftly and stood up as the magistrate approached their pew. Adam stood up beside her. If Master Hargrave had noticed their intimate positioning when he entered the church, he gave no sign.

'Did you learn anything, sir?' Lucy asked, heading back out of the church.

'I spoke to Professor Gordon. He was still serving as master just before the murders occurred. It seems that there had been a set of altercations between the two men prior to the murder that were settled by the university. They will do this when dealing with the affairs of privileged persons, such as Hammett de Witte and Philip Emerson.'

'Earlier skirmishes, Father?' Adam asked as they walked out of the church. They began to walk back to High Street.

'Yes, it seems that Mr Emerson had been watching the pair for some time, and had threatened Mr de Witte with a knife once before. I read the testimony that had been collected by my friend, when he was still master. Emerson had

193

claimed drunkenness and youthful folly, which is a typical young man's ploy. The Cambridge authorities threw him in jail for an overnight stay, to cool his heels. After that, Mr Emerson had promised the master that he would stick to his studies. His father was a well-known benefactor of St John's, his college, and they preferred to keep the matter from spreading. Of course, local gossips likely still knew the tale.'

'He doesn't seem to have stuck to his studies,' Lucy said. 'The serving maid at the Two Doves said Eleanor had asked Philip to read a letter that Hammett had written to her, which may well have triggered his rage. Then, when Ellie accepted Hammett's ring, he fell into a great fury and killed both of them. He fled, but it seems that he was quickly picked up by authorities on his journey back to London.' She paused. 'It makes me wonder what happened to him after he was set free from Newgate during the Great Fire,' Lucy said, finally breaking the silence. 'Did he stay in London, I wonder? Or forge a new life somewhere else?'

'Probably easier for him if he did,' Adam said. 'He may have taken on a new identity, just as Jack Campbell did when he took on the identity and livelihood of Paul Corbyn.'

'What kind of identity could a Cambridge-educated man take on that no one recognize him?'

'It is unlikely that he would have become a lawyer. He couldn't risk someone from Cambridge recognizing him, unless, of course, he pretended he was from Oxford,' Adam said, considering the question. 'There is only so long someone might mask that identity.'

'I wonder if there is any way he might be found?' Lucy mused. 'Although he truly could be anywhere.'

The carriage they had hired pulled up then, with a fine pair of dappled grey horses for the drive home. 'We should make good time back to London,' Master Hargrave said, looking at the spirited pair with approval. He looked at Lucy's bulging sacks. 'It looks as if you did well with your trades and purchases, Lucy?'

'Yes, I believe Master Aubrey will be pleased I could procure these volumes for Miss de Witte and Professor Wallace at a great price indeed.'

Adam handed Lucy into the carriage, and when they had settled in, Lucy passed the volumes she had got at the Hoddesdon bookseller to Master Hargrave. 'Please, sir, feel free to examine these if you would like,' she said.

As she handed them over, she glanced out the window. Her breath caught. There, standing outside, was Dev, an odd smile on his face. Their eyes met, and he touched his cap in mock salute. *I know who you are*, she could almost read on his face.

With a lurch, the carriage pulled away, and Dev soon moved out of sight.

For the rest of the journey home, Lucy stayed silent, thinking about the way Dev had touched his cap. There was no doubt that he had seen her. What would he do? She kept craning her head out of the window, trying to determine whether they were being followed. She thought about

195

telling Adam and Master Hargrave, but hesitated. *Why worry them unduly? There's nothing that can be done now.*

As they approached home, the Hargraves discussed the matter more fully, not noticing the distress she was doing her best to hide. 'We need to speak to the constable about this,' Master Hargrave said, glancing at Lucy. 'That is certain.'

Lucy nodded but squirmed uncomfortably. She knew that Duncan would not be pleased that she might have put herself in harm's way.

'We need to question them,' Master Hargrave declared. 'Find out what those innkeepers know about Paul Corbyn's death. If anything.'

'What if they flee?' Lucy asked.

Adam shook his head. 'The Two Doves Inn is fairly well established. I cannot imagine that they would take flight. They are more likely to claim that you were mistaken – or lying.'

'I wasn't lying!' Lucy said hotly.

'Of course you were not,' Adam said, patting her arm. 'I know that, my—' He broke off abruptly. Lucy had the feeling he was about to use an endearment, and she flushed. She had not yet had a chance to sort out her feelings, and all she knew now was that she wanted to be alone with her thoughts and her heart. 'I know you were not lying,' he said.

'Unfortunately, it is as Adam says, Lucy. I wish it were not so,' Master Hargrave said. 'I fear that identification from a witness, even one as true-hearted and virtuous as yourself, may only go so far. They may simply deny it or pay someone to say they were somewhere else that morning of

Corbyn's death. Right now, they are two against one, and the case is already so fantastic that I do not think their guilt will be easy to prove.'

'I told you all of their names, Dev and Pike, before I met the one named Dev at the Two Doves Inn. How could I know their names otherwise?'

'Indeed, that is so,' the magistrate murmured. 'There is no question that they were there. The question is, why kill the guard? Why not the murderer himself?'

'Perhaps they have not been able to find Philip Emerson,' Lucy said. 'That ring, hung around Corbyn's neck – could it have been a warning of sorts? To someone else, I mean?'

Master Hargrave stroked his beard. 'An intriguing premise, to be sure. How, though, would their intended recipient know about such a warning? I'm afraid, for now, we still have more questions than answers.'

Eighteen

After supper that evening, Lucy walked quickly over to the Wallace household, gripping her pack and holding a lantern high. The note Mrs Wallace had left for her was in her pocket, though she'd mostly memorized it already, given how many times she'd read it in the hours since she'd returned from Hoddesdon.

> *Dearest Lucy,*
> *Master Aubrey has informed me that you are in Hoddesdon today, procuring some new treatises and books for my husband. I cannot tell you how timely this is. My husband has a few of his scholars over to dine tonight at seven o'clock, and I'm certain that they would welcome any new mathematical tracts to explore over their sherry. He will pay you well for your troubles, I will insist upon that. Please do come, Lucy.*
> *Yours, Joanna W.*

Even though Lucy had wanted nothing more than to crawl into her bed after the long journey and the fright she'd suffered in Hoddesdon, she'd accepted the request. Besides, Master Aubrey would not let her miss out on such an important sale. So here she was now, bracing herself against the chilly December winds and wet fog.

'I hope I do not take ill from these travails,' she muttered after three sneezes in a row. Although she liked Mrs Wallace quite well, this felt an unnecessary excursion.

When she arrived, the maid whisked her cloak away, before ushering her to the drawing room where the Wallaces were entertaining four guests, all of them men, dressed in a range of dining attire. All appeared to be gentlemen with their noble bearing, although judging from their threadbare finery, some looked as if they had experienced more prosperous days. For a moment, Lucy stood there, gripping her pack, not sure what to do.

A few of the men began to cough and sputter when they noticed her, causing Mrs Wallace to turn around and give her a warm smile. As before, although her dress was well crafted and expensive, her hair was a bit sloppy. 'Oh, Lucy,' she said, moving to take her arm, 'I'm so happy that you received my message and were able to come. Everyone, this is Lucy Campion, apprentice to Master Aubrey, printer and bookseller. Lucy, these men are all scholars.' She nodded towards each man in turn. 'Mr Quayle is a specialist in the histories of the ancient Greeks and Romans, Mr Newman studies musical theory and rhetoric, and Mr Jacobs is a student of astronomy.' The men she introduced were all tall and gangly, with the sickly pallor of those who rarely ventured out of doors. Mr Quayle had bright red hair and freckles, and when he gave her a mischievous smile, he reminded her of Lach. Mr Jacobs looked a bit surly, while Mr Newman managed a small sad smile.

She paused, indicating a fourth darker-skinned man in the corner whose goblet was full of honeyed water. 'Mr ibn Mohammad is a scholar from Cairo.'

Lucy nodded at the men in turn, her arms at her sides as none of them extended their hand in greeting, glancing back at Mr Mohammad. She'd met a few Muslims in the pursuit of her trade, although his presence here seemed unusual.

'I heard tell that you were in Hoddesdon today,' Professor Wallace commented. 'Did you stop in Master Barnaby's shop?'

'Yes, sir. Indeed, I did, sir,' Lucy replied, holding up her pack. 'I managed to procure a few of the titles on your list.' Here she hesitated, looking at Professor Wallace's outstretched hand. *Don't give anything to them until they've paid you*, Master Aubrey admonished her. *Those gentlemen sorts can be the worst, running up their debt, never remembering that such things have actual costs.*

She was relieved when Mrs Wallace nudged her husband. 'You need to pay her first,' she whispered, handing him his purse.

'Ah, yes, of course. Certainly,' he said. 'Step over this way, would you, please, Miss Campion?' There he handed her the money with a little extra for her trouble, while the scholars began to exclaim over the books with reverence.

'Please let me know if there is anything else I may procure for you,' she said, giving a little

200

curtsy to the room. 'Although I suppose you may all journey more often to Hoddesdon than I do.'

'Ah, Lucy, would you like to stay for a glass of sherry? My good friend Thomas Hargrave thinks so highly of you,' Professor Wallace said. He'd clearly been in his cups for a while.

She glanced uncomfortably at Mrs Wallace. 'I do need to get going. It is late.'

'It's quite all right, Lucy. Just one,' Mrs Wallace replied, handing her a small glass. 'Do stay a moment.'

'Says you are quite a clever lass!' Professor Wallace continued, slurring his speech a little. 'A stout heart with a keen sense of justice. Thomas says you even helped catch a criminal once or twice!'

The scholars looked up in interest at his words. 'Do tell,' said Mr Quayle.

'Oh, there's not so much to those stories,' she demurred, taking a tiny sip of her sherry.

'I met her because she had discovered a cipher. On a dead body, no less!' Professor Wallace enthused. 'Can you imagine such a thing?'

The scholars all looked impressed and began to clamour for more details. Conscious of her host's expectant smile, Lucy hid a sigh. *Entertain us, Lucy*, she could almost hear the mathematician say.

When she didn't speak, Professor Wallace jumped in. 'Someone tried to make his death look like a suicide by hanging him at the crossroads. And he had a secret message on his person.'

Lucy's heart sank. She wasn't sure that Duncan would like this information to be so publicly known. She looked at Mrs Wallace's face which had turned a little red at her husband's words.

'I think we've bothered poor Lucy enough for tonight, don't you think?' she said. 'Lucy, would you come with me? There's something I wanted to show you before you leave. If you'll excuse us, gentlemen.' Grabbing Lucy's wrist, she led her out of the room.

To her surprise, Mrs Wallace led her up the stairs to her own bedchamber and sat down on her bed. 'I have something to tell you,' she whispered, looking about to burst, 'and I didn't want to take the chance of anyone overhearing. The *true* reason I asked you here tonight!'

'What is it?' Lucy asked.

Mrs Wallace grasped both her hands, pulling her down beside her on the bed, looking like a delighted child. 'I found it, Lucy!' she exclaimed. 'Would you believe it? I scarcely can believe it myself.'

'Found what?'

'The key to the cipher!'

'What? Where did you get it?' Lucy asked, gripping the top of a chair to keep herself steady. Excitement was making it hard for her to breathe. Would they be able to decode the messages? Would they learn the secret of the murder?

Mrs Wallace spoke quickly. 'I'm not proud to tell you this, but I searched my husband's possessions again and found it hidden away among his belongings.' She made a disgusted face. 'I didn't want to say before, but I have had the oddest feeling that they might still be corresponding using the cipher. Even if they weren't, I did not think that he could bear to get rid of something she created.' She sighed. 'I was right in this regard, even though I most desperately wish I were not. See how it's torn there? I think he started to destroy it but then changed his mind and kept it hidden away instead.'

Seeing Mrs Wallace brush away a tear, Lucy looked down at her feet. Secrets between a husband and wife always brought ill will, she'd come to discover.

'Let us not mind that,' Mrs Wallace said, pressing a piece of paper into Lucy's hands.

Lucy looked down at the paper, rolling it between her thumb and fingers, noting that it was a finer quality than the paper they used to print broadsides and ballads. The sheet, which had been ripped diagonally in half, contained rows of hand-printed letters and symbols. 'This is the cipher? How do we make sense of it?'

Mrs Wallace's face fell. 'I don't quite know. From hearing my husband talk about ciphers, I believe that these letters get substituted. Therefore, if you see a letter M in the message, you look at the cipher and it tells you that an M is really a J and then you write down J, and so forth.'

Lucy nodded. That made sense. 'I shall look at it more closely later. Thank you, Mrs Wallace.'

'Please, Lucy. As I instructed the other day, call me Joanna. Somehow, these last few conversations with you, I feel we've become friends,' Mrs Wallace said, sounding hesitant. 'I do not have many friends, you see. My husband spends so much time with his books and his scholar friends. Miss de Witte was a friend once . . .' Her voice trailed away.

'Thank you, J–Joanna,' she said, stumbling slightly. She felt she was crossing into a world that had always seemed so distant to her. 'I have something to tell you as well,' she said briskly, trying to change the mood. 'As you know, we went to Hoddesdon, and we located the coaching inn where Miss de Witte's brother was murdered.'

Mrs Wallace raised an eyebrow. 'I was wondering why you went to Hoddesdon. A rather morbid pastime to indulge in, Lucy.'

Was her tone faintly scolding? Lucy hastened to explain. 'When I saw the portrait, I was struck by the fact that he had been painted wearing a ring that was very much akin to a ring the corpse had been wearing on a chain around his neck. It's an unusual piece, and the coincidence was too much to be borne.'

'So you set out to Hoddesdon to discover the connection? Lucy, I am ever impressed with your resourcefulness. Pray tell, what did you learn?'

Lucy quickly recounted the tale, and then showed Mrs Wallace the ballad she'd traded with the bookseller. 'We did learn from the servant there that Philip Emerson took Hammett's ring off Eleanor's finger and fled with it. How, then, did it get around the neck of the dead man?'

Mrs Wallace pondered the question. 'Philip must have given it to Mr Corbyn. Or Mr Corbyn stole it. Or—'

'Or what?' Lucy asked.

'Or Miss de Witte gave it to him. I believe

that she demanded the ring back from the authorities during Philip's trial. She convinced the
judge at the time that it was hers, because it had
belonged to her deceased brother, as part of his
property.'

'Wouldn't such a ring be considered the
property of the betrothed?' Lucy asked. 'Wasn't
it considered the property of Ellie Browning, or,
more accurately, her brothers?'

'I don't know if Eleanor's brothers made a
claim for it. I believe, if I recall correctly, that
Lucretia even used the portrait of her brother
wearing the ring as evidence that it belonged
to her. If the ring was returned to Lucretia, could
she in turn have given it to Mr Corbyn? That
would mean she had been in contact with him.'
Mrs Wallace shook her head. 'How would they
have known each other?'

'This makes me think that Miss de Witte *was*
involved in some way,' Lucy said, opening the
cipher again. 'It is too much of a coincidence
otherwise, don't you think? The presence of a
message using her cipher already suggests this.
The ring is still a mystery. I wish there were a
way to find out if she did get the ring back in
the first place. If so, was the ring then stolen
from her or did she give it to Mr Corbyn?' Lucy
stood up. 'I must head home now. Master Aubrey
will be wondering what has happened to me. I
imagine that you must get back to your guests.
I am glad that Professor Wallace was so happy
with the books I provided to him.'

'Lucy,' Mrs Wallace said, embracing her. Lucy
could feel her trembling. 'I trust you with the

cipher. But I beg of you, do not share the messages my husband exchanged with that woman. I should be mortified if they fall into other hands. It chagrins me greatly to think of you reading his loving words to another woman. Pray, just use it for the message found upon that poor soul's body.'

'I can't believe that I have the cipher,' Lucy whispered to herself, clutching her cloak against the chill. The cipher was tucked carefully into her pocket hidden beneath her skirts. 'I'll start working on deciphering the messages as soon as I've completed my evening chores. I just hope they are not in a language I can't read, such as Latin or Greek.'

As she walked, the light from the lantern caused the shadows around her to skip and dance. It was then that she realized how silent and solitary the street was. At eight o'clock, most of the buyers and sellers had long found their way home. The fog that had been drifting in all day was now thick and oppressive. She could barely see a few feet in any direction. She stopped abruptly, suddenly confused by her surroundings. She held her lamp higher, trying to get a sense of the landmarks around her. *Did I make a wrong turn?*

She began to move back in the same direction from which she'd come when the sound of a step behind caused her to whirl around. 'Is s–someone there?' she asked.

No one answered, and Lucy began to walk quickly again, hoping this time that she had regained the correct direction. A moment later, she heard another step behind her and she stopped abruptly. The sound stopped too, causing a chill to run over her. 'Don't be a goose, Lucy,' she whispered. 'There's nothing—'

Suddenly, a strong hand clapped over her mouth, silencing her panicked scream. She began to struggle with all her might, elbowing and kicking, and trying to shout. The assailant's other hand closed itself around her neck, pressing against her windpipe, and her mad struggles increased. She tried to bite the hand at her mouth. 'Hush. I don't want to kill you,' someone growled into her ear, a harsh throaty voice. Was it a man or a woman? She couldn't tell. 'I will, though, if you interfere again.'

'Mmmfff!' was all she could utter in response.

'Next time—' The menacing words ceased at the sound of a crashing noise at the end of the street. Then, just as suddenly as the person had accosted her, she was released.

She slumped to the ground, still gasping and holding her hand to heart as the person ran away. Who was her assailant? Dev? Had her visit to the Two Doves Inn prompted this? She shuddered, still feeling the hands wrapped around her mouth and neck. Had he followed her all the way from Hoddesdon? Suddenly, she felt ill and wanted to lie down in the middle of the dirty London street.

Forcing herself to move, she stood up. *Don't think about this now*, she scolded herself. *Get back to Master Aubrey's.* She heard the same crashing sound she'd heard before, causing her to jump. As the fog broke, she could see some dogs licking at a tin of slops that had been thrown out of a tavern. In that moment, she realized where she was and took off, not even bothering to brush off her cloak or skirts, running all the way back to Master Aubrey's without stopping.

Nineteen

Next time. Lucy could still hear the harsh voice in her ear, and she swallowed, putting her hands to her throat. She could still feel the impression of the person's hands there. An hour had passed since she had arrived back at Master Aubrey's and her trembling was growing worse. She was supposed to be washing the supper dishes, but she had to stop, for fear she'd drop and break them all. 'Lucy, get a hold of yourself,' she said, after splashing cold water on her face. 'You've got the cipher. Focus on that! Soon you'll learn what that message says once and for all.' When the trembling didn't abate, she took a few swallows from a jug of red wine that Master Aubrey kept in the storeroom.

She hadn't told the others what had happened. She thought about it and very nearly did so. Then she thought about how they'd react. Will would demand that she stop her investigations, and Master Aubrey might start confining her movements for fear that she might be harmed. What would that mean for her life as a bookseller? No, she'd decided. Too much was at stake. *I wasn't harmed and I'll just be more observant.*

When the tremors subsided, she finished up the dishes and retired to her bedchamber, placing the outdoor lantern on her little table to improve the lighting in her room. Carefully, she pulled out the cipher key she'd received from Mrs Wallace and placed it alongside the other messages and the note found on Mr Corbyn's body.

She examined the cipher key. Although it was torn in half, the part that remained was legible. It was similar to the cipher key that had been published in the Babington tract, displaying a grid of columns and rows. The first column consisted of the alphabet in order, with each letter neatly printed in turn. Then below the alphabet there were several double letters – 'tt', 'ee' and 'nn'. Across the top row, the alphabet looked to be written out again, although it stopped at the letter H, where the paper had been torn diagonally in half. Then the rest of the grid was filled out with a jumble of letters and some symbols.

How to begin? she wondered. 'There's a way to figure out which cipher to use,' Lucy muttered. 'Professor Wallace told us that. What was it he said?'

As she racked her brain, she began to study one of the shorter exchanges between Professor Wallace and Miss de Witte. He had written:

E C XKVJT RBI BIANR AJT LGIAPI RBI IZI. RI ᛁ: HI XBAR C AH EZ AJT EZ.

Beneath it, was her reply:

L UANYX ✝.

Lucy took out her quill and a fresh piece of paper. 'All right, if I substitute each letter, then the first letter E would be substituted as a D.' She wrote that down. 'Then there's a space, and then there is the letter C which substitutes for K.' She wrote that down as well. 'Then the next five letters together, XKVJT, which become, let's see – YQWPF.'

She tapped the pen harder against her paper, surveying what she had written. 'This is all nonsense. Unless . . . could it be a different language now? There's nothing I could do about that. Or maybe it's a double substitution, where I take these deciphered letters, and decipher them again.'

Rubbing her chin, she continued to stare at the cipher key and the messages, trying to control her rising sense of frustration. 'If the message is a double cipher, does that mean that there is a second key? How would the recipient know?' She began to examine the key in more detail. 'There has to be a way that the recipient would know this.' She began to study the first column under A again, the one she had already tried. For the first time she looked at the first eight letters. 'Q-U-A-E-S-T-I-O,' she read out loud. 'Then a triangle. Then the letters B-C-D-F. No E. Why skip E?' Then she looked at the first letters again. 'Don't be a dolt, Lucy, the E was already used. Let's see, what's next. F-G-H-J. So, no I, because the I was already used. I think I see what's happening here. K-L-M-N, no P, no Q or R, no S, no T, no U, V-W-X-Y-Z and then some other symbols.' She looked back at the beginning. She'd seen that word before in some of the tracts she'd printed.

'*Quaestio*. I think that's Latin. Does it mean question?' She looked at the column labelled B. 'R-E-S-P-O-N-U-M and then a square. I've also seen the word "responsum" before. Could this mean response? Perhaps the second S was removed to avoid confusion in the cipher.' She started to grow excited. 'Question and response? Could there be two different codes?'

She looked at the third column, labelled C. 'This one starts with a U, not a Q. Where's the Q?' Her eyes travelled up and down the column. 'Oh, I see. The Q is at the bottom.' Her heart started to beat faster. 'Good heavens, I see it now. All the odd columns follow the *Quaestio* order, just switching one, while all the even columns follow the *Responum* order. Question and response.'

She looked back at the exchange between Professor Wallace and Miss de Witte. 'Even if the first line is written as a question, and the second one works as a response, I already tried to decipher that one.' She snapped her fingers. 'Maybe the cipher is found in a specific column? I just need to know where to start, Professor Wallace said. How could someone know?'

She closed her eyes, trying to remember what the scholar had told them that night. 'There was a way to know where the start was. Usually with the first letter, he said!'

She looked at the message again. 'The first letter is E, which would be one of the *Quaestio* columns. Do I start with the letter E, though? That would be "B" then an "I". Then "XKVJT" is "WOUND".' She stopped and stared at what she had just written. 'B. I. Wound. I wound – I wound? Let me keep going.' She continued piecing it together.

A few minutes later, she was staring at what she had written in amazement. 'I wound the heart and please the eye. Tell me *something* I am by and by. That missing word has to be "what". I think it's a riddle.'

She straightened back up. 'What is the response? L-U-A-N-Y-X-✝. So that means the cipher will be found in the L column, except that part has been torn away. What of the message found on Mr Corbyn's dead body?' She looked at it again.

M YGHX HX YGC MIN ✝GP XCY YGC
& DWA

'Let's see. It starts with the letter M. I'd wager anything that the answer falls in the M column. Except that part of the cipher key has also been torn away.' A sense of exhaustion and despondency flooded over her, and she blew out the candle and collapsed on to her bed. Overcome by disappointment, she pulled the blanket over her head, finally ready to submit to the need for sleep.

'If only we had the whole cipher . . .' she murmured.

Then she sat bolt upright. 'I can just create the other columns!' she whispered. 'Why didn't I think of that before? Each column just started by switching out one letter! I can recreate the cipher myself.' For a moment, she thought about hopping out of bed and lighting the candle again. Then

213

she came to her senses. 'Lucy Campion,' she told herself sternly, 'you can work on this after you get some sleep.' Hugging herself, she soon fell asleep, pleased that she might have moved one step closer towards deciphering the message.

Several hours later, Lucy could hear the roosters starting to crow. She'd woken before the first light had begun to stream through her shuttered windows and, after eating some cold porridge, had seated herself at the workroom table. In another hour, she'd have to start doing her early-morning chores, but right now she'd begun to carefully write out the rest of the code by hand. 'If I can just figure out the M column, I can decipher the message!' It was tedious work, though, and she had to rub her hand several times.

'What in the world are you doing, Lucy?' Lach asked, his voice tinged with annoyance and curiosity. 'We've no tracts to print today.'

'Why has breakfast not been tended to?' Master Aubrey, close behind him, added.

She looked up, startled. The sun had climbed higher in the sky, and she could tell she was late to get breakfast started. 'Forgive me, Master Aubrey. I will get the hearth going.' Walking into the kitchen, she said over her shoulder. 'You'll not believe it!'

'Tell us after you get our porridge ready,' Master Aubrey said, scowling. He didn't see when Lach made a rude gesture at her behind his back. In return, Lucy mimed spitting into his bowl.

When the porridge was ready to eat, Lucy

hastily placed bowls on the table, making sure to give Master Aubrey the heftiest portion. Will came ambling in then, running his fingers through his unruly thick hair, and she hurried to fill his bowl as well.

'So much clamouring today,' Will commented, watching her rush about.

After Master Aubrey took a bite, he set his spoon down. 'All right, lass, I can see you are itching to tell us something. What is it you discovered?'

'Hang on, I'll be right back.' A moment later she placed the original torn cipher and the part of the cipher she had recreated alongside the copy of the corpse's message with a bang. 'Behold! I have deciphered a message.'

Everyone jumped up to look at the riddle that she had deciphered. 'See, this is the cipher key. This first letter indicates to the person receiving the message which column to use.'

'Ingenious,' Master Aubrey said.

'So I figured out that this first line had to be deciphered using the E column and then the response is using the L column. Because the full cipher key is missing, I had to make my best guess on what a few of the characters mean.'

Will gave her an approving look. 'That's some thinking, sister,' he said, clearly impressed.

'So, they sent riddles to each other?' Master Aubrey said, rubbing his cheek. 'I suppose that is one way for a romance to unfold.'

Lucy nodded, feeling a pang at her broken promise to Mrs Wallace. *Don't share what my husband wrote to that woman*, she had pleaded.

I won't share any more than I have to, Lucy reasoned. *It's all to help ensure I have the code right.*

Even Lach looked amazed as he peered down at the deciphered message. Swallowing, he said, 'You don't know if it will work.'

'It will work. It just takes time and I haven't got to the M column yet. Once I have worked out the M column, I should be able to read the message.'

Master Aubrey rubbed his hands. 'I suppose you'd like to work on this instead of your actual work?'

Lucy rubbed the sides of her skirts. 'Yes, sir. I do believe it's important.'

'Why don't you just show it to Master Hargrave or the constable? They can work it out, now that you've got it started.'

'Yes, that's true,' Lucy said, feeling crestfallen. She had really hoped to be able to decipher the message for herself.

Catching sight of her expression, Master Aubrey relented. 'However, it will be a better story coming from you,' he said gruffly. 'Just be quick about it. In the meantime, Lach, you can go to the market, I've some new pamphlets for you to sell.'

For the next several hours, Lucy worked meticulously at piecing together the missing cipher. Finally, she created the cipher for the M column.

'This is it,' she whispered. With growing excitement, she dipped her quill in some ink and took a clean sheet of paper. She dabbed at the ink so

216

that she would not blot the letters in her nervousness. She looked at the first line.

M YGHX HX YGC MIN ⊹GP XCY YGC
& DWA

Slowly, she began to write down each corresponding letter. 'This is the man who set the Devil free,' she whispered.

Her heart started beating quickly, and excitedly she went to the next line. But that line quickly showed itself to be nonsense. She muttered an oath. The next line started with the letter P. 'No,' she said. 'Each line must correspond with a different column. Let's see.'

Sure enough, the next was Y and the last was Z. She pushed away the pages in annoyance. 'This means I have to create the cipher all the way through to the Z column.'

Slowly, carefully, she continued to write out the cipher for all the remaining columns, until finally she had completed the last column. With shaking fingers, she carefully deciphered the whole thing, and then read it out loud.

This is the man who set the Devil free.
Make him lead us to the Devil.
Hang the ring from the Devil's neck.
Punish him for his deed. Send him to the
gallows.

Lucy stared at the message, before quickly writing out several copies. She hid the original and a copy in her pocket. 'I must take this to

Constable Duncan,' she told Master Aubrey, who read it over in unveiled astonishment.

He just waved his hand at her, before mopping his forehead. 'What kind of apprentice do I have here, anyway?' she heard him mutter as she sailed out the door.

Twenty

As she rushed out of the printer's shop, she collided with Lach who had just returned from a delivery, her elbow going sharply into his chest.

'Ooof!' he exclaimed. 'Dunderhead! Why have you got to knock a man down?'

'Pardon, Lach! I'm in a hurry!' Lucy cried. 'I've got to see the constable at once!'

'Back to the constable,' he said, tutting. 'Tired of the noble life already, eh?'

'Actually, I should like to see Master Adam, too. Could you go and see him? Tell him I'm away to the constable's and—'

'Uh-oh! He's not going to like that,' Lach commented.

'Lach!' she exclaimed. 'Tell Master Adam that I deciphered the message that was on the corpse and—'

'You did?' Lach interrupted, his mouth hanging open. 'What did it say?'

'Lach! I don't have time for this. Just go and tell him, would you?'

'Certainly. I'm on my way. See me running there already? Knock knock knock, I'm at their door.'

'Lach! Stop your jests,' she scolded. 'I don't have time for this. Just say you'll tell Master Adam about the message. Please, it's important.'

'What's in it for me?'

'What's in it for you?' Lucy exclaimed, getting thoroughly exasperated.

'There must be something in it for me. I'm hungry and you're asking me to do this during the time I take my noon meal.'

'Fine! I'll do your morning chores for a day! No, a week! Is that good enough?' Inwardly, she sighed. She had no trouble beating down merchants and vendors in the markets, but Lach just wanted to torment her and there was very little room to negotiate.

'My night chores as well.'

'Lach!'

'Promise. Or I won't go.' He grinned, his freckles sticking out across his cheeks.

'Fine, I'll do it! Now, just go!'

Lucy turned to go and was gratified to see Lach stop his ambling stride and take up a rapid trot towards the Hargraves' home.

'Duncan!' Lucy called, entering the jail. She leaned over, her hand to her chest, trying to catch her breath.

'What is it?' he replied, walking out of the back area. Seeing her doubled over, he rushed to her side. 'Lucy, what's wrong?'

Straightening up, she declared, 'I deciphered the message that was found on Mr Corbyn's body.'

'What?' he exclaimed. 'How ever did you do that?'

'I went to Professor Wallace's house last night to deliver some mathematical books I picked up for him in Hoddesdon. Mrs Wallace gave me half the cipher.' She pulled out the coded message and read it out loud.

> This is the man who set the Devil free.
> Make him lead us to the Devil.
> Hang the ring from the Devil's neck.
> Punish him for his deed. Send him to the
>   gallows.

He stared at her. 'I can't believe you worked this out!'

'Well, I had a portion of the cipher,' she said modestly.

Duncan turned his attention back to the message and frowned. 'Something seems off about it, though, don't you think?'

'How do you mean?'

'Well, the message seems to be speaking of two people.' He tapped the page. 'See here. "This is the man who set the Devil free." That's Paul Corbyn, or Jack Campbell, who let Philip Emerson and the other men out of Newgate that day. The Devil must be Emerson. Stands to reason since the men you saw at the crossroads were Eleanor Browning's brothers and the cipher was created by Hammett's sister.'

'Yes, that's true,' Lucy said. 'However, the message then says, "Hang the ring from the Devil's neck." So why was the chain with the ring around Paul Corbyn's neck?'

'Lucy, Duncan,' Adam said from behind them. He was panting slightly from his exertions. 'What is it you've learned? Lach told me that you deciphered the message?' There

221

was more than a bit of pride and admiration in his tone.

Lucy handed him the cipher and the message. 'I worked the full cipher out from the partial one that Mrs Wallace gave me,' she explained.

'That's truly incredible, Lucy,' Adam said, looking at the reconstructed key she had created. Then, more seriously, he added, 'You must not tell anyone about this.'

Her mind flashed to the man who had come after her last night. *Next time*, he had whispered. *I will kill you if you interfere again.*

She shuddered.

Seeing this, Adam looked at her sharply. 'What is it?'

Reluctantly, she decided she'd better tell them what had happened. 'I think that the innkeeper of the tavern, Dev Browning, may have figured out who I was. Someone came after me last night, after I left the Wallaces' house, telling me not to interfere. I think it may have been him.'

Duncan and Adam both stared at her, wearing equal expressions of horror. 'What?' they both exclaimed at once.

Adam grasped her gently by the shoulders. 'Slow down! Someone came after you? Are you all right?'

'Yes, yes, I'm fine.' Quickly, she recounted everything that had happened the day before, including how Dev had seen her getting into the carriage with the Hargraves. 'I think he figured out who I was. Maybe he enquired at the booksellers in Hoddesdon. I had shown them Master Aubrey's seal, to make sure they would be willing to bargain with me. I think it would have been easy enough to discover my identity. They had already guessed I was a bookseller when they ran me over with the cart that morning on Drury Lane.'

'This man, Dev Browning,' Duncan broke in, 'is someone we need to speak to again. Immediately. You've already identified Dev, but I should like to know about the other man you saw as well – Pike? We shall question them both, and likely arrest them.' He paused. 'I should like you to accompany me back to Hoddesdon, Lucy. This afternoon, if possible. We do not wish them to flee, even if, as you say, the inn is so well established there.'

'I will accompany you, Constable,' Adam said grimly. 'Those men do not need to face their accuser until trial. There is no need for Lucy to be there.'

'I am coming,' Lucy said, taking a step forward. 'Master Aubrey will not mind, as Professor Wallace and his scholar friends gave me another list of books to procure on their behalf. Besides, I think the constable does need me there to identify them both.'

'I can see you will not change your mind,' Adam said. 'We shall set out this afternoon.'

'Why do you need to go?' Duncan asked Adam.

'If you are bringing those men into jail, I will not have Lucy travel with them, and I won't have her travel alone.'

Lucy looked from one man to the other. Neither seemed happy. 'It is settled then.'

Within the hour, the three were travelling back to Hoddesdon, in a rickety carriage that Duncan had managed to summon with some alacrity. Hank was also there, and Lucy found herself talking mostly to him along the journey. The other two men stayed quiet, listening, but hardly talking, clearly wary of one another.

Lucy remembered something that had been bothering her for a while. 'Duncan, what happened to Philip Emerson? After he escaped from Newgate?'

Duncan shrugged. 'Who's to say? Disappeared, it seemed.'

'Did anyone ever check his home?'

'Well, that I don't know. The world was in chaos during the Great Fire and those weeks that followed. No one knew up from down. At the time, soldiers were sent to round up those that had escaped, I believe, but if he was smart, he would have long fled.'

'Or perhaps he has returned home. Is he from London?'

Duncan frowned. 'I have no idea.'

'We have speculated that he might have taken on a new identity, in the same way that Jack Campbell assumed Paul Corbyn's,' Adam intervened. 'Perhaps it is worth sending an inquiry to Cambridge. Emerson's address should be in their rolls. I'll dispatch a message when we arrive in Hoddesdon.'

Duncan grunted his thanks, and they all fell into an uncomfortable silence.

Then Hank asked Lucy a question about bookselling. Gratefully, she began to tell some of the silly stories that filled her days as a bookseller. Just as she was regaling them with the time that Master Aubrey had caught Lach setting the type forward instead of backwards, they arrived back at Hoddesdon.

Twenty-One

As before, the Two Doves Inn was dark inside but more of the windows had been opened to let in the last bit of afternoon sun. Peeking in through the window, Lucy could see Tabby inside, passing out some ales. She didn't see either the innkeeper or his wife.

When they entered, Tabby gave them a little wave and walked over. 'You again! I thought you were returning to London. Or did you end up staying with your sweetheart?' She winked at Adam, causing all of them to shift uncomfortably.

'Let's sit here,' Duncan said, gesturing to an open table close to the entrance.

'Some ales?' Tabby asked. 'I can't drink with you again, I'm afraid. Mrs Browning boxed my ears for that.'

'I'm sorry,' Adam replied.

She shrugged her shoulders. 'No matter. Worth it for the extra coins.' She looked hopefully at Adam.

'Does a man named Pike work here, too?' Duncan asked.

'Pike? Of course! He owns the inn with his brother.'

So they *were* brothers. Lucy remembered thinking there had been a family resemblance.

'Pike's right over there, with that customer.'

Before they could stop her, she had called out to the man. 'Pike! Someone's asking for you!'

When the man turned, Lucy darted a quick glance at him before ducking her head. It was definitely the other man she'd seen at the cross-roads. 'That's him,' she whispered.

Pike came over. 'What can I do for you, gents?' he asked, and then stared at Lucy. 'You!'

He turned then and walked out, nearly running into Dev who was just entering the inn with his hands wrapped around a small barrel of ale. 'What the—' Dev started to say before catching sight of Lucy.

Before either man could flee, Hank had caught hold of them both by the upper arm. 'We've got some questions for you,' he said gruffly. 'Sit down.'

The two brothers sat down with a constable on either side of them. Lucy and Adam remained standing, Adam standing slightly in front of Lucy.

'What kind of questions?' Pike asked.

'I'd like to ask you some questions about the death of Paul Corbyn of London.'

'Who's that?' Pike asked, spitting on the ground.

'The man you hanged.'

'We did no such thing,' Pike said.

'You saw us hang a man?' Dev asked, his brow rising. 'Who claims such a thing?'

'On the morning of the twenty-fifth of November, Paul Corbyn was found hanged,' Duncan said. 'Tell us what you know about his death.'

'We don't know anything. We weren't even there,' Dev said.

'A witness placed you at the gallows where the man was found.'

Pike looked up at Lucy. 'What witness? Her? We saw her on the road to St Giles-in-the-Fields, peddling papers, some distance from the gallows. That man was already dead when you saw us.'

Dev punched his brother. 'Dunderhead.'

Adam's stare hardened. 'Thank you for confirming your presence at the scene.'

'All right, we saw the man hanging there. We had nothing to do with his death,' Dev conceded. 'Besides, he had clearly committed self-murder.'

'I saw you steal some things from his body. His pocket, shoes and a watch,' Lucy said. She pointed at Pike's shoes. 'I believe you are wearing them now!'

Dev and Pike stared at her. 'So you *were* there!' Pike said. 'You probably stole the ring around his neck.'

Dev slapped his head and then punched his brother again. 'Stop talking,' he hissed at him. Turning back to Duncan, he said, 'We've said all we know.'

'That is most certainly not true,' the constable replied. 'Given that the man who died was Jack Campbell, the Newgate jailer who freed your sister's murderer during the Great Fire.'

'What?' The man tried to feign innocence.

'We know nothing of that—' Dev began, but Pike interrupted him.

'He came to us! He felt guilty! He said he deserved to die. So we, er, helped him.'

Dev punched his brother in the face. 'What does it take to shut you up?'

228

'According to the physician, this man was murdered,' Duncan said. 'He was struck on the head before being hanged. You did not help him to commit self-murder; you killed him. You are under arrest.' He beckoned to Hank. 'We're bringing you in to stand trial.'

'It wasn't just us!' Pike cried.

They all stopped and stared at Pike. Dev just groaned. 'Just stop talking!'

'Explain yourself,' Duncan growled. 'We may go easier on you.'

'Someone told us to do it. She sent us a message. Said it was the only way to get the revenge we sought.'

They all sat back down, looking at each other. Lucy recalled the message that had been found on the guard's body. *This is the man who set the Devil free. Make him lead us to the Devil.*

'Who was it?' Duncan asked.

'It was the woman. Hammett's sister. She told us to do it.'

Hammett's sister? Lucretia de Witte.

'Tell us everything,' Adam said.

'Hammett's sister came here after it happened, before the trial. She kept saying she couldn't wait until Philip Emerson was dead. We saw her again at the trial and she was so pleased when the verdict was read. We wanted him dead, too. She didn't seem quite right in the head. Addled, you know.'

Lucy frowned. Lucretia had not seemed so confused to have lost her wits. Perhaps she'd not been herself after her brother was killed. Such a thing would hardly have been surprising. Could she not remember those moments of numbness and fury? Yes, she most certainly could. 'Tell us. What did this woman look like?'

'Noble born. White-blonde hair. Green eyes. Small build. Smaller than you,' Pike said.

They described Lucretia perfectly. Adam and Duncan looked to her for confirmation. 'Yes,' she whispered. 'That does sound like her.'

'Seemed at first as if she was sculpted from an icicle. Until she saw the bloodstain on the floor. She lay right down on the floor and started screaming and weeping. Then the icicle was fully melted,' Dev added.

'She started writing to us, a few months after the Great Fire. At first we could not make any sense of the message, but then we realized it was in cipher – the same cipher that her brother had used to write messages to Ellie. I still had the key in my possession.'

'Why did Hammett de Witte use a cipher to write messages to Ellie?' Adam asked. 'Was your sister's mind great but untrained?' He glanced at Lucy.

Dev frowned. 'I asked him the same thing, after the first time she came to me. Poor lass could not work out how to decipher the messages, even with the key. She hadn't much ability with reading and writing as it was.'

'What did he say?' Lucy asked.

'He couldn't fathom that anyone, even a merry light-hearted lass like our sister, wouldn't be able to read such a thing!'

'He had her on a pedestal, he said,' Pike said,

sounding scornful. 'Said he could not bring himself to address her in an ordinary way.'

'I ended up having to figure it out,' Dev replied, anger rising in his voice. 'The first time he sent her the message, I read it to her, but his words – all romantic gibberish – shamed her and made me angry. Suffice it to say, she did not have me read it again. I think the next time she asked Philip Emerson to read it for her, bringing the fate into motion.'

Both men shook their heads. 'The cad!' Pike exclaimed. 'My sister did not deserve such a fate. It's those godforsaken, good-for-nothing scholars that are the leeches of our society. Living off others and contributing nothing. We were better off without them, and we are heart-sick that Ellie was taken in by their handsome countenance and fell for their nonsense.'

'I will say that Mr de Witte was not one of the usual sorts we had to protect her from at the Two Doves,' Dev said, a look of regret passing over his features. 'I believe that his love for her was true. As true as anything can be between a man of means and a serving wench like her.'

Adam's jaw tightened, but he didn't say anything.

'Tell us about Miss de Witte's messages. What did she write?' Lucy asked hurriedly.

'A few weeks ago, she wrote to us that she'd located the guard, which was the next best thing to finding Emerson,' Dev replied. 'She said she'd send him to meet us outside St Giles-in-the-Fields and that he'd be carrying a message from her.

That she'd send along some spirits that would get him talking.'

Lucy nodded. That explained the whiff of alcohol she'd smelled when she first encountered the corpse.

'Sure enough, we were waiting there at first light and he came right up to us with his handcart full of goods and handed us the message, along with two bottles of wine,' Pike explained. 'He told us she'd paid him handsomely to make the journey, but that he hadn't minded as it was part of his regular trading route.'

'As soon as we deciphered it, we knew what to do,' Pike added. 'In her message, she told us to hang him with the ring around his neck.'

'You went along with it,' Adam said, his voice even. 'Why did you agree to carry out her wishes – to murder a man?'

'At first we didn't want to,' Pike said. 'Then we remembered how he had given that murderer a chance to live when our dear sister was in the ground, never to live or love again.' He wiped away a tear. 'We thought it best to make it look like suicide. So we took him to the old hanging tree at the crossroads.'

'How did you get Mr Corbyn to the crossroads?' Duncan asked, pushing on.

'We got him drinking. Miss de Witte had marked the bottle for him. It made him tired. We struck him over the head, hid his mercer's goods, and rolled him there in the cart,' Pike said. 'The hardest part was getting him over the tree branch and pushing him off.'

Dev sighed. He seemed to have given up reining in his brother.

'Why did you place the ring around his neck?' Lucy asked. This point was still puzzling her, especially since it was different from what the sender of the message had instructed.

'The ring was cursed,' Pike said. 'Hammett had given that dreadful thing to our dear sister, and Emerson took it off her hand as she lay dying. We all wanted to be done with it.'

'Yet you went back to rob him,' Lucy said, her lip curling. 'Why were you planning to take the ring back if it disgusted you so?'

'Well, we thought we might as well make some money off him.'

Ignoring him, Lucy softly recited the message from memory. '*This is the man who set the Devil free. Make him lead us to the Devil.*'

Pike stared at her. 'You know the message?'

'*Hang the ring from the Devil's neck. Punish him for his deed. Send him to the gallows,*' Lucy continued in the same soft tone. 'You fools. She wasn't telling you to murder the guard. She wanted you to make the guard tell you where Philip Emerson was. It was Philip you were supposed to hang, not the guard.' She took in the men's shocked faces and continued. 'Did the man you killed tell you where to find Mr Emerson?'

Both men shook their heads vigorously.

'Time to go,' Duncan said, gesturing to Hank to seize Pike's arm. He pulled some ropes from his bag and handed one to Hank. 'Tie him up. Let's get these men to the jail.'

233

Lucy and Adam followed the men back to the carriage. Lucy still had questions. She turned to Dev. 'It was you who came after to me in London, wasn't it? You're the one who threatened me!'

'Don't know what you're talking about,' Dev replied. Pike shook his head as well.

Confused, Lucy stepped back. *If it had not been Pike or Dev, who else would have threatened her in such a manner?*

She watched as Duncan and Adam tied the men to the back of the cart so that they would not be able to make an escape on the journey back to London. They would be in jail before nightfall.

Duncan came back over to speak to them. 'After I lock them up for evening, I will need to speak with Miss de Witte about these accusations. To do this I will need an entry.' Irritated, he looked up at Adam. 'That means you. Men of your kind are always allowed in such places.'

'I have an idea,' Lucy said. 'She might be willing to speak to me again.' Straightening up, she added, 'I can be of help here. Let us go together in the morning. Right now, we can stop back at Master Barnaby's before we head back, to pick up some tracts that might entice Miss de Witte.'

Adam and Duncan looked at each other with a sense of shared exasperation. 'I don't think there's any stopping her,' Duncan said, while Adam just watched her ruefully.

'Are we really going to be able to prove that Miss de Witte helped those men murder Paul Corbyn?' Lucy asked Adam as they settled into the carriage that Adam had acquired for the long drive back to London. She placed the full pack of books she'd procured at Master Barnaby's on the seat beside her. 'I can scarcely believe it myself.'

Adam scratched his chin. 'We will have to approach our quarry delicately, or we'll frighten her away.'

For a few minutes more they discussed what they had learned from Pike and Dev. Then Lucy pulled out the copy of the cipher and several of the messages that had passed between Miss de Witte and Professor Wallace. 'It may be a good idea to understand her thinking,' she said. 'Perhaps we should figure out the rest of these messages as well.'

They spent the rest of the journey deciphering the remaining messages together. A few turned out to have been in Latin, which Adam studied in some detail as well. They all seemed to be flirtatious riddles, mostly consisting of Professor Wallace praising Miss de Witte, followed by Miss de Witte's coy replies.

'They had quite a flirtation,' Lucy commented, after reading through them all. She tucked them back into her small embroidered pocket.

'That seems to be the case,' Adam agreed, sounding a bit disgusted. 'He doesn't seem to have thought too highly of his marriage vows.'

'I can understand why Mrs Wallace felt wronged and why she insisted that her husband destroy their correspondence.'

'Yes, I can understand that, too,' Adam said. 'Although it is good that she had a change of heart and kept them from being destroyed. She told you it was out of duty to her husband's work, but I wonder if she may also have pondered the professor's admiration for the woman he seemed to favour.'

'She said she never deciphered the messages, and I can see why.'

'I don't know if I'd have been able to do that myself,' Adam commented. 'If one is fair, one will see many good and admirable qualities. How could someone you love be in love with someone bad or lacking in virtuous traits?' He looked out of the window. 'Sometimes it is very easy indeed to see what draws someone you love to another.'

For a moment they stayed silent. Then he spoke again. 'I meant to tell you,' he said, back to his regular conversational tone. 'I received a letter from Sarah yesterday. In the excitement, I forgot to tell you about it. A Friend dropped it off. Said it had been passed to him in Bristol. It's from a month ago, written just after I saw her.'

'What did Sarah have to say? Does she fare well?'

'I'll let you read it,' he said, pulling it from his pocket.

Smoothing out the crumpled letter, Lucy struggled to read Sarah's careless script. Though Lucy could read print quite well, sometimes handwritten letters still gave her pause. The ink had smeared in parts as well, making some of the missive nearly unintelligible.

'*My dearest Brother Adam,*' she murmured Sarah's words out loud. '*I give thee the most*

236

truest love from my heart and wish you blessed of mind and spirit.' She smiled at the exhortations in the opening, which were typical of the Friends' speech. She could still remember Sarah as a rather merry and silly girl, clamouring for ribbons from her brother and to be taken to the local fair. 'Sometimes it's still hard for me to believe she has become a Quakeress,' she murmured.

'I know what you mean,' Adam replied, watching her as she continued to read.

She continued to whisper Sarah's words softly to herself. *'I did find it in my most tender conscience to protest some of the King's most recent petitions as they had come to the New World. I know that it upset thee to see myself in the stocks, but thou should be pleased that my dearest heart's content is being fulfilled.'* Lucy sighed. It always worried her to think about Sarah getting punished by authorities who did not appreciate the Friends' expression of their Inner Light and conscience. *'I do hope that thou hast given some thought to my words when I last saw thee. I hope too that thou will find thy way—'* Here she abruptly stopped reading out loud – *to Lucy. Will all my love, thy sister Sarah.*

Lucy passed the letter back to Adam who carefully folded it before replacing it in his pocket. *What did Sarah mean?* she wondered. *I hope too that thou will find thy way to Lucy.*

As they pulled down Fleet Street, Lucy finally brought herself to ask Adam the question she'd been thinking about. 'What did Sarah mean? What words does she hope that you've given thought to?'

Adam leaned forward, placing his hands on her knees. 'She saw my sadness at our separation.'

'Oh,' Lucy said, her heart starting to beat more quickly.

'My travels through the New World have helped me see things I have not seen before. The rampant injustices of society. The privilege and reputation given to a man based upon his birth and parentage.'

Lucy nodded, not sure what to say.

Adam seized her hands. 'Lucy, I know that our worlds are uneven, but perhaps there is a way forward?' At her silence, he looked at her more closely. 'Unless, you have given your heart away in my absence?'

'I have not,' she said, pulling away.

'Are you under a spell, lass?' Master Aubrey said, snapping his fingers at her. 'I think you didn't hear a word of what I just said.'

Lucy blinked, realizing that both the master printer and Lach were staring at her. The words that Adam had just uttered as she stepped out of the carriage were still whirling around inside her head.

'I said it looks as if you did well at Master Barnaby's. Mrs Wallace was very excited earlier when I told her you'd gone back to Hoddesdon. She said she would invite the scholars back to their home this evening, in case you picked up something interesting for them to review.' He looked at her sternly. 'You *did* pick up something interesting for them to review, did you not?'

'I–I did,' she faltered. Master Aubrey was

looking unusually stern. 'Also for Miss de Witte, whom I plan to see in the morning if that is all right.'

'Certainly,' Master Aubrey said, visibly relaxing. Then, unexpectedly, he boxed Lach's left ear. 'How come you don't bring in business like Lucy does?'

'Maybe because I don't go looking for dead bodies like her— Ow!' he cried, as his cheeky response was met with another light boxing of the ears.

'I don't look for dead bodies,' Lucy muttered as she pulled on her cloak. 'I just bring victims to justice.'

Twenty-Two

For the second time in two days, Lucy found herself standing outside the Wallaces' drawing room, pack in hand, waiting to be acknowledged by her hosts. As before, Professor Wallace's scholars had already gathered, appearing to be the same four who had been there the other night, already deep into the wine. This time, Mrs Wallace seemed to be keeping an eye out for her, giving a little squeal when she appeared. 'Lucy, come here!' she said, taking her arm and bringing her to Professor Wallace who was engaged in conversation with one of the men. 'Neville, I invited Lucy back as a surprise. Tell me you have some good pieces for us!'

'Ah, so,' Professor Wallace said, looking flustered. 'Very good, very good. The thing is, well, we've still been studying the ones you delivered the other day, and here you are with a few more precious tomes.' He patted his pocket and glanced at his wife. 'Perhaps we might wait a few weeks or even months between your efforts. I do thank you kindly, my dear.' Although he seemed genuine in both his interest and thanks, Lucy could read between the lines. *This is too costly a hobby to have the bookseller come twice in one week.* 'But, since you're here, let's see what you brought.' He moved aside the decanter and glasses and patted the long wooden sideboard.

Carefully, she pulled the books from her pack one by one for all to see. This time she had brought several related to musical theory, which included the application of mathematics to the playing of the violin. The other scholars clustered around as Mrs Wallace once again pressed a glass of sherry into her hands. With a satisfied sigh, Professor Wallace began to peruse one of the books, admiring the gilded pages and embossed cover before running his finger down the table of contents.

'I fear my wife is spoiling me, asking you to procure such fine items on behalf. I thought the list would take you more than a year to acquire, not three days!' Professor Wallace said, looking more jovial.

'Ah, 'twas no trouble at all,' Lucy replied, accepting the glass but not taking a sip. 'I was in Hoddesdon again for a short spell. I stopped at Master Barnaby's and picked a few more off your list.'

'Another journey to Hoddesdon? Were you not just there?' Professor Wallace asked, looking a bit alarmed. 'I hope you did not return on my account.'

'I haven't been to Master Barnaby's in so long,' one of the men commented. He was the man with red hair. Mr Quayle. 'His store was always so well stocked.'

'He can be quite a bear, though,' Mr Jacobs replied. His clothes looked properly tailored and expensive. He reminded her of the itinerant scholars who used to teach Sarah. 'Very protective of his books.'

Lucy nodded, although that only improved her opinion of the bookseller. All the booksellers she knew were highly protective of their stock.

'I've heard tales of Master Barnaby, though I've never met himself. He seems quite fearful indeed,' Mrs Wallace said, giving a mock shiver. 'Did he make you wait on him very long, Lucy? I know that he tends to do that.' She nudged her husband, who coughed. 'I should think we should give you some extra coins for your troubles.'

'Yes, of course,' he replied. 'I'll add some pennies.'

Suddenly, Lucy felt a little embarrassed and confused. She was being treated like a guest and a servant in the same moment. *How would Master Aubrey handle this type of transaction?* she wondered. 'Oh, it did not take so long,' she said, setting the glass of sherry down, still untouched. 'I just stopped into Master Barnaby's because I was already in Hoddesdon. The constable had asked me to make the journey so that he could arrest the innkeepers from the Two Doves Inn for murder.'

'What?' everyone exclaimed, pausing what they were doing. They all stared at her.

'Arrest the innkeepers?' Mr Newman asked. He, like the other men, had a pale and cheese-like countenance, owned by those who rarely spent much time outdoors or in healthful pursuits. His threadbare suit hung awkwardly on his lanky body.

'Yes,' Lucy replied. 'They were believed to have

helped murder a man – an old Newgate guard who set some criminals free during the Great Fire. Paul Corbyn. The innkeepers are in jail now, awaiting trial.' She paused. 'The constable needed me to identify them. After that was done, I was able to slip over to Master Barnaby's shop and procure these in no time. As I said, 'twas no trouble at all.'

Mr Newman suddenly did not look well. Bowing his head in turn to Professor and Mrs Wallace, he said, 'Pardon me, I am feeling very ill. I should take my leave of you now. I should like to return to my room at the Hare and Pony to rest.'

'Of course, my good sir,' Professor Wallace said, not even looking up from the treatise he was examining. 'Return to us when you are recovered.'

Mrs Wallace extended her hand in farewell. 'You must come back when you are better.'

'I will,' he said, swallowing. He darted an odd look at Lucy before exiting the drawing room.

Something about that furtive gesture caught Lucy's attention. She sidled over to Mrs Wallace. 'Who was that man?'

'Roland Newman,' she replied. 'As I mentioned before, he is a tutor of Greek, Latin and musical theory, from what I understand. Why do you ask?'

'I suppose you have known him a very long time?' Lucy asked.

'Not so long. If I recall correctly, he started to reside at the Hare and Pony Inn with the other scholars a few months ago. Neville and I have only recently made his acquaintance. We

243

have found him to be quite knowledgeable, although moody when his opinions are questioned. Out of Oxford, he said. Fancies himself quite the scholar. I know that Neville thinks highly of his intellect, which contributes greatly to my measure of the man.' She drew Lucy to the back of the long room, away from the other scholars. 'What is it? I can tell something is disturbing you.'

'Well,' Lucy began, struggling to put her half-formed impressions into words. 'It's just that Mr Newman seemed distressed when I mentioned Hoddesdon. Even more so when I said that those two innkeepers in Hoddesdon had been arrested for Paul Corbyn's murder.' She paused. 'Why would that bother him? He seemed quite unwell when he left. Or was he more concerned with the murder itself?'

'For some men, the thought of murder can be distressing,' Mrs Wallace replied. 'What are you thinking?'

'He also seemed to start when I mentioned the Two Doves Inn,' her voice dropped. 'Could it be—'

Mrs Wallace leaned in. 'What?'

'I know it's preposterous, but could that man be Philip Emerson?'

Her eyes widening, Mrs Wallace covered her mouth with her hand. 'Philip Emerson? You must be jesting!'

'Yet, could he be so disguised? Wouldn't your husband or one of the other scholars know him from Cambridge, if he were indeed Mr Emerson?'

Mrs Wallace shook her head. 'I can tell you that Neville and I never met Philip Emerson. The other scholars move around between London, Oxford and Cambridge, when they are not travelling abroad. There is no reason to think they would have known the man.' She bit her lower lip. 'From what I understand of the matter, Mr Newman would certainly be about the correct age. He is of the same moody character that I heard tell defined Mr Emerson. Yet scholars tend to have a melancholy presence, from which only my own dear Neville appears to have been exempt.' She pressed her hand to her forehead, beginning to sway. 'Forgive me, Lucy, I am feeling quite faint.'

'Pray sit down,' Lucy said, leading Mrs Wallace to a seat. 'Drink your wine. I do apologize for having given you this fright. I am sure that I am jumping to conclusions, for such a fantastical thing could hardly be true.'

'I am indeed horrified by the thought that we have been harbouring a vicious murderer in our midst,' Mrs Wallace whispered fiercely. 'Not just harbouring but protecting, and plying with drink, merriment and pleasurable discourse. We have even helped establish his reputation – I know that Neville has recommended him as a tutor to several noble families. He has benefitted greatly from consorting with us.'

'We should not condemn him unjustly,' Lucy said quickly, touching the woman's wrist. 'I should like to identify him as Philip Emerson first, so that he may be arrested and punished for his crime. See justice restored once and for all.

Duncan wouldn't want to take the chance of having the innkeepers identify him, for fear that they would lie and say they could not remember him. He could send for someone from Cambridge or even Hoddesdon, but that will take some time. As such, I am at a loss.'

Mrs Wallace looked thoughtful. 'You said that the constable invited you to Hoddesdon to point out the innkeepers, so that he could arrest them – correct?'

'Yes,' Lucy said. 'I understand what you are saying. We need someone who could identify Philip Emerson. Who could do that?'

'That is the question. Not Professor Wallace or I, since we never met him as Emerson. Nor do the other scholars seem aware of his past. However' – she paused, a distasteful look crossing her thoughts – 'Miss de Witte would know him. She attended the trial after all. Besides, he and her brother were once friends. She might even have known him – before.'

'That is true. She would likely be able to identify him,' Lucy said. *Except, would she? If she had been involved in Mr Corbyn's murder – if she had written those messages, why would she identify Philip Emerson? What would she gain from such an act? On the other hand, even if she is guilty of the other crime, would she deny herself the chance to point out her brother's murderer to the constable?*

'Lucy?' Mrs Wallace asked, trying to peer at her face. 'You appear deep in thought. What are you thinking?'

'You say that he and the other scholars have

taken up residence at the Hare and Pony Inn,' Lucy mused. 'Perhaps I can find a way to bring Miss de Witte to the tavern tomorrow and see if she could identify him for the constable. That is, if he has not been unnerved and fled already. I hope that she would be willing to identify him.'

'I should think so,' Mrs Wallace replied. 'Her fury towards Mr Emerson, and the man who set him free, is unchecked. I should not think it would be so hard to convince her to come with you.'

Lucy crossed her arms. 'We shall see. The trick now is how she can identify Mr Emerson without him knowing. We should not want to bring her into any danger.'

'Lucy, you must stop putting yourself in the way of harm,' Duncan said. He had just finished listening to her breathless account of what had occurred at the Wallaces' the night before. She had darted over to the jail early that morning after getting Master Aubrey's resigned approval. In addition to chores, she also had to promise she'd write another true account for him.

'To be fair, I did not know that one of the scholars could be a murderer. I agree it seems quite far-fetched, but I believe it is worth pursuing.' Lucy kicked a rock. 'You will have to be very careful in how you approach her now.'

'What do you mean?'

'Well, Dev and Pike claim that she is the one who told them to kill Mr Corbyn, even if they misunderstood her message. Obviously, we know that the individuals involved used her cipher. She can simply deny this.'

Duncan sighed. 'That is so. Moreover, if we anger her, she might not wish to cooperate with us and identify Mr Emerson. We must tread carefully.'

'Perhaps you should have her identify Mr Emerson first, without bringing up the ciphers or the claims made by Dev and Pike,' Lucy said. 'I have a thought on how to proceed, if you'll allow me.'

At Duncan's knock, the same servant who'd been there before cautiously opened the door. 'Is Miss de Witte in?' he asked courteously. 'We'd like to speak with her.'

Seeing the woman's hesitation, Lucy jumped in. 'I'm Lucy Campion. I was here recently with Mrs Wallace, if you may recall. I have some more of the tracts she asked for, which I'd very much like to share with her. You are Mavis, are you not?'

Relaxing a bit, Mavis nodded. 'This way, please,' she said, leading them to the same room where Lucy had first met Miss de Witte.

'Look at the portrait,' she whispered to Duncan. 'That is Hammett de Witte. See the ring? Look, too, at the piece of paper sticking out of the book. I think that's part of the cipher as well.'

Duncan was still studying the portrait when Lucretia de Witte sailed into the room. 'Lucy!' she started to say in a delighted way, before stopping short at the sight of Duncan. She took in his red uniform, confusion quickly turning to anger. 'What is this? Why have you brought a soldier to my home?'

'Miss de Witte,' Duncan said, stepping forward. 'I am Constable Duncan. I have some questions for you about Philip Emerson, the murderer of your brother Hammett.'

She blanched. 'I don't wish to discuss that monster.' Reaching for the embroidered pocket around her waist, she pulled out some coins and spoke coolly to Lucy. 'I see you have brought those tracts for me, Lucy. Will three shillings suffice?' Accepting the tracts, she added, 'I'll bid you good day and thank you for your troubles. Pray, do not return, Lucy. I do not appreciate the misleading pretext for your visit. Furthermore, I do not wish to know why you sought to involve yourself in my family's tragedy, and I certainly do not appreciate such *people* being brought to my home.'

Beside her, she could feel Duncan stiffen at the slight. *This is a mess*, Lucy thought as she handed her the tracts. 'Miss de Witte,' she blurted out, 'we came here today because we have learned the whereabouts of Philip Emerson, your brother's murderer.'

'What?' Miss de Witte said, growing pale. She grasped the edge of a chair for support. 'Whatever do you mean?'

'He is here, we believe, in London,' she explained. 'However, there is good reason to believe he has assumed a new identity.'

'A new identity?' Miss de Witte said. She went

over to the sideboard and poured herself a glass of sherry, even though it was still morning. 'Who is he?'

Lucy glanced at Duncan, not sure if she should provide his name outright.

'Would you remember what he looked like?' Lucy asked instead. 'You may be the only person who could identify him, unless the constable sends for someone from Cambridge. That could take too much time and he might learn of the inquiry and flee.'

Miss de Witte's eyes grew hard. 'I remember every line, expression and feature of that murderer's villainous face,' she said, practically spitting. 'I have no doubt that I could identify him. Where is the scoundrel hiding?'

'We believe Mr Emerson is living among some other scholars and tutors at a nearby tavern, the Hare and Pony,' Duncan said easily. 'You would not need to speak to him. We just need to confirm his identity before I can arrest him again. If you were willing, I was hoping we could venture there now.'

Miss de Witte stood up. 'Let us out this vicious murderer once and for all. I would see him hanged for his crimes.'

Just then there was a tap at the door and the servant appeared, bearing a small salver with a letter. 'A message for you, Miss de Witte.'

'Thank you, Mavis.' Miss de Witte quickly slit open the seal, a huge smile on her face as she opened it.

'Good news?' Lucy asked.

Ignoring her question, Miss de Witte folded up

the note and slipped it into her pocket. 'Just let me fetch my things. I shall meet you at the front door and we can walk over together.'

To their surprise, Miss de Witte did not call for her carriage, preferring to walk. Given that she had already taken more than fifteen minutes to ready herself, Lucy thought she would have preferred to move in a more urgent manner.

'Why draw attention to ourselves?' she'd said reasonably, a point to which Duncan and Lucy readily agreed. Her entire mood had brightened, her tone was no longer so clipped and chilled, and her steps were brisk and light.

She seemed pleased now to speak with Lucy. 'You have become more acquainted with the Wallaces of late? Tell me, how does Professor Wallace fare?'

Lucy spoke cautiously. 'He fares well, from what I can see. He told me that he was working on a new mathematical treatise.'

'Is that so? You are wondering about my interest, I can tell. There was a time, when he was still my tutor, that we were very dear acquaintances.'

'I see,' Lucy said, trying to sound noncommittal. She did not wish to betray Mrs Wallace's confidence, although she was hoping to learn as much as she could from Miss de Witte. She certainly did not wish to let on that she and Adam had deciphered several of the riddles that Miss de Witte and Professor Wallace had exchanged.

Miss de Witte glanced at her. 'She told you

251

what happened, didn't she? I suppose she portrayed me as a seductress, stealing her husband's affections away.'

'Er . . .' Lucy began, not sure how to reply.

'Of course she did. I'm guessing, though, that she didn't tell you that she'd cuckolded him first.'

Lucy cocked her head. 'Is that so?' Sometimes she felt hard-pressed to think of any marriage that had not been betrayed on some level.

'The Hare and Pony Inn is just ahead,' Duncan said, pointing at the stone structure with the painted sign of a rabbit riding a horse above the door. 'Shall we go in? See if the scholars are there?'

As soon as they walked in, they saw a number of scholars playing cards, another softly playing a lute. Lucy recognized the scholars she'd met at the Wallaces' home, including Mr Newman.

'Do you see him?' Lucy whispered. She took care not to identify the man directly, so that Miss de Witte would do so herself.

Yet Miss de Witte had already spied him. 'That's him,' she exclaimed, clutching Lucy's arm, pointing to the man known as Mr Newman. 'That's Philip Emerson. I'd recognize him anywhere.'

'All right,' Duncan said, his old soldierly side taking over. 'Let's not act too hastily—'

'What are you waiting for?' Miss de Witte hissed at him.

'I just need to get a little closer. Be patient—'

Before he could finish his sentence, however, Miss de Witte violently shoved Lucy to the ground.

'Murderer!' she screamed, and before anyone could stop her, she withdrew a knife from her skirts and lunged towards Mr Newman.

Duncan made a grab for her but missed, and Miss de Witte flung herself forward, driving the knife into Mr Newman's shoulder. 'Kill my brother? I'll kill you!'

Then, while everyone stood frozen as statues, Mr Newman pulled out his own knife and plunged it into Miss de Witte's gut, the wrenching movement making a sickening sound.

Then, in unison, both clutched their wounds, Miss de Witte slumping to the floor while Mr Newman began to stagger off. Screams and shouts filled the room as confusion abounded.

'Murderer!' people began to scream, although no one seemed quite sure where to point their finger or how to fathom what was happening.

Lucy crawled over to Miss de Witte. 'Don't let that scoundrel get away again,' the woman pleaded, reaching her hand out. 'If he lives, he must hang.'

Half turning, Lucy could see Mr Newman stumbling towards the tavern door, about to take flight. Before he could escape, Duncan had lunged forward, pinning the scholar's hands behind his back and wrestling him to the floor.

Seeing that blood was starting to seep through Miss de Witte's dress, Lucy caught the hand of a serving maid who was bending over them anxiously. 'Give me your apron,' she said. Without a word of protest, the young woman untied it and handed it to her. Lucy pressed the material against Miss de Witte's stomach, trying helplessly to staunch the flow of blood. The injury looked fearful.

'Why in heaven's name did you stab him?' Lucy asked Miss de Witte, who had started to tremble. 'The constable was here to arrest him!'

'I don't know. I suppose a rage came over me at the sight of him,' Miss de Witte whispered, blood trickling from her mouth.

Lucy frowned. 'How is that so? You brought that knife with you. You must have planned this.'

'He deserved what he got,' Miss de Witte whispered, her face flushed. Then her eyes rolled back and she passed out.

'We must get them to Doctor Larimer's surgery straight away,' Duncan cried. He pointed at a bald man dressed in labourer's clothes, who, like everyone else, was looking stunned. 'You there! Call for a cart!'

Hearing the authority in the constable's voice, the man hopped to do his bidding, and within moments two carts had arrived. Both Miss de Witte and Mr Newman were loaded into the carts, and they quickly headed to Dr Larimer's, Lucy whispering a small prayer that they would survive.

Twenty-Three

The mile-long journey to the physician's surgery was as swift as it could be. Duncan led the curious procession, brandishing his stick, Mr Newman's cart directly behind him, followed by two men pushing a handcart containing Miss de Witte's supine body, Lucy at her side.

'Clear the way! Clear the way!' Duncan called out, so that the other carts and people would step aside. 'Official business!'

Well-wishers and gawkers alike walked along either side of the cart, helping push people out of the way and ensuring that none of the cart-wheels got stuck in the muddy, cluttered paths. Lucy kept an anxious watch over Miss de Witte as they moved to the physician's, trying to keep her wound covered and making sure she was still breathing. Some kind soul had even handed her a blanket, which after being placed over the woman's lying form had grown blood-soaked in moments. Mercifully, she had not revived, as the pain was surely unbearable.

When the entourage arrived at Dr Larimer's, there was a quick flurry as the constable rapped at the door with his stick and members of the crowd began to bang on the shutters. 'Summon the doctor!' one loud-mouthed man called. 'Come out! Come out!' others clamoured.

Mrs Hotchkiss, the housekeeper, threw open

the door. 'Lucy!' she exclaimed, taking in the crowd with uneasy eyes. 'Explain what all this shouting is about!'

The constable touched his hat and indicated the two bodies in the carts, both starting to moan as they revived. 'Stabbings. Bring the physicians, quick.'

Mrs Hotchkiss, used to patients arriving at their door in all forms of distress, just gave a tight nod. 'Follow me,' she said, and Duncan and another man wheeled the two injured souls towards the surgeries.

Lucy turned back to the crowd of people who were still gaping in fascination. Spying one of Dr Larimer's servants crouching against the wall, holding a barrel of water in each hand, she called to him. 'Tom! I need you.'

'What happened there, miss?' he asked, looking a bit green. 'That woman – there was a lot of blood.'

'Tom, please. I need you to send a message to Master Aubrey and tell him I'm here. Do you remember where his shop is on Fleet Street?' She pulled a penny from her pocket. 'Be quick about it, and I'll give you a second one when you return?'

'The water is for washing them,' he said, holding the barrels to Lucy.

'I will bring it in directly,' she said, accepting both barrels. 'I will also let Mrs Hotchkiss know where you are.'

Following the din at the end of the corridor, Lucy walked as quickly as she could, carefully balancing the overly full barrels of water, trying to keep them from sloshing over. Duncan was nowhere to be seen. Setting one of the barrels down, she opened the first surgery door. Dr Larimer was looking grim as he bent over Miss de Witte, whose eyes were mercifully still closed, though she was moaning. Mrs Hotchkiss was cutting open her dress so that the physician could examine her wound. They looked up when she entered.

'Ah, Lucy, bring that water here. We need to clean off some of this blood,' the physician said. 'Grab those bandages, would you?'

For the next thirty minutes, Lucy followed the physician's instructions, helping Mrs Hotchkiss take care of Miss de Witte.

'Will she recover?' Lucy whispered. The woman's face had taken on a deathly pallor as if almost all of her lifeblood had drained from her body.

Dr Larimer grimaced. 'We'll know soon enough. She has certainly lost a lot of blood, but I do not believe any of her organs were injured. If she makes it through the next few hours, her chances of recovery will improve greatly, unless her body becomes polluted by infection.' He shook his head. 'There may be little we can do if such a thing comes to pass.'

'What about the other man?' Lucy asked. 'Do you know how he fares?'

'Mr Newman will probably be all right. Doctor Sheridan is looking after him.'

'I should tell you that this man, Mr Newman, has just been identified as Philip Emerson. He is a murderer. Miss de Witte, your patient, is the one who identified him.'

'Yes, Constable Duncan informed me of that fact and is, I believe, guarding him now.' Turning back towards his housekeeper, he said, 'Mrs Hotchkiss, please watch over Miss de Witte until I return. I wish to check on our other patient.'

Since it did not look as if Miss de Witte would awaken any time soon, Lucy followed the physician out of the room and slumped into a chair in the long corridor. Dr Larimer disappeared into the other surgery to check on Mr Emerson. Her thoughts whirled as she began to think over everything that had happened earlier at the tavern. What was it that Miss de Witte had said? *I suppose a rage came over me at the sight of him.* Except, that didn't explain why she had brought along a knife.

'Had she even wanted Duncan to arrest Mr Emerson?' Lucy whispered to herself, tapping her fingers on her leg. It was then that she noticed she had blood on her skirts. She took out her handkerchief to scrub it away. 'Or had she planned to kill him the whole time?'

Lucy closed her eyes, trying to shake off the sickly image of Miss de Witte and Mr Emerson slicing into each other with their knives. Once again, she wondered why Miss de Witte had brought the knife along. What about Mr Emerson? 'Does he always carry a knife with him, even though he has been trying to pass himself off as a scholar?' she asked herself. 'Perhaps, as a criminal who has murdered two people and taken on

258

a different identity, he might always carry a weapon.'

Dr Larimer's front door opened then, and Adam appeared in the doorway, panting from exertion. The boy Tom was at his side, rosy-cheeked and sweaty.

'Lucy!' Adam called, his eyes dropping to the blood-stained handkerchief tucked in her fist. 'How do you fare?'

'I am well,' she replied. 'Though it was a sickening business to be sure. Mr Emerson and Miss de Witte stabbed one another!'

'I heard! I was at Master Aubrey's when he received your message from Tom here,' Adam explained, nodding at the servant who was still hovering nearby. After tossing Tom a coin, he drew a chair next to hers. 'What is the news?'

'Miss de Witte was stabbed in her stomach but apparently all vital organs were missed. Mr Newman was stabbed in his shoulder. His is the less serious injury.'

'How in the world did this happen? How did you come to be there?' He leaned towards her. 'Please, Lucy, explain from the beginning. Help me understand what transpired.'

Being in Adam's presence strengthened Lucy. Taking a deep breath, she quickly filled him in on how they had discovered Mr Newman's true identity, and why they'd been at the Hare and Pony with Miss de Witte.

Adam ran his hand through his dark hair. 'They stabbed each other? How fantastical.' At her shudder, his gaze grew concerned. 'I'm so sorry you had to witness that sight.'

'Will Miss de Witte be arrested for attempted murder, then?' she asked. 'If she survives?'

'That seems likely, yes. Have you learned anything more about her involvement in Paul Corbyn's death?'

Lucy shook her head. 'No. Duncan didn't ask her about it. I assume that he didn't want to scare her off before she'd first confirmed that Mr Newman was indeed Philip Emerson. Once we arrived at the tavern, everything happened so quickly. She is still unconscious, I am afraid.'

Duncan came out then, catching the end of their conversation. 'Ah, Mr Hargrave. You're here.' He seemed tired. 'I agree, we should question Miss de Witte as soon as we can. None of this happened the way I expected when I asked her to identify Mr Emerson.'

'I'll never forget the manner in which she stabbed him with that knife,' Lucy said, swallowing down the bile that suddenly threatened to cause her to gag. 'Her fury was something to behold.' She paused. 'Duncan, were you surprised that she brought that knife along? She claimed she'd attacked him after being overwhelmed by rage, but this makes it seem as if she planned to do it ahead of time.'

Adam whistled. 'That seems deliberate.'

'I think so, too,' Duncan agreed.

Dr Larimer stepped out then. 'I'll try to revive Miss de Witte in a few hours, if she does not wake up on her own. Lucy, perhaps you could tend to her so that Mrs Hotchkiss can return to her duties.'

'Let us first speak with Mr Emerson,' Adam

said. 'I should very much like to hear what he has to say.'

Dr Sheridan straightened up when they walked into the room, having just completed wrapping a bandage around Mr Emerson's shoulder wound. 'I've given Mr Newman here—'

'That's not his name,' Duncan interrupted, giving the man a hard look.

'I've given *this man* some medicine to soothe the pain, but he needs to rest.' He shook his finger at Lucy when he said the last, and then turned to Duncan. 'Just a few questions, Constable.'

'Constable? Constable! You need to lock up that wretched woman who stabbed me!' Mr Emerson shouted, before pointing at his arm. 'I'm a musician and tutor to several fine families. Just look what she did to me! I was just defending myself from her attack!'

'Of course,' Duncan said, giving the man a stern look. 'First, I have several questions for you.'

'Go ahead,' Emerson replied.

'How long have you been passing yourself off as the scholar "Mr Newman"?' Duncan's tone was flat, brooking no nonsense. Dr Sheridan clucked his tongue as he exited the room.

'Er, uh, what?' Mr Emerson asked, starting to sputter. His indignation seemed manufactured, weak. 'I don't know what you mean—'

'There's no point in denying it. We know that your real name is Philip Emerson. We know that you murdered Hammett de Witte and Ellie Browning. We *also* know that you fled from

261

Newgate Prison when the Great Fire broke out, and that at some point you took on a new identity of "Mr Newman, tutor".'

'That's not so,' Mr Emerson whispered, although his denial fell flat.

'New-man – fairly obvious, is it not?' Lucy smiled at him sweetly.

'It's no matter now. You've already been identified as Philip Emerson by a witness.' Duncan shook his head. 'It will be simple enough to have someone confirm your identity, so you might as well surrender. Face your punishment.'

Emerson slumped back in the bed, looking resigned but still sullen. 'I have nothing more to say.'

'I can make sure your hanging is quick and merciful, or it can be prolonged and torturous,' Duncan said. Lucy looked at him, startled. She'd never heard him sound so harsh before. His words had the intended effect.

'That woman tried to kill me!' Mr Emerson protested. 'I want to see her hanged alongside me.'

'It truly matters not a whit what that woman has done to you. Besides,' Duncan said, 'she's more likely to die from her wounds than you. Only time will tell.'

Lucy stared at Mr Emerson, not feeling particularly sympathetic towards the murderer. 'Why did you have that knife with you anyway? If you were trying to pass yourself off as a scholar, surely such a thing would raise questions.'

'I don't always carry a knife. But I knew she was going to kill me. I had to protect myself, did I not?'

'What do you mean?' Lucy asked. Something about the man's indignant fervour was surprising. 'Why did you think she was going to kill you? Did you recognize her?'

Emerson grimaced. 'I received a message telling me so, that's why. However, I'm afraid you'll have to take me at my word on this point.'

'A message? Whatever do you mean?'

Grimacing, the man reached into his pocket and held out a blood-stained paper to Lucy, who accepted it gingerly. Adam and Duncan crowded around her, craning their heads over her shoulders. Inside, there was a familiar cipher, containing a single line of carefully printed text.

C B UG OJBHO PJ DB✢ YJR IJM P△T GRMSTMTM YJR UMT

'It's a C cipher!' Lucy exclaimed. 'What does it say?'

Mr Emerson stared at her. 'You know it's a C cipher?'

'Yes. Tell us what it says,' Duncan replied. 'Mind you, we have a key and will decipher it for ourselves later. So, there's no point in lying to us.'

Mr Emerson looked defeated. '"I'm going to kill you for the murderer you are."'

'"I'm going to kill you for the murderer you are,"' Lucy repeated softly, exchanging a quick glance with the others. Why would Miss de Witte have warned him in such a fashion?

'Tell us more about this message. Who sent it to you? When did you get it?' Duncan asked.

'A boy stopped by the tavern around ten o'clock this morning, asking for me by name. He ran off before I could find out who had paid him to deliver it. When I saw the cipher, I was dumbfounded. I had not seen such a thing in more than a year – since Ellie Browning had brought the wretched thing to me, pleading with me to decipher Hammett's message, as it was beyond her capability to discern.' He clenched his fist when he said their names.

'How were you able to decipher it?' Lucy asked. 'Surely you were no longer in possession of the key?'

Mr Emerson scowled. 'You noted yourself it was a C cipher. After a bit of thinking, I was able to recreate the cipher fairly well because I remembered how it worked. That the A column began with *QUAESTIO* and was followed by the rest of the alphabet and a handful of symbols. I remembered that the C column simply removed the Q from *QUAESTIO* and the rest of the same, and ended with a Q. It was not so difficult to decipher.' He straightened up. 'I did not know if it was written as some sort of odd jest, but I kept a knife on me, which now I'm glad that I did. That woman, my murderess—'

'Miss de Witte,' Duncan supplied. 'Hammett de Witte's sister. I imagine you recognized her.'

'Only as she bore down on me, knife in hand, did I realize. It all happened so quickly, and I only remembered her from the trial.' He gave them a wry humourless smile. 'I suppose I understand why she wants to kill me.'

'She's been planning to kill you for some time,

264

it seems,' Duncan said. 'She's been pursuing you, and she worked with two accomplices to determine your whereabouts.'

'Accomplices?'

'Dev and Pike Browning, the innkeepers at the Two Doves Inn. Ellie's older brothers. She even enjoined them to commit murder in this dogged pursuit of you.'

'I wasn't aware that Miss de Witte and the Brownings even knew each other. Hardly the same social *milieu*, one would think.'

'Murder tends to arrange for strange bedfellows,' Adam said drily.

'They tracked down Jack Campbell, the Newgate guard who freed you during the Great Fire, and hanged him,' Duncan said. 'Perhaps he gave up your whereabouts before he died. He'd taken a new identity this past year – that of Paul Corbyn, mercer. Perhaps he was aware of your identity as well.'

'I see. Why hang Jack Campbell?'

'As far as we understand, to help atone for the sin of setting you free – you, the murderer of their sister,' Duncan replied. 'He was your accomplice, in their mind, and, as such, deserved to die. They hanged him, as they wanted you to hang.'

Emerson sucked in his breath. 'Can't say I'm all that surprised. Their love for their sister was deeply possessive.'

'You managed to ingratiate yourself with the Wallaces,' Adam commented, changing the subject. 'How did that come about?'

Emerson frowned. 'I was with the other scholars

265

at the Hare and Pony. I could not hide my scholarly self. They discovered me reading some pieces of music theory one day and invited me along. They were good enough companions, and I was pleased to indulge in some spirits, particularly if I did not have to pay. I did not know the Wallaces very well, so I do not believe *ingratiate* is quite the right word.'

'Had you known that Miss de Witte developed the cipher to converse in secret with Professor Wallace?' Lucy asked.

'I didn't know anything about that,' Mr Emerson replied. 'This matters not one whit to me.'

Another thought occurred to Lucy. 'That night, when I stopped by the Wallaces' household with the tracts, you heard me talking about the innkeepers at the Two Doves Inn in Hoddesdon,' Lucy said slowly. 'Are you the one who came after me? I thought at the time it was Dev or Pike, but now I wonder . . .' A sinking feeling stole over her, as she thought about having been at the mercy of a murderer.

Emerson shrugged. 'I had to deter you from your search.' At his words, both Duncan and Adam tensed up. 'I left you unharmed, did I not?'

Lucy suppressed a shiver, remembering his harsh words in her ear, and turned away.

'That will do,' Duncan replied. 'I'll just tie you down. Make sure you don't go anywhere.' Deftly, he tied the man to the bed frame, being careful of his bandaged shoulder. He then pulled back the blankets and tightly bound the man's feet to the post at the end of the bed.

Emerson turned to the wall. 'I have nothing

266

more to say.' His voice sounded strained. 'Indeed, I'd like to be alone to ponder my visit to the Tyburn Tree.'

When the three stepped out into the hall, for a moment they all looked at each other. 'Very perplexing,' Adam said.

'Vexing, too,' Duncan added.

'*I'm going to kill you for the murderer you are,*' Lucy said, frowning. 'Was the message from Miss de Witte? How could that be? We were with her, were we not? There was no time to have sent the message.'

Adam frowned. 'Also, why attack him outright then, when she knew Duncan was there to bring him back to jail? Something seems amiss here.'

'We need to speak to her more, and soon,' Lucy said. 'I shall tend to her now, to be there should she wake.'

Twenty-Four

For the next two hours, Lucy sat beside Miss de Witte, watching her chest rise and fall, waiting for her to revive. She was lying back in the bed, her head propped up by two pillows. Her long blonde hair had been loosened from its bun and now spilled out from a white knitted cap. Unlike Mr Emerson, she did not appear to have any of her limbs tied. Probably not necessary when she was so deep in her deathly slumbers. Dr Larimer was seated beside her on another chair, writing his observations of her appearance in a little book.

'Please revive her if you would, Doctor Larimer,' Duncan said, as he and Adam entered the room together. Lucy looked up sharply, wondering what they had been discussing for so long. 'I still have some questions for Miss de Witte. We cannot delay this inquiry much longer, particularly if she is to pass through death's tunnel.'

Dr Larimer nodded. 'This is against my medical advice, but for the sake of the law I shall abide by your request.' After Lucy moved away to give him some room, she watched the physician place something under Miss de Witte's nose.

A few seconds later, her eyes opened, full of confusion and pain. 'What is happening? Where am I?' she murmured, tears streaming down her cheeks.

'Drink this,' the physician said, holding a cup to her lips. 'Slowly.'

They all watched her gulp down the wormwood tea, which would soon work its magicked solace upon her pain-ridden body. After a moment she calmed down, and stared up at the ceiling, ignoring or unaware of their presence in the room. As she sighed, it appeared the pain was passing away, at least for a short while. She still kept tight hold of the grey blanket that was spread over her body.

Dr Larimer touched her forehead and cheeks, and then turned towards Duncan. 'Not too long,' he warned. 'Her condition is serious. She needs to rest in order to live.' As he exited the room, he whispered to Lucy, 'Find out if she has any family members, would you? I'll be right outside if she needs me.'

At his voice, Miss de Witte rolled her head languidly in their direction. She seemed surprised to see the figures in the room, squinting a bit in the dim light.

'Lucy? Is that you?' she asked. 'Pray, sit by me. Tell me what has happened.'

At Duncan's nod, Lucy sat down in the chair by the bed. He and Adam hung back so as to not overcrowd her. 'Do you remember being stabbed by Mr Emerson?' she asked gently.

Miss de Witte's eyes widened in fear and remembrance. 'Oh, yes, it was terrible.' She gripped her stomach. 'Am I going to die?'

Lucy patted her hand. 'Doctor Larimer is the

best physician in London. He has been tending to you. He believes that none of your organs were injured in the attack.'

'What of *him*?' she asked through clenched teeth. 'Will that bastard live?'

'The wound he sustained from you is more of an inconvenience than a death blow, unless it should grow infected. Regardless, his life is not for long. Justice will be meted out, and his original sentence will be served. I promise you that,' Duncan said. 'Now, I should like to ask you a few questions.'

Her eyes flicked towards Adam. 'Who are you?'

'Adam Hargrave,' he replied simply. 'The constable asked me to be here.'

Miss de Witte made a futile gesture, clearly resigned as she looked back at Duncan. 'You said you have more questions for me?'

'What do you know about the death of Paul Corbyn?' Duncan asked.

She blinked. Clearly, this was not the question she was expecting. 'Who? I don't know anyone by that name.'

Is she putting on an act? Lucy wondered.

'He was a mercer of pots and pans,' Duncan replied.

'Never met him,' she said, more impatiently. 'Why are you asking me about him?'

'Perhaps you remember him by his true name. Jack Campbell. He was a guard at Newgate Prison before the Great Fire.'

This time there was more of a response, as a pained expression crossed her face. 'Jack Campbell? Was he the one who—'

'The one who set your brother's murderer free, instead of letting justice be served? Yes, that guard.' Then, driving the knife in deeper as Miss de Witte's breath grew more ragged, Duncan continued. 'Not only did Mr Campbell take on a new identity after the Great Fire as a wealthy mercer of pots and pans, but he allowed Philip Emerson to take on a new identity as well. Indeed, he allowed Emerson to live carefree in the world.' His eyes narrowed. 'Imagine! You wouldn't have been stabbed today if Mr Campbell had not set that murderer free.'

'How did Jack Campbell die?' Miss de Witte whispered, still clutching her abdomen. Her face had grown paler and she seemed startled by the news. Was she such a good actress?

'A few days ago, he was found hanging at a crossroads on the way to St Giles-in-the-Fields.'

They all watched her closely as she leaned back against the pillow. 'Found hanging at a crossroads? Self-murder to be certain. His guilt over what he did must have got to him. May he suffer long for his sins. I shall not pray for his soul.' She bit her lip. 'Why are you asking me about his death?'

'The physicians believe that he was murdered,' Duncan said.

'Is that so? Serves him right.'

'Why do you say that?' Lucy asked.

'That man freed my brother's murderer, with nary a qualm, rather than letting that devil hang for the crime as the law of the land decreed. Justice has not been served.'

271

'Has it been served now?' Adam asked.

'I'm not sorry he's dead. I'm not going to hide my anger at that man, nor will I hide my joy in learning of his fate. His soul will find no mercy from me.' She swallowed painfully.

Lucy poured a cup of light ale from the pitcher on a small table and held it to the woman's lips.

Strength returning to her voice, Miss de Witte asked, 'Who killed him? Why are you asking me about his death? Why would you think I'd know anything about it?'

'We have reason to believe that Mr Campbell – or Mr Corbyn, as he came to be known – may have been killed by Dev and Pike Browning, the elder brothers of Eleanor, your brother's lady love,' Duncan replied. Then, more gently, he added, 'I believe you know them?'

'What? No, I don't know them. I mean, I saw them at the trial, of course, but I was hardly in a place to converse pleasantly with others. Particularly not with *innkeepers*.'

'I understand. Perhaps when you came to the Two Doves Inn,' Duncan said. 'They claim to have met you there.'

'Met me at the Two Doves Inn? How curious,' she said. 'I recall travelling to Hoddesdon shortly after the tragedy happened. I suppose I wanted to see where my dear brother drew his last breath.' Tears began to slip down her cheeks. 'The serving maid showed me where the horrific deed had transpired. The blood had hardly been scrubbed away. I laid my body down upon that bloodstain, weeping and cursing the devil who murdered them.'

'Did you speak with the brothers then?' Lucy asked, tucking a small towel into Miss de Witte's fist.

Miss de Witte dabbed at her eyes and nose. 'I suppose I did. I think the serving maid summoned the innkeepers and I believe they took me around to the back of the inn. We wept together there.' She blinked. 'They swore revenge. I just wanted Philip to hang. My brother and their Ellie deserved that bit of justice provided on this earth. We drank a few pints and then they sent me home in a carriage. That was all.'

'Other than that visit, did you meet with either Dev or Pike Browning again?' Adam asked.

'Naturally, I saw them at Philip's trial. We were all there when he was condemned to hang, like the vile scoundrel he was. However, I did not speak to either again. Why would I? Did they say I did?'

'Did you otherwise communicate with them? Through letters, perhaps?'

Unexpectedly, Miss de Witte's eyes filled with tears. 'I've had no dealings with any of these men you've mentioned since I left that trial. Those days were among the worst of my life, and now this horror has been dredged up for me again. I do not thank you for this.'

Duncan seemed to be considering her tearful outburst. 'They claim that you've sent them messages.'

'What? That's a malicious lie! A complete and utter falsehood!'

'They said the messages were written in the cipher that you created,' Lucy said, watching

273

Miss de Witte's eyes grow wide. 'The same cipher that your brother used at first to communicate with Ellie.'

'What? That cipher was never meant for . . . anyone else!' she exclaimed, flushing. 'I showed it to Hammett because I thought he might enjoy the novelty. It was meant to be private!' She pressed her fingers against her forehead. 'I don't understand. They say I sent them messages? What did the messages say?'

From memory, Lucy recited the message that had been found on Mr Corbyn's corpse. '*This is the man who set the Devil free. Make him lead us to the Devil. Hang the necklace from the Devil's neck. Punish him for his deed. Send him to the gallows.*'

'Anyone could have written that message!' Miss de Witte exclaimed. 'You already said that Hammett used it to send Ellie messages. Someone must have helped the poor girl decipher the messages, don't you think? Is that how the Brownings used it?'

'Yes, that's so,' Duncan agreed. 'However, who else but you would care about killing Mr Corbyn?'

'You said he let a few prisoners go free! Maybe the family of another victim did it?'

'The other prisoners were rounded up soon afterwards and duly executed at the next public hangings. Only Philip Emerson has kept himself at bay.'

Duncan said. 'Besides, how would they know your special cipher and why would they send it to the Brownings?'

'I don't know. I'm so tired.' Miss de Witte's voice began to fade. 'The messages were only meant for Neville. It's been so long since he wrote to me. Until—' Before she could finish the thought, her head began to sink back and her eyes began to flutter.

Dr Larimer stepped back into the room. 'That's all for now. I'll let you know when she wakes up if you still have questions for her later.'

'How odd that she claims not to have known Dev and Pike,' Lucy said, pacing about Dr Larimer's study. They had adjourned there to discuss what Miss de Witte had just conveyed to them. Duncan leaned against one of the walls, while Adam perched on the edge of Dr Larimer's table. 'That she'd only been to the Two Doves Inn once after the murders occurred,' Lucy continued. 'That she didn't remember talking to them at the trial. How striking, too, that she denied exchanging messages with them, when they so fervently agreed that she had.'

'She may well have been lying about that,' Duncan replied.

'Or *they* were,' Lucy replied. Duncan bowed his head, acknowledging her point.

'She was certainly angry enough to have killed Emerson, there is no doubt about that,' Adam added. 'She referred to him several times as "devil", which was similar to how he was referred to in the message found on Corbyn's body.'

'She seemed genuinely distressed by the idea that her cipher had been used by others,' Lucy said, remembering how upset the woman had

275

seemed. 'It seems surprising she would use it to communicate with the Brownings.'

'We are clearly dealing with a very shrewd and brilliant woman,' Adam said. 'I think that we have to weigh all of her statements as possible truths and possible lies.'

'How can we ever get at the truth, then?' Lucy asked, feeling disheartened. Something was still nagging at her. She still felt as if they were forgetting or missing something. What was it? It was really bothering her. 'Wait a minute!' she cried, snapping her fingers. 'Didn't Miss de Witte get a message, too? Just this morning.' She looked at Duncan. 'You were there. She put it in her pocket.'

'Yes, that is so,' he replied. 'It may be worthwhile looking at it.'

'Doctor Larimer usually stores patient effects over there,' Lucy said, pointing at the desk. 'I imagine he would have stored Miss de Witte's pocket there for safe keeping.'

Sure enough, when she opened the drawer, Miss de Witte's embroidered pocket was at the top. She handed it to Duncan. 'I'll let you look.'

Untying the strings, the constable looked inside and withdrew a small folded message. For a moment he stared at it. 'You won't believe it.' He held it up, the single line of cipher easy to see.

A VOUN FQG VQDCM TLZ VOH MOPDE US OQGSE

'Another cipher? Who would have sent it to her? The Brownings are still in jail,' Duncan said.

'Unless she sent it to herself.' He gave a half-snort, but Adam looked thoughtful.

'She smiled when she received it,' Lucy said, thinking back a few hours ago. 'Indeed, I recall thinking that she seemed delighted.'

'Yes, I agree,' Duncan replied. 'I remember having the same thought,'

'A smile like that – the message was written by someone she knows.' She continued to examine the folded-up missive. 'It uses an A cipher. It's not very long. I can work it out without needing to run home to get the key.' Without waiting for either man to respond, she seated herself at Dr Larimer's desk and pulled over a piece of paper and uncorked a bottle of ink. Quickly, she wrote the alphabet vertically down one end of the paper.

'Let's see, how does it start?' She looked up at Adam. 'What's that Latin word for question again?'

'*Quaestio,*' Adam replied. Then after she paused, he spelled it out for her. They watched as she wrote down each letter in a long vertical column, and then added the remaining unused letters of the alphabet below. Biting her lip in concentration, she began to work it out. Within a few minutes she was staring at it in awe. 'Another riddle!' She held it out to them. '*What man walks free who should be hanged?*'

'Clearly, the answer to that riddle was Philip Emerson,' Adam replied. 'This is very odd indeed.'

'It seemed very much like the riddles exchanged between Professor Wallace and Miss de Witte,' Lucy mused. 'I wonder if it might be the same hand. As we both noted, she seemed pleased to get this message. I think she did recognize the sender.'

'You're suggesting that Neville Wallace sent this message to Miss de Witte?' Adam asked. 'Why would he send her a riddle of this nature?'

'He knew of her quest to kill her brother's murderer,' Duncan surmised. 'He was reminding her of her conviction. Perhaps he overheard Lucy speaking with his wife. Or perhaps Mrs Wallace informed him of their discussion. Either way, it is not hard to see that he might have learned of the morning plan to have Miss de Witte identify Mr Emerson. Perhaps he even partnered with Miss de Witte to kill Emerson in the first place.'

Lucy rubbed her brow. 'Why would he do that?'

'Love? Obligation? A sense of duty? Who knows? Think about it,' Duncan said. 'Miss de Witte *did* seem genuinely surprised to hear about the coded letters that the innkeepers swore she'd exchanged with them. Perhaps he was the one who sent the message to Pike and Dev, to direct them through the plan, not Miss de Witte.'

'You've known Professor Wallace for some time,' Lucy said, turning back to Adam. 'Does he have such a calculating nature?'

Adam considered her question. 'Certainly, Father and I have known Professor Wallace for a few years, and his reputation as a mathematician has not been surpassed. Still, Father would also be the first to say that even the most affable and educated demeanour can mask the hardest and most murderous of hearts. You've known that to be true as well, Lucy.'

'That is so. However, why send the message to Philip Emerson? Why warn him that Miss de Witte was on to him? Would Professor Wallace have wanted Miss de Witte to be killed?'

'I cannot see why,' Adam mused. 'Still it cannot be a coincidence that both Philip Emerson and Miss de Witte received such messages on the same morning. It's almost as if someone wanted them to act violently towards each other. That's a riddle in itself.' He straightened his back. 'We must cease this speculation. Let us speak with Professor Wallace. Get to the bottom of this peculiar thing.'

Duncan nodded. 'Let me just speak with Hank. Have him maintain a keen eye on Mr Emerson. We must not allow him to flee again.'

Twenty-Five

The Wallace household was quieter than it had been on Lucy's last few visits. This time when they were led into the drawing room by the servant, she found Professor and Mrs Wallace seated on chairs at either end of the long room. Mrs Wallace was seated before a large embroidery frame, while Professor Wallace had a small book in his lap. The brocade curtains were still open, revealing a bleak overcast sky that matched the dark mood of the room. Without the laughter and animated voices of the scholars, and without the steady flow of wine, the room had little of the crackling vitality she'd witnessed before, and now simply seemed devoid of any energy or life at all.

Mrs Wallace rose when they were announced, while Professor Wallace set his book aside with a sigh. 'Three visits in three days, Lucy?' He walked over and shook both men's hands. 'What brings you here? I must say, Lucy, I'm a bit relieved that you do not have your pack. While I do view myself as a scholar of high intellect, you have provided me with several weeks of thought to digest, and I would be quite ashamed to say that I cannot keep up.'

Lucy smiled slightly. 'That is not why we are here, Professor Wallace.'

'Ah, more questions about ciphers? Find a new message, did you?'

'What makes you say that?' Duncan asked, stepping forward slightly.

At the constable's soldierly bearing, Professor Wallace stepped back and his grin faded. 'N–no reason,' he stammered. 'I just thought, given Mr Hargrave and Lucy's interest, they might have more questions. Similar to what they asked me before.'

'Pray, tell what has happened?' Mrs Wallace asked, twisting her fingers in her skirts. 'I can see on your faces that there is something serious to discuss.'

'We should like to speak to your husband for a moment,' Duncan said.

'Oh, they must be here about our guest Roland Newman, dear,' Mrs Wallace said, leaving her embroidery frame to come and sit beside him. 'Did you see him at the Hare and Pony? Was Miss de Witte able to identify him?'

'Yes,' Lucy said, glancing at Duncan. She didn't want to say too much. 'She did. She was able to confirm that Mr Emerson had been passing himself off as the scholar Roland Newman.'

'Newman,' Professor Wallace scoffed. 'Not a lot of imagination with that name, eh? How do you think he came up with it? "I'm planning to create a new identity for myself, so I won't be hanged for murder, and the best name I can come up with is 'New-man'." I thought he was a more original thinker than that.' He looked disgusted. 'Just shows how willing to mock and trick us that man was.' He wiped his brow. 'My God! I've even recommended him for his grasp of musical theory to some of the finer families in town. I've spoken his praises, detailing his disciplined mind and form. What a blow to my reputation this shall be.'

'Such treacherous behaviour indeed,' Mrs Wallace said, her face growing flushed. 'He's made a mockery of us! I still cannot believe that we invited that murderer into our home. Such indignations should not be suffered!'

'Is he back in jail, then, Constable?' Professor Wallace asked. 'I imagine he'll be hanged soon – is that not so?'

'He is under guard, although he is currently being treated by Doctor Larimer. Miss de Witte, too, although her condition is far more serious and it is not certain if she will survive,' Duncan replied.

'Good heavens!' Mrs Wallace exclaimed. 'What on earth happened?'

At Duncan's nod, Lucy quickly recounted all that had occurred earlier that day. The Wallaces listened intently, occasionally making shocked sounds and emitting soft gasps. Only when Lucy described how the two had stabbed each other did Mrs Wallace clutch her chest. 'You must be jesting!'

'I'm afraid I am not,' Lucy replied, before continuing her story. Professor Wallace, she noticed, kept his face buried in his hands.

When she finally stopped relating the outlandish events, Mrs Wallace put her hand on Lucy's. 'What a strange ordeal,' she said, patting her hand. 'I'm so relieved that you were not injured in any way.'

'Thank you,' Lucy replied. When she glanced

at Professor Wallace, she could see he was trembling. 'Sir, are you unwell? Shall I have the servant fetch some ale? Or perhaps some sherry?'

Mrs Wallace stared at her husband and gave a brittle laugh. 'You seem upset, dear,' she said.

'The idea that we invited that murderer into our home. Bestowed upon him our hospitality, provided him with drink and victuals and good company. To have been the scurrilous ruffian who murdered the brother of a dear acquaintance! Such an indignity shall not be easily borne, nor forgotten.'

'You're claiming that you did not know Mr Newman's true identity?' Duncan asked, his earlier friendliness slipping away.

Professor Wallace gulped. 'Of course not!'

'You never saw him when he was still Emerson?' Adam asked. 'You did not attend his trial?'

There was a clear change in the room. Professor Wallace looked decidedly uneasy. 'No, I don't recall doing so.'

Mrs Wallace darted him a quick look before casting her eyes down. 'I believe you did go to the trial, Neville.' she said quietly. 'How could you not recall? I remember perfectly. Miss de Witte, your *pupil*, needed someone she could rely on, as she had no other relative or friend who might dispatch such a duty. Of course, I know no one took such care with her as you.'

Professor Wallace coughed. 'I suppose, yes, I was there.' The red spread painfully across his cheeks, coming out in a chequered pattern beneath the greying brown of his beard. 'I do

283

not remember Mr Emerson in such detail. I swear I did not recognize Mr Newman as Mr Emerson. Perhaps he changed his hair or his clothes or air!' At the continued silence, he pounded his fist on the arm of the chair. 'Damn it all! One simply would not expect to see a convicted murderer show up at one's door, speaking so elegantly on the mathematical origins of musical composition.' He rubbed his jaw with vigour. 'I know that makes me an unobservant fool, but so be it. I did not recognize him, and I'm sorry I did not. He'd not have walked free for so long, nor cause the damage that he has done, had I recognized him for who he was.'

'I see,' Adam said. 'You told us last week of the cipher that Miss de Witte created. Are you still sending her secret messages?'

'No!' he sputtered. He grasped his wife's elbow. 'Dear, you know that I am not. Such an accusation is simply unfounded.'

'Is it? Can you explain this?' Mrs Wallace opened the sideboard and removed a small silver box. Inside there were several messages. She held them out, her fingers trembling. At a glance, Lucy could see they were all written in cipher. 'Why must you continue to b–betray our marriage in this way?'

Her husband stared at them in horror. 'Where did you get those?'

'Several times now a messenger has brought me notes, thinking that I was the correct recipient.' Mrs Wallace pressed her hand to her stomach as if enduring a physical blow. 'After I intercepted the first, I came to realize that your betrayal has continued, even though I forgave you when I believed that you had broken it off.'

'What? No, that is not so! I did end it, over a year ago.'

'She's had my husband under a spell,' Mrs Wallace said, beginning to sob quietly. 'How shameful this is!' Lucy came over and grasped her hand. Mrs Wallace gave her a grateful look. 'I am not strong like you, dear Lucy,' she murmured. 'I wish I could find a livelihood of my own, instead of being at the mercy of my husband's wishes and foibles.'

'Joanna!' her husband cried, sounding half strangled. 'Truly, I erred, I did! But I have not been with Miss de Witte in so very long. I have fully restored the sanctity of our marriage.'

'Miss de Witte received a message from you this morning,' Duncan declared, watching him carefully. 'Miss Campion and I were on hand when she received it. It seems you have still been communicating with her. Your wife told Lucy of her suspicions that this may be the case.'

'What? No!'

Duncan continued, 'This suggests that you may have been aware of her interactions with Dev and Pike Browning, the innkeepers at the Two Doves Inn in Hoddesdon. Perhaps you wanted to help her in some way?'

'What? No!' Professor Wallace exclaimed. 'I never knew them! I may have seen them at the trial but I swear I never spoke with them.'

'Were you not in Hoddesdon at the Two Doves Inn with Miss de Witte?'

Tears welled up in Mrs Wallace's eyes. 'You went to an inn in Hoddesdon with her?'

'Yes, he did,' Duncan interrupted before Professor Wallace could speak. 'I was informed that a man accompanied Miss de Witte to the inn soon after her brother's murder. The description they provided clearly matched your own. Do you deny travelling with Miss de Witte to Hoddesdon?'

Professor Wallace's eyes filled with tears. 'I do n–not deny going with her,' he whispered, looking desperately at his wife. Mrs Wallace stared stonily ahead.

'I do not love her, my dear! You must understand that,' Professor Wallace pleaded.

'That may actually be the truth,' Adam commented. 'You grew tired of your involvement with Miss de Witte. You wanted to see it ended!'

'Yes! Adam, you must believe me! While I was besotted with Lucretia's mind, I did not seek a relationship with her. She would still send me messages, but I swear I stopped communicating with her.'

'I see,' Duncan said, exchanging a look with the others. 'You are no longer in love with her. The relationship with her is a burden.'

'Precisely,' Professor Wallace said. He stood up. 'If you'll excuse me, I should very much like to have a private conversation with my wife.'

'She has kept you wrapped around her finger for months!' Mrs Wallace burst out. 'I hid that from them, out of shame as well as wifely devotion. I cannot hide anything more. I heard you call that messenger around this morning. I know you sent Miss de Witte a note!'

286

'What? No!' Professor Wallace tried to deny.

The constable stood up then. 'I have heard enough. Professor Wallace, I am arresting you as an accomplice in the murder of Jack Campbell and the attempted murders of Philip Emerson and Lucretia de Witte.'

Mrs Wallace gave a small shriek and fell into a dead faint. Professor Wallace tried to lunge towards his wife before being restrained by Duncan and Adam. 'Joanna!' he cried hoarsely. 'You must believe me! None of this is true!'

'I will tend to her,' Lucy said to the other men, as she touched the recumbent woman's forehead. 'You take Professor Wallace into the jail. I will look after Mrs Wallace and make sure she is comfortable. That was a dreadful blow indeed.'

After Lucy called for a restorative, Mrs Wallace was soon sitting up again. Lucy had sent the servant away, finding her anxious puttering and cooing more distracting than soothing. 'I shall have you send for a physician, should she not improve,' Lucy promised the servant, before closing Mrs Wallace's bedchamber door.

'You've had a terrible shock,' Lucy said, trying to soothe her. 'Several of them.'

'Whatever shall I do?' Mrs Wallace cried. 'All of this is so terrible. I never wished Miss de Witte ill, you know, even though I despise how she adored and seduced my husband. Thank the heavens we have no children to see the shame that has been brought upon my marriage. Still, I will pray for Mr Emerson and Miss de Witte. Certainly, I hope they can both recover.'

Lucy nodded. She was not sure she could be so gracious in a similar situation.

'I am so very confused,' Mrs Wallace said, standing up and opening both shutters in the window. 'I need some air.' A rush of cold air swept over and Lucy breathed in deeply. The deathly stillness of the room had oppressed her more than she realized. Mrs Wallace pressed her hand to her own face, and Lucy stood beside her. 'Lucy, what is it that they think my husband did?'

'Both Miss de Witte and Mr Emerson received a cipher this morning, inciting them to injure the other,' Lucy explained. 'You said yourself you saw your husband send the message to Miss de Witte.'

'Can it be so?' Mrs Wallace put her hand to her forehead. 'Neville was entranced by her, since the day they met. I place much of the blame on Lucretia. I have no doubt that she manipulated my husband, delighted in doing so. I believe that she may well have manipulated those men who killed the Newgate guard. She's the one who has held murder in her heart this past year.' She began to weep softly then, burying her head in her hands.

Lucy touched the woman's arm. 'Mrs Wallace, did you tell your husband what we discussed last evening? About asking Miss de Witte to identify Mr Newman as Mr Emerson? Did he know she would be going to the Hare and Pony, where Mr Emerson had taken up residence?'

'Yes, I told him so,' Mrs Wallace said, slumping back. 'What does that mean?'

288

'It means your husband may have incited both Miss de Witte and Mr Emerson to murder,' Lucy replied. 'Moreover, it may not have been the first time he managed such a thing.'

'But he s–sent the note to Mr Emerson as well, knowing that he might kill her—'

'I know, it's odd.' She patted Mrs Wallace's hand. 'Perhaps it was his strange way of ending the infidelity with Miss de Witte once and for all.'

Mrs Wallace brushed away a tear. 'I have been injured but will not be so again.'

Twenty-Six

In the darkened room, Miss de Witte groaned again, and Lucy reached over to wipe her brow. She'd been at Dr Larimer's for several hours already, having offered to keep an eye on the woman in case her condition worsened during the night. Dr Sheridan had returned to his own home, and Dr Larimer was finally resting from the day's travails. *There might be an important deathbed confession as well*, Lucy had thought. It was not the first time she'd sat vigil at the bedside of someone who might be dying, and those final tragic utterances often contained secrets. Nonsense, too, but sometimes important things could be learned.

Master Aubrey had given her permission for the vigil on the promise that she would write up a whole true account of the surprising tale. Besides, they had tried to locate a relative and it seemed that Miss de Witte had no other friends or family members who could be bothered. At least Miss de Witte's servant Mavis had promised to stop by in the morning to see how her mistress was faring.

At Mrs Hotchkiss's cough, Lucy looked up from the tract she'd been writing. The housekeeper had a tray with two steaming mugs and a bowl of soup. 'The wormwood is for her, if she can take it. The soup and hot mead are for you,' Mrs Hotchkiss said. For a moment, Lucy was reminded of the bond they'd shared earlier that year, as another patient was nursed back to health.

'I hate to wake her,' Lucy whispered, staring down at the pale face gleaming in the candlelight. 'I don't know if she has indeed incited men to murder, but she was certainly pitiful today.'

'That other man killed her brother, did he not?' Mrs Hotchkiss asked, jerking her head in the direction of Mr Emerson's room.

'Yes. He should be hanged, since that was the sentence. No doubt about that.' She took a sip of the soup. 'Delicious. A new recipe?' Then, without waiting for the housekeeper to reply, she continued, 'I believe that he will be moved back to Newgate in the morning and will be executed at the next hanging. He will not stand trial again, I know that.'

The housekeeper nodded. 'Good riddance, I say.' She gestured towards the door. 'The constable came a while ago. I guess he and Hank are going to take turns watching him, since Doctor Larimer didn't want him to leave yet.' She shuddered. 'To think we have to have that murderer in our house!'

After Mrs Hotchkiss left, Lucy quickly downed the soup and mead. She began to try to write again, but waves of tiredness overwhelmed her. Laying her head down, she soon drifted off to sleep.

Lucy awoke abruptly to a sharp din. Groggily, she looked around, her head pounding and a heaviness to her body as she tried to figure out where she was.

'Where did he go?'

'The prisoner escaped!'

Where am I?

Her eyes flitted around the darkened room, trying to get a sense of what was happening. Details came back to her. Dr Larimer's house. Watching over Miss de Witte. 'Oh, that's right,' she said, a wave of nausea coming over her as she moved her head. *What was wrong with her? Had she been overcome by illness?*

The door opened then, bathing the room in light. Duncan was standing there, holding a glass lantern in each hand. 'Are you all right?' he asked, casting one of the lanterns around. The dancing shadows made Lucy feel a bit sick. 'Is Emerson in here?'

'Emerson? Why would he be here?' Lucy asked. Her thoughts seemed unusually fuzzy, and she rubbed her eyes furiously, trying to rid herself of the sleepy feeling. 'What's going on?'

'Looks as if the rat escaped,' he said, punctuating his irritation with a full-forced oath.

'What? Weren't you watching him?'

Duncan grunted, looking a bit sheepish. 'I drifted off. Not sure how that happened,' he said, clearly irritated with himself. 'When I woke up just now, he was gone! I've no idea where he is. No one has seen him.' He handed her the other lantern and gestured to the chair that Dr Larimer had been seated on earlier. 'Put that chair in front of the door, under the handle, when I leave. It'll keep the door tight.'

'Is that necessary?'

'Lucy, we don't know where Emerson is. As far as I'm concerned, he's an escaped murderer and we need to find him straight away. Please, I need you to stay here with Miss de Witte. Don't let anyone inside until you hear from me. Do you understand?' Seeing her nod, he touched his hat, pulling the door shut behind him.

Lucy sat there for a moment, trying to gather her thoughts. 'Escaped?'

Then, remembering what Duncan had told her, she dragged the chair over and propped it under the knob. *That won't hold for long if someone tries to break down the door*, she thought. She glanced at the clock. It was around nine o'clock. In her groggy state, it seemed as if the full night had passed.

'Lucy?' a small voice whispered from the bed.

When she turned around, she could see Lucretia de Witte staring out at her from under the bedclothes, her brown eyes large with fear. Her forehead was covered with sweat and her mouth was scrunched in pain as she clutched the blankets protectively to her chest.

'Oh, Miss de Witte! You're in pain! Let me help you.' She poured a bit of Dr Larimer's tonic into a spoon and held it to the woman's lips.

After obediently swallowing the spoonful of medicine, she clutched Lucy's hand. 'Did Emerson really escape?'

'It looks that way,' Lucy replied.

'I think someone helped him,' she whispered. 'I don't think he's alone.'

Lucy drew back from her. 'Why do you say that?'

'A few moments before the constable stopped in here, I heard something in the hallway. A banging sound. Voices.'

'What were they saying?'

'I'm not entirely sure. At first, I thought I was dreaming. It sounded like a woman and a man talking, arguing maybe. I think one must have been Mr Emerson.' She paused. 'I could not wake you at all.'

'I was quite tired,' Lucy said. 'Still, that is strange, as I am not usually one to sleep so heavily.' She turned her attention back to Miss de Witte. 'They were arguing? Tell me, what were they arguing about?'

Miss de Witte closed her eyes. 'He said, "You have set me free. Now let me go in the direction I please." She said, "You must accompany me somewhere first. Where the end is the beginning."'

'*Where the end is the beginning*. How odd. Did you recognize the woman's voice?'

'No, it was muffled. Then I heard a sound as if the man might have been pushed or hit, because I heard him give a little yelp of pain. Then he said, "Very well. Let us go." That was all I heard.' She made a fist. 'Who would have set that man free?'

'I don't know,' Lucy replied, pressing her hand to her forehead. The room was still spinning, and she had to push her foot hard on the floor to regain a sense of balance. *What on earth is going on?* 'A friend or relative must have caught wind he was here. Although "You must accompany me somewhere first" suggests something else.'

Grimacing, Miss de Witte pulled herself up. 'I say, Lucy. Are you quite all right?'

'To be honest, I feel a bit strange.' Her eyes fell on the cup with the mead she'd drunk earlier that evening. 'You said I was hard to rouse?' She picked up the cup and smelled it. 'Could I have been drugged in some fashion?' She thought about what Duncan had said about falling asleep as he watched over Mr Emerson. 'Maybe the constable was as well.'

After pacing about, Lucy went over to the window. She opened it up and allowed the cold air to cool her flushed cheeks and bring order to her jumbled thoughts. *Who would have helped Mr Emerson escape but force him to do something else first?* That did not sound like something a loving friend or family would do.

She breathed deeply, as a memory from earlier in the day surfaced. Mrs Wallace, standing by her drawing-room window, flushed and upset, trying to calm herself as her husband was led away by the constable, protesting his innocence. The accusations she had hurled – it was clear that she had believed her husband had been duped and manipulated by Miss de Witte.

'Mrs Wallace hated you,' she said slowly. 'She truly hated you.'

Miss de Witte flinched. 'I know,' she whispered, sounding contrite. 'It was wrong of me to go after her husband in such an unladylike fashion. I should not have pursued him as I did.' She put her hand to her forehead. 'I thought we had made

295

amends when you two came to see me that day. Certainly, I was wrong.'

'Is it because you are still committing adultery with Professor Wallace?'

'No! I swear it! It ended long ago!' she exclaimed. 'That's why I was so pleased to receive his note this morning. It made me feel – as if he still cared for me. After so many months of darkness, I was grateful to know that he still thought about me from time to time.'

Lucy shook her head. Something wasn't making sense here. Mrs Wallace was clearly mistaken about her husband's inconstancy. She thought about what Mrs Wallace had said after she'd revived from her faint. *I have been injured but will not be so again.* She began to tap her fingers on the windowsill. Something disturbing was coming to her. She shook her head, trying to piece some things together. 'Mrs Wallace knew that you were going to identify Mr Emerson to the constable,' she said. 'In fact, she was the one who suggested that we ask you to do it.'

'So?'

Lucy sat abruptly down in the chair, thoughts churning as memories overwhelmed her. 'Mrs Wallace was always the one with information and suggestions, now that I think about it. She told me everything I needed to know these past few days. She fed me knowledge like one might feed an apple to a horse,' she said, turning her gaze back to Miss de Witte. 'She gave me the cipher that you created, both the messages and the key. She was the one who told me about your brother's murder. About Hoddesdon. Every time

I didn't know what to do next, she gave me more information.' She put her hand to her forehead still trying to steady herself. 'Why would she do that? Why would she care? What were Hammett and Ellie to her?'

'Nothing,' Miss de Witte replied. 'Are you thinking that Mrs Wallace is the one who has helped Mr Emerson escape? Why would she do such a hateful thing?'

'Why would she? Except—' The thought that was coming to her was preposterous. 'If she wasn't seeking justice, what was her aim? Vengeance?'

'Vengeance?'

'Think about it. Mrs Wallace hated you for your infidelity with her husband – is that not so? Could she have deliberately sought to frame you for Paul Corbyn's murder?' Yet hearing the thought expressed out loud caused her heart to sink. 'Who would do such a thing? There has to be an easier method of revenge.' Lucy stood back up. 'We'll have to sort out the motive later. We need to find out if she is involved, and if she is, we must stop her and Mr Emerson!' She pulled the chair away from the door in a single scraping move. 'I'll be right back.'

'Duncan!' Lucy called, running into the corridor, searching for the constable. Seeing the house-keeper at the end of the corridor, her arm draped protectively around Tom, Lucy cried out to her. 'Mrs Hotchkiss! Where is the constable? Has he left?'

'He's gone, miss,' Tom replied. 'He told us to lock the doors while they go to raise the alarm.'

Lucy put her hand to her forehead, trying to think.

'This all happened because that constable fell asleep on his watch,' Mrs Hotchkiss grumbled. 'Too much mead, I don't doubt.'

'Did you taste any of this mead?' Lucy asked.

Mrs Hotchkiss smiled. 'Just a nip myself. So kind of Mrs Wallace to bring it over. Said she'd heard you'd all had a rough day, and she thought it would do you a heap of good. Help keep you warm.'

So it *was* Mrs Wallace. 'It kept us warm – and sleepy,' Lucy said. 'That's for certain. She drugged it so that we wouldn't wake up while she set Mr Emerson free.'

'W–what? The mead was drugged? Why would Mrs Wallace do such a terrible thing?' Then, without waiting for her to reply, Mrs Hotchkiss stepped close and put her hand on Lucy's brow. 'Are you all right? Shall I fetch Doctor Larimer?'

'I am fine, I think,' Lucy said, trying to shake off the heaviness she was feeling. 'Did you hear anything? Miss de Witte said she heard Mr Emerson speaking with a woman in the corridor. It must have been Mrs Wallace.' She put her hand to her forehead. Time was slipping away. 'I'll go and see if there's anything to be learned in Mr Emerson's room.'

Cautiously, Lucy held up her lantern to look around. Mr Emerson's room appeared very much as it had earlier. A basket of rolled bandages in one corner. Some blood on the sheets of the bed

– probably from where his shoulder wound had seeped.

As in her room, there was a bottle of mead and a cup on the side table. This bottle was bigger but less full. Duncan must have drunk a bit more of the honeyed drink than she had.

On the floor was a rope that had been cut through. She remembered how Mr Emerson had been tied up earlier. Perhaps that was the rope that had been used to tie him to the head-board. 'His feet and hands might well still be tied,' she said out loud.

Tom appeared behind her then. 'Say, miss, I can see that one of the handcarts is missing from out back. Usually, there's three. I know the physicians didn't take them.'

'I see,' Lucy said. If Mr Emerson was still tied up, he might need to be moved in a handcart. 'Where would Mrs Wallace have taken Mr Emerson? What did she need to show him?'

She sighed. Opening her peddler's pack, Lucy picked the ropes off the floor and placed them inside. For good measure, she took a few of the cleaned bandages from the basket and stuffed them in as well. *How far could they have got if she is pushing a man in a handcart? Not very far*, she thought. Then out loud she lamented, 'I don't even know what direction to go.'

What else had Miss de Witte heard? *I'll take you to where the end is the beginning*. What could that have meant?

She followed Tom into the courtyard, pulling the cloak around her more tightly to ward off the evening chill. She held the lantern out. She could see deep indentations in the muddy courtyard from the missing handcart. She followed the grooves until they got to the back gate. They appeared to turn west, but she could not track them very long once she got on to the main road.

'So they're going west,' she thought. 'What is west from here?'

'This road runs into Drury Lane.'

'Drury Lane?' She snapped her fingers. 'That's it! Perhaps she's taking him to the hanging tree, where Mr Corbyn was killed.'

'You're really going to the hanging tree? This time of night?' Tom whispered. 'My mates and me – we don't like to go there much, on account of the ghosts.'

Lucy nodded. 'That's where I'm heading. Don't worry, I won't let them see me.' She picked up her lantern and turned to head out.

Tom started after her. 'I'm coming with you,' he said, puffing out his chest.

Though touched, Lucy patted his shoulder. 'Tom, you can't come with me. I need you to go over to Fleet Street and leave a message at the jail for the constable. It's vital that you do so.' She paused. 'Be careful and mind the cold.'

'At least take this with you,' he said, holding out a small spade from the garden with shaking fingers.

After tying her pack across her body, she accepted the spade. With that, she set out, clutching her lantern and spade in her hands almost as talismans, on her way to the hanging tree at Drury Lane.

Twenty-Seven

Lucy walked quickly, shivering as light snow began to fall. She pulled her cloak around her body, holding the lantern low so that its light was only cast a few feet ahead. 'Is this a bad idea?' she whispered to herself. Neither Adam nor Duncan would be very happy if they knew she was following Mrs Wallace and Emerson on her own. *I just won't let them see me.* 'It could be too late if I wait for someone else,' she whispered to herself. *At least that's what I'll say if someone scolds me about it later.*

As she hurried by the Hargraves' residence, which was just a few dwellings away from the Larimers', she saw a familiar figure making his way from the back entrance. 'Sid!' she called. 'Come here! I need your help with something.'

Sid trotted over to her. 'What do you need my help with?' he asked, giving her a cocky grin. 'I knew you'd need me one day.' Then, when she didn't slow down, he grabbed her arm. 'Can you stop for a moment while you tell me?'

'I need you to tell the Hargraves that Mrs Wallace helped the prisoner escape and that I think she's taking him to the hanging tree up by Drury Lane.' When he stopped and stared at her, she banged the spade on the ground. 'Hurry! I don't know what she's planning to do to him!'

'I'll go with you,' he said, looking serious for once. 'You can't do this alone.'

'What if something happens to both of us?'

'Someone should lock you up in Bedlam, you know that?'

'Just do it! I don't have time to explain.'

'Don't get yourself in any more trouble,' he said, before running to the Hargraves' servants' entrance.

She continued to walk quickly and as softly as possible so as to not draw any attention to herself. There were not too many people outside at this time of the evening. As she entered Drury Lane, she could see a single lantern bobbing in front of her. Still keeping to the side of the road, she was ready to dart behind a tree at any second.

Is that them? She strained to distinguish the figures in front of her. Mrs Wallace appeared to be pushing Mr Emerson in the handcart. *Is he all right?* she wondered. He did not appear to be moving. *Was he still alive? Maybe he's been drugged as well. Why else wouldn't be he moving?*

She didn't dare get too close. Although it was foggy, the light snowfall was making everything a little brighter and more visible at this time of night, making her feel more vulnerable as well.

Then a hand reached around her arm and she nearly screamed. 'Hush!' Sid's familiar voice hissed in her ear. 'It's just me. I can't believe I caught up with you!'

'Did you tell the Hargraves?'

'Of course! Annie told me they were out looking for an escaped murderer. Did you know that there was an escaped murderer in the area?'

'Yes, and that's him. The one being pushed in the handcart. The woman who is pushing him has plans to take him to the gallows. I assume she might be planning to kill him, but I'm not entirely sure why.'

When Mrs Wallace started to move again, Sid pulled her back. 'Give her a little more space,' he whispered. They moved silently together, Sid holding her elbow to keep her from slipping on the softly falling snow. She would never tell him so, but she was grateful for his presence.

When Mrs Wallace reached the crossroads, she stopped by a large tree stump, a few feet from the hanging tree where Lucy had found Mr Corbyn's corpse. With a sudden sharp movement, she pitched the handcart forward, dumping Mr Emerson out. Since his hands and feet were still bound, he could not brace himself in time, and they heard him groan as he hit the ground with a painful-sounding thud.

'At least he's alive,' Sid whispered in her ear, echoing her thought. 'I was starting to wonder.'

'Over here,' Lucy whispered, pointing to a tree with a large trunk and blowing out the candle in her lantern. Sid crouched behind the tree with her so that they were about twenty feet away from Mr Emerson and Mrs Wallace.

Mr Emerson raised his head, and Lucy could see he looked confused. His mouth had been tightly wrapped with a cloth, and it appeared that another cloth had been stuffed inside his mouth so that no one could hear if he shouted for help. 'What's goin' on?' she heard him mutter.

'This is the old hanging tree,' Mrs Wallace

303

explained, her manner pleasant and friendly, pointing to the long-standing oak tree as if she were describing a fine painting. She gestured towards the branch where Mr Corbyn's body had been found hanged. 'Although you deserve to die in front of a crowd, paraded and mocked as a spectacle to others, I could not in good conscience run the risk that you might flee again and once more escape your fate. Such a thing could not be borne. So I decided to take matters into my own hands.'

Mr Emerson stared up at her, his brow furrowing. His gestures seemed to take an enormous effort. Lucy could relate to the sense of confusion he seemed to be experiencing.

Mrs Wallace continued to speak to him, in the same conversational tone that was so chilling to hear. 'I wager you are wondering what I'm going to do.' She pulled out a long knife from the belt at her waist. 'I'm going to kill you here, so that your soul will be lost and attach itself on to an unsuspecting passer-by.' She laughed again. 'Assuming you believe such nonsense.'

Beside her, Lucy felt Sid stiffen. She didn't know if he was more unnerved by the talk of ghosts or by murder. Both continued to watch the scene unfolding before them. Mrs Wallace had knelt down beside the trunk and suddenly grabbed Emerson under his arms and hauled him upright, pushing him so that he sprawled across the wide tree stump, like an animal awaiting slaughter.

He still appeared to be in great pain, his body trembling. He didn't have a coat, Lucy realized.

The temperature was dropping. She blew on her hands to keep them warm. Beside her, Sid was quietly stamping his feet, trying to keep them from growing numb.

Mrs Wallace reached out to touch Mr Emerson's face. 'You look so frightened,' she said. 'I'm sorry that we have no one here to record your last dying speech.' She ran the tip of his knife along his face. 'Can you feel how sharp it is? I plan to plunge it into your body, kill you as you have yourself killed.'

Lucy hefted the spade in her hands, wondering what to do. When she looked up at Sid, he gave her a warning look. *Stay here!* she could almost hear him say. She shook her head at him. *I can't let Mrs Wallace kill him. Perhaps I can sneak up behind her and knock her to the ground.*

Mrs Wallace had continued talking. 'You're not so very handsome, you know,' she sneered, looking down at the man. 'You look quite piteous indeed, with your muddied hair and without your scholar's robes.' She laughed again. 'I don't wonder that Ellie Browning preferred Hammett de Witte to you. Oh, does that hurt? Don't like me talking about that? I bet he was smarter and kinder, too.'

Mr Emerson had begun to shake, although it was impossible to know whether it was due to the deepening chill or Mrs Wallace's cutting words.

'Don't you worry, kind sir,' she continued with the same mocking tone. 'Even though you're not very handsome, I still intend to give you a gift.' She then withdrew something from her pocket

305

and held it in front of him. 'Do you recognize this?'

Both Sid and Lucy craned forward, trying to make out what the woman was dangling from her hand. Whatever it was, Mr Emerson grew horrified at the sight of it and emitted a muffled shout.

'That's right. I see you recognize this ring,' she said. Then, as Emerson tried to crawl away, she kicked him. 'Stop your struggling! I just want to put the ring around your neck, since you do not deserve to have it on your finger.'

That ring! A chill travelled down Lucy's spine as she remembered how she'd found Mr Corbyn dead, with that ring around his neck. *How had Mrs Wallace got it? Was it not with Duncan? Had she stolen it from the constable?*

Mrs Wallace kicked him hard, in the ribs, so that he doubled over, trying to breathe. In the shadows, Lucy slipped her pack to the ground and hefted the spade in both hands. Could she close the distance between herself and Mrs Wallace in time? She would need to keep the element of surprise on her side.

'Don't bother trying to escape again,' Mrs Wallace warned. 'There's nowhere to go, no one to help you.'

With her victim now stilled, she was able to crouch down and easily place the chain with the ring around his neck. Lucy could feel her body sweating as she listened to the woman spit out her next words. 'This ring, once a symbol of love, now means death and betrayal,' she said. 'It is fitting for a man such as yourself.'

Then, without warning, she yanked Emerson's head back by his hair, exposing his throat. Her back to Lucy and Sid, she then held the gleaming knife high in the air. 'Any last words?' she asked Mr Emerson in a mocking way. 'No? Then, I'll—'

'No!' Lucy shouted, snapping herself from whatever spell she'd been under, and raced towards them, her spade held high. Before Mrs Wallace could plunge the knife into Emerson's neck, Lucy had swung the metal and wood staff against the back of the woman's head with all her might.

Mrs Wallace released Emerson and sank to the ground, senseless. Emerson began to shake and weep in earnest until Sid moved over and slapped his face, bringing him out of his hysteria. Lucy and Sid stared at Mrs Wallace's unmoving form in dismay.

'Uh, Lucy,' Sid ventured, 'I wonder if you may have hit that woman too hard—'

Lucy stared at the lifeless body. She could see blood on the back of the woman's head where she'd been struck by the spade. Slowly, she and Sid crouched down beside her. With a shaking hand, Lucy rolled her over, causing her to groan.

'She's alive!' Sid confirmed with relief.

Too overwhelmed by relief to speak, Lucy took a deep breath, trying to control her racing heart.

Then they heard a sound beside them. Emerson was trying to crawl away again.

'Sid, stop him! I'll stay with her.'

As Sid jumped on Mr Emerson to keep him from getting away, Lucy raced back to the tree to grab her pack. Mrs Wallace had revived and

307

was in the process of trying to stumble away herself.

'Oh no, you don't,' Lucy cried, tackling her. She quickly found that she had misjudged Mrs Wallace's ferocity, and she was knocked flat on her back, the woman on top of her.

'Why couldn't you leave well enough alone?' Mrs Wallace cried, wrapping her hands around Lucy's neck. 'Why did you follow us here? This had nothing to do with you!'

'You brought me to this,' Lucy said, gritting her teeth. With all her strength, she continued to kick and struggle. Finally, she managed to roll them both over so that she was back on top of the flailing woman. 'Sid!' she called. 'Help me now!'

In the distance, she heard people shouting. Suddenly, there were lots of helping hands all around her, trying to pin the crazed woman down. Sid. Adam. Duncan. They all grabbed hold and managed to subdue Mrs Wallace. Grimly, Lucy pulled out the rope and wrapped it around the woman's legs. Then, without speaking, she rolled the woman over, quickly wrapping some of the bandages she'd brought around the woman's wrists so that she was immobilized.

Finally, she sat back and pointed at Mrs Wallace. Still panting, she said in halting words, 'Constable. This woman brought about Mr Corbyn's death. She brought Mr Emerson out here in order to kill him.'

Duncan hauled the woman to her feet. 'Let us all head back to the jail. We shall sort everything out there. Hargrave, you've got Emerson? Sid, help me out, then.'

Sid gripped Mrs Wallace's other arm. As Sid and Duncan began to haul the woman to the cart, Lucy went and stood in front of them, looking Mrs Wallace straight in the eye. Then, without another word, Lucy raised her hand and slapped the woman, hard, across her cheek. 'That's for the falseness of your friendship,' she said. She didn't say another word for the whole cold journey back to the jail.

When they arrived at the jail, Lucy perched herself on top of one of the old barrels that the constable had salvaged from the old Cheshire Cheese public house after the Great Fire. She'd draped an old blanket around her shoulders and helped herself to a bit of the mead that the constable kept in the back room. Dr Sheridan had arrived to check Mr Emerson's wounds, and once pronounced fit, the murderer was led to the cell next to the one occupied by Mrs Wallace. Throughout, Sid had helped Duncan and Hank handle the prisoners. 'Nice to be on the other side of the arrest for once,' he'd jested, his statement causing them all to glare at him. Adam had moved next to her, not speaking, but she could tell he was watching her closely.

'All right, Lucy,' Duncan said. 'Time to explain everything.'

'We were drugged by that woman,' Lucy said, pointing in the direction of Mrs Wallace's cell, 'so that she could free the prisoner and kill him at the hanging tree, as she wanted to do all along.'

'I'm afraid, Lucy, my dear, you are quite mistaken,' Mrs Wallace said, coming to stand at the bars, peering out at them. Her hair looked more bedraggled than usual and she looked quite forlorn. Her face still bore the mark where Lucy had slapped her. 'Please, Adam. Constable. This is all a terrible misunderstanding. I should like to get a chance to defend myself. I do admit that I had taken it in my head to set Mr Emerson free, but that was out of a misguided attempt by a wife to save her husband.'

When Lucy's eyes narrowed, Adam touched her arm. *Don't say anything*, he seemed to be telling her. 'Explain yourself,' he said. 'Start with why you freed Emerson.'

Mrs Wallace gave them all a teary smile. 'I know it was wrong to set that murderer free. I know it! I do admit to having drugged your mead, but it was just to help you sleep while I got him out. I injured no one – I certainly harbour no ill will against any of you.' She looked at the stony faces staring back at her and sighed. 'You have to understand, my husband has been accused of being an accomplice to *murder*, for heaven's sake. I thought the arrest would be dismissed once Emerson was not around, and Dev and Pike were hanged for the murder of Paul Corbyn. I thought there would be no further connection to my husband. It was foolish, I know.' She bowed her head, tears beginning to fall. 'What woman is not foolish around the man she loves?'

'Why take Emerson to the hanging tree?' Duncan asked. 'Why not just give him a purse and send him on his way?'

'I wanted to make sure he fled the city, so I thought to send him on his way to Westminster.

We had just stopped there as I was tired, and the stump was as convenient a place as any for me to rest.' She wiped a tear. 'As I said, I was just doing this for my husband, but I understand that there must be a punishment for my ill-thought deed. A few nights in jail, perhaps, or a stint in the stocks. I will bear it because I know that I am innocent in all respects.' The purity of love in her words rang through, and Hank shifted uncomfortably. Lucy glanced at Duncan and Adam, who were looking thoughtful. *Surely they are not fooled by her?*

'Liar!' Sid exclaimed, bringing them back to their senses.

Lucy jumped off the barrel. 'You framed your husband and Miss de Witte for the murder of Paul Corbyn,' she declared. 'You sent both Miss de Witte and Mr Emerson messages, hoping that they would kill one another. Is that not so?'

Mrs Wallace gave her a tight smile and cast an imploring look towards Duncan and Adam. 'Lucy's words are quite fanciful; do you not agree? It is no wonder that she excels as a seller of books. She tells a convincing tale.'

'Hey, we saw you about to murder that man!' Sid declared. 'With our own eyes!'

'Well, I've seen you in the stocks, more than once,' Mrs Wallace replied. 'Everyone knows you are a liar and a thief. As for Lucy, you're a former chambermaid who tells stories for a living. Certainly, if I was not the subject of her rather wild accusation, I should be quite amused. Indeed, I would ask her to publish this as *Strange News*.' Her tone grew hard. 'However, this is all

311

absolutely false, I assure you. I beg you not to continue this farce. Set me free at once.'

Adam and Duncan exchanged an inscrutable glance, then they looked towards Lucy. She knew what they were thinking. *We want to believe you Lucy, but what is the evidence here? What is the truth?*

'Tell us about the ring around Mr Emerson's neck,' Lucy said. 'Sid and I saw you put it there. How did you get it? Did you steal it from the constable?'

'What ring?' Duncan asked, standing up. Before waiting for her to explain, he pulled out the keys to the other cell and stepped inside. A moment later he returned, holding out two rings on chains, one in each hand so that everyone could see both of them 'This ring was the one that Lucy retrieved from around Paul Corbyn's neck. *This* ring was around Emerson's neck. Where did this other ring come from?'

Lucy touched both lightly with her index finger. The rings were very similar, but the two faces on each face were drawn slightly differently. 'The jeweller told us these were usually made in pairs, as sets,' she said. 'Hammett de Witte had one. *You* had the other,' she said to Mrs Wallace. 'Why is that?'

When the woman remained silent, Lucy started to sort it out loud. 'Wait a minute. Did these rings belong to you and Hammett de Witte?' Everything began falling into place. '*You* were in love with Hammett de Witte yourself!'

Everyone stared at Mrs Wallace, whose face had suffused with blood. 'How can you say such

312

a thing? I love my husband and am committed to our marriage.'

'I see. After all, what would a handsome and scholarly man like Hammett de Witte see in a woman like you?' Lucy said, deliberately goading her. 'I mean, he was surrounded by scholarly minds, including his own sister, so he would not hold you in particularly high regard.'

'But he did—'

Ruthlessly, Lucy went on. 'It was no wonder that he was fascinated by Ellie Browning, who, by all accounts, was a merry and beautiful girl.'

'He did love me! He did! He told me that being with me gave him solace! We did have many a fine conversation. He even asked me about leaving my husband!'

'That seems so far-fetched,' Lucy said. 'Tell us. How did it happen? Did you fall in love with him when you discovered your husband was being unfaithful to you with his sister? Or did it happen before that?'

'Before that! He came to our house, seeking a mathematics tutor for his sister.' Her voice softened at the memory. '"She has a brilliant mind," he said. "She deserves to be educated." I remember at the time being so impressed that someone could love his sister with such devotion and tenderness. He would accompany her while my husband tutored her, and we became' – here she paused – 'most dear acquaintances.' She laughed bitterly. 'It was clear by then that my husband, who had only cared for me out of necessity and duty, had his heart touched by Miss de Witte. In my foolishness, I thought that perhaps we could annul our loveless marriage.' She bowed her head, her earlier defiance gone, and more agitation setting in as she sought to explain. 'I bought the rings from the jeweller and gave Hammett one, to pledge my love, before he returned to Cambridge—' She broke off.

'However, you didn't know that he had met Ellie Browning at the Two Doves Inn and gave her the ring that you had given him,' Lucy said softly, filling in the gaps. 'That must have been a terrible realization.'

'It was!' Mrs Wallace exclaimed, her eyes filling with tears. 'Oh, that foolish girl! Yes, Hammett gave my ring to her in a moment of infatuation. A wretched act of betrayal, indeed. Still I loved him and I know he loved me, too. He knew that my marriage to Professor Wallace was a loveless one, and he had to have known that Ellie would never have loved him as deeply as I did.'

'That's why you swore revenge on the man who killed him,' Lucy said.

Mrs Wallace gripped the bars, her voice trembling. 'That filthy rat, Emerson! He killed my Hammett!'

'How angry you must have been when he was set free by Mr Corbyn. You wanted revenge on both men, did you not?'

Mrs Wallace shook the bars, her ire rising. 'Of course I was angry with both men! When I found out they had both taken on new identities in London, their lives and livelihoods intact, I was—'

She dropped off, but Adam filled in the missing part of her sentence. 'Furious.'

314

'You wrote those notes to Pike and Dev,' Lucy said. 'Pretending to be Miss de Witte.'

'Yes.' Her answer was straightforward, sounding neither embarrassed nor ashamed. She was so caught up in telling the story that she seemed unaware of what she was confessing. 'Their grief was strong enough and they were well committed in their vengeance. I simply thought that they required direction. Although the fools still managed to mishandle everything.'

'Was your intention to frame Lucretia de Witte for the murder?' Adam asked.

'Why not? She committed adultery with my husband – with their stupid ciphers. I never loved him so well, but I despised how he viewed *her* as his intellectual match. He thought I was too foolish to understand, and perhaps I was, but once I found his cipher key, everything was easy enough.'

'You continued to send messages between them?' Lucy asked.

'To her, yes. I forged them, so that it would appear that their infidelity continued.'

'How did you come to learn of Mr Corbyn's whereabouts, given his new identity?'

'I saw them both by chance a few months ago. At one of the new coffee shops built after the fire. I could scarcely believe my eyes when I saw them together, seated at a table outside.'

'They were friends?' Lucy shook her head. Could a murderer and his jailer have such accord? Of course, Mr Corbyn had also freed him from Newgate and released him from divine execution by fire. Perhaps the jailer had

315

a fondness for the man. Stranger things have happened.

'I do not know.' Her knuckles whitened around the bars. 'When they set aside their cups, I followed them both for a while. Unfortunately, they separated, taking opposite paths before very long. I only had a moment to decide which man to follow. I followed Mr Corbyn.'

'Why?' Lucy asked. 'Wasn't Emerson the object of your hatred?'

'It was as if fate had intervened in that decision,' Mrs Wallace said, shrugging. 'Naturally, I wanted to follow Philip as the bigger prize, but he walked too quickly. Paul Corbyn was far easier for me to pursue, since he was heavily burdened with all of his mercer's goods.' She folded her arms. 'It was quite easy to follow him to his shop and figure out that he had stolen the mercer's identity and that his wife was installed in the other woman's place.'

'Why not just confront Mr Corbyn then and there?' Lucy asked. 'Why go to the trouble of working with Pike and Dev to kill him?'

'That wouldn't work with my plan, now would it?' Mrs Wallace said. 'My main goal was to find out where Mr Emerson was. I assumed when I first heard he'd been set free that the murderous fiend had likely fled London altogether. Later, though, when I thought about where he could have gone, it occurred to me that he might strive to forge a new identity for himself, as so many others had done. Then I wondered what kind of identity such a man could adopt. Surely he had no useful skills. I thought he might seek to be a tutor, so that he would not have to dirty his hands with real work. I congratulate myself on having read him so well.' She sniffed.

'As for Paul Corbyn,' she continued, 'I knew he had no reason to know me from the trial, so I just contracted him as a mercer. After I'd purchased a few objects from him, I gave him the ring and the letter, and paid him a handsome sum to take it to Dev and Pike, along with some other household goods. Delivered him to them! The foolish man! Who would have thought he'd make a copy of my message and keep it in a second pocket!'

'The message you wrote to Pike and Dev, in which you pretended to be Miss de Witte, did not instruct the men to kill Mr Corbyn,' Lucy said.

'I most certainly did not instruct them to kill that guard,' Mrs Wallace insisted, sounding peeved. 'Those idiot innkeepers took matters into their own hands. I thought they would just beat Mr Corbyn until he told them where Philip was staying.' She shook the bars. 'Those idiots – they went and killed him with the death I wanted for Emerson! I had to track him down myself.'

'How did you do that?' Lucy asked.

'I knew that it would just be a matter of time, assuming he was still in London. I convinced Professor Wallace to begin cultivating the scholars in the area, with the hope that one might know Emerson and invite him to accompany him one evening. That came to pass just recently.'

The sound of a man weeping interrupted them. It was Professor Wallace, who'd evidently been

317

listening to the conversation from the back room. 'Oh, Joanna!' he cried, tears streaming down his cheeks. 'How can you have done such a terrible thing? Frame Lucretia? Frame me? Your own husband, whom you purported to love. How could you do such a thing?'

Mrs Wallace's eyes grew cold. 'You brought this on yourself by behaving in such an abandoned way with Miss de Witte after we were already married. When I married you, I knew that we had little love between us.' She sighed. 'You'll find your solace in your books soon enough.'

Swallowing, Lucy finally asked the question she'd been wanting to know all evening. 'Why did you treat me as you did?'

Mrs Wallace sighed. 'You were a means to an end, Lucy. At first, I was terrified when I realized you'd met Pike and Dev – those idiots – at the hanging tree, especially after you kept looking for information about Mr Corbyn's identity. Then I thought how perfect it all was. I could feed you bits and pieces of information, and control what secrets you discovered and when. With your help, I was able to convince you that Miss de Witte and my own husband were to be blamed.'

'You thought I was willing and gullible,' Lucy said.

Mrs Wallace laughed, although the sound lacked mirth. 'That may be so, but clearly' – she gestured to the cell – 'I underestimated you, which I most heartily acknowledge and regret.'

Twenty-Eight

When Adam declared it high time for Lucy to return home to Master Aubrey's, she did not demur. They walked in silence through the quiet foggy streets. At some point, Adam drew Lucy's arm in his. The snow from earlier was already melting into puddles that sparkled under the dancing light of the lantern.

'I was tricked by that terrible woman,' Lucy said, after taking a deep breath. 'How could I not have realized it? She took advantage of my trust in her and my fervent belief that the friendship she offered was true.' She gulped. 'It is difficult to realize that when I thought she was helping us, she was in fact using us to throw suspicion on Miss de Witte, and even her husband.'

'Lucy, you are berating yourself unnecessarily. Mrs Wallace tricked a lot of people, Father and me included,' Adam replied. 'Her duplicitous nature caused many a despicable and wanton act, which will be hard to recover from, but she will be brought to justice for her crimes.'

'She spoke of me as her dear acquaintance, her dear companion. I truly believed that she had a high regard for me.' Here Lucy gulped. 'Her falsehoods inspired in me a false pride.'

Adam gently patted her hand where it rested in the crook of his elbow. 'Those who know you

319

well only have the highest regard for you. Pray, do not view her treachery as commonplace.'

'Sometimes I wonder how we can ever really know people, Adam!' she exclaimed. 'False identities. Liars. They're all around us.'

'That may be true. However,' he said, stopping and putting his hands on her shoulders, 'that is not true of all people. Let us be who we are to each other, Lucy. Let us not be Master Adam and Lucy the Hargraves' servant.' His gaze was intense, capturing her completely.

'Other people won't accept that,' she said, tears coming to her eyes. 'They'll always say I'm not of your station. That I'm not worthy of you.'

'Lucy, Lucy! The people who matter to us will know,' he replied, wiping her tears away with his fingers. He placed his hands on her cheeks and inclined her face toward him. 'Besides, it is I who am not always worthy of you. You are so quick to care, so quick to do what is just – there is so much I have learned from you.' Leaning down then, he kissed her. As she closed her eyes, a sense of hope and love flooded over her. *Perhaps there is a path forward.*

Several weeks later, Lucy set the type for the piece that Master Aubrey had approved the night before. As usual, the title was quite lengthy and in a larger italicized font.

Order Restored – The Strange and True Account of Three Murderers, Who Will Hang in Accordance with the Law. One Escaped Murderer and Two who Killed the

320

Newgate Guard who set him Free on the Night of the Great Fire, namely Philip Emerson, a Cambridge scholar, and Pike and Dev Browning, two innkeepers from Hoddesdon.

Below that, in smaller font, was another headline.

Additionally, two attempted murderesses sentenced to prison. Mrs Joanna Wallace, wife of the mathematician Neville Wallace, sentenced to ten years for attempted murder, and Miss Lucretia de Witte, three months for assault.

Lucy shivered as she placed the woodcut in the top right-hand corner; it was an image they used with some regularity, depicting two witches and two criminals. She was grateful not to have to attend the hanging. Lach would go instead, selling all three pieces at Tyburn – the piece she'd written describing Paul Corbyn's death, this *True News* they were currently setting, and the *Last Dying Speech of Philip Emerson.*

She'd spoken to Emerson a few days earlier, before he was transferred to Newgate Prison to await his execution. Many of his words she'd used to put his final confession to paper as the *Last Dying Speech.* 'I only ever wanted to be a musician,' he'd told her. 'My father, who died during the plague, insisted that I get a university education. Hammett de Witte was one of my only friends. But when I met Ellie Browning, she was singing. Her voice was light and beautiful, like a bird, and I was enchanted. I just wanted to have that beautiful voice to myself. When she brought me the love messages from Hammett, I was enraged, as I was the one who introduced them. Mrs Wallace was quite right when she said I was an ugly man. I am an ugly man, not just on the outside, but that I could take two such beautiful souls out of this world will be a regret.' Here he'd paused in his speech to wipe his tears, which were flowing easily now. Lucy had handed him a handkerchief but did not say anything. When he was ready, she dipped her quill in the ink and began to write again.

'When Jack Campbell – you know him as Mr Corbyn – set me free on the night of the dreadful conflagration, I thought the good Lord had thought fit to give this sinner a second chance. I lived in fear of discovery, so it was not a life worth living. No love, no life – and very little song. When I received the message that fateful morning, which I now know was from Mrs Wallace, I was overwhelmed by my fear and anxious thoughts. When Miss de Witte attacked me with the knife, I had no other thought than to keep her from destroying the very little life I had regained.' He concluded then, in the typical vein of many of these speeches. 'I repent of my sins and ask for forgiveness. In this way, I end my last dying speech, full of repentance and a warning to others to avoid my sinful and shameful ways.'

* * *

'The crossroads are just a little distance ahead,' Lucy said to Mrs Corbyn. The woman had come to her the day before, dressed from head to toe in black, and asked Lucy if she might accompany her to the hanging tree. Although she did not wish to return to that site, Master Aubrey had overheard the request. 'Go and sell at St Giles-in-the-Fields,' he had said. 'Those pieces will sell well there.'

The woman nodded. She'd been silent for much of the journey, only breathing harder as she pushed a small cart through the mud. The cart did not appear to hold any of Mr Corbyn's household goods, but rather bags of different weavings and colourful clothes. 'I'm going to try my luck at the market, too,' she said, when she'd seen Lucy looking at the pack. 'I'm going to be Mariah Campbell again. No longer Mrs Corbyn. I never even knew who that was. No sense being something I'm not. I've left the house and everything behind. Besides, I'm certain the good Lord will punish me for our misdeed, even more than we've already been punished. Thank the Lord that the priest saw fit to bury him as Jack Campbell – that is my only solace in this whole matter.'

At the hanging tree, Mrs Corbyn kneeled down in prayer. 'You foolish man!' she cried. 'Why did we have to steal to better ourselves? Look at the world in which you've left me in. I cannot survive in that false role another moment. Why did you ask me to do such a wrongful, immodest thing?'

During the woman's teary tirade, Lucy hung

back. As she listened to the woman rant, some of her words started floating in her world. 'A new world doesn't come without hard work! No one is going to hand you a new life! You must work for it! Become someone. You can't make society accept you just by telling them you belong.'

Lucy found herself nodding. In many ways, Mrs Corbyn was echoing some of the thoughts in her own heart as well and reminded her of the conversations she'd had with Adam, and with Duncan, too.

'Are you certain, Lucy?' Duncan had asked her, earlier that morning, when she'd tearfully told him of her decision. 'I can give you a good home, a family. You can still work at Master Aubrey's as you please. Can Hargrave offer you the same?' She'd stood there, twisting her skirts, unsure how to explain her heart more fully. 'Never mind, Lucy,' he'd said, his voice gentle. 'I can see that you are still besotted with him. Should anything change, please come back to me. I will wait for you until the day I see you wed.'

Mrs Corbyn straightened up. 'I'll take my leave of you now.'

Lucy turned away from the hanging tree and stared around her at the crossroads. She could turn back and take the road to London. She could go north or east and end up in Covent Garden or St Giles-in-the-Fields, two places she'd already been. She eyed the path leading to the east. 'Time to make some decisions! Spitalfields market is that way,' she said to herself. 'Let me try something new. Who knows what awaits?' Hefting her pack over her shoulder, she forged ahead.

Author's Note

I was inspired to write *The Sign of the Gallows* after I had the image of Lucy standing at a crossroads, which felt apt, given the big decisions still ahead of her. Crossroads also occupied an interesting space in early modern European folklore generally. The bodies of people who had committed suicide could not be buried in consecrated ground, and so it was not uncommon to bury them at crossroads, so that their restless spirits would not find their way back home. Such practices led to a common apprehension of crossroads, especially those in more secluded locations. However, I wanted Lucy to be braver and less superstitious than many of her contemporaries, which seemed reasonable to me, because she had spent many years with the magistrate, a man whose attitudes and behaviours aligned with the rational, scientific precepts associated with the emerging Enlightenment.

I was further inspired when I began to research the new developments in mathematics, especially those focusing on ciphers and cryptography, that had been steadily advancing throughout the sixteenth and seventeenth centuries. The story of Sir Francis Walsingham, who successfully deciphered an encoded message between Anthony Babington and Mary, Queen of Scots, which resulted in her demise, demonstrated how seriously the Crown and scholars alike took the new field of study. I drew particularly on the life of English mathematician, John Wallis, to inform the background of my character Professor Neville Wallace, who, among other things, deciphered Royal missives captured by Parliamentary forces during the English Civil Wars. By the mid-seventeenth century, coded messages were becoming more common, not just for concealing military secrets, but also for communications between merchants and in some cases, romantic partners. I spent many hours working out the ciphers in this book, using some of the more common principles discussed in popular tracts, such as Frances Bacon's exploration of ciphering, which was an intriguing, if a bit daunting, task.

Lastly, I've also always been fascinated by what happened to the inmates of Newgate prison during the Great Fire. Until recently, there was a long-standing narrative of the so-called 'miracle' of the Great Fire, drawn from Dryden's *Annus Mirabilis*, in which there were only six or so confirmed deaths, despite half the city being destroyed. Recently, this narrative has been questioned, and indeed, there is no clear record of what happened to the inmates. An orderly evacuation seems unlikely, although it seems possible that some may have escaped before the notorious prison succumbed to the flames. Collectively, these are the kinds of questions and details that drive my story, and I do my best to be as faithful as possible to the larger social, cultural, political and economic trends of the period.